THE DEEPEARTH
TALES OF MIURAG

BY
A.S. ETASKI

Published by Corpus Nexus Press
ISBN: 978-1-949552-21-8

etaski.com
etaski.com/sister-seekers
miurag.etaski.com
www.patreon.com/etaski
www.goodreads.com/etaski
www.bookbub.com/authors/a-s-etaski
www.facebook.com/asetaski
mastodon.online/@etaski

Cover Design by Eris Adderly
Book layout by DocKangey

INTRODUCTION

My main published series, *Sister Seekers,* begins underground with *No Demons But Us*, where Dark Elves live and die in darkness. Sirana, a novice Red Sister, leads us through most of the story through her eyes, but there are many others with stories of their own to share.

Tales of Miurag: The Deepearth is a same-world anthology collection of novellas and short stories. They reveal critical moments in the history of the Davrin of Sivaraus, the Dark Elves of the Red Desert now fallen to the Abyss.

The stories appear in chronological order for Miurag's timeline but not the order I'd written them as extras for my patrons between 2015-2017.

The major story of this collection is the first novella, *House Aurenthin*. This is a tragedy within which we witness the origin of the lowest-ranking House in Sivaraus and see hints of its future.

The next three stories are a mix of tales.

In the erotic horror tale, "Auranka the Keeper," we see the chilling origin of the present-day Mistress of the Driders.

Next, we explore a surprisingly romantic tale of Sirana's Matron and mother in "Rohenvi."

Finally, in "Gaelan," we witness the early connections formed between two youths yet to become Red Sisters.

Warning: This book contains mature and disturbing themes and is intended for adults only. These stories contain explicit sex and violence some readers may find disturbing.

A glossary is available at World Anvil where I keep my series lore!

HOUSE AURENTHIN

A TALE OF MIURAG
BY A.S. ETASKI

CHAPTER 1

1600 S.E., THE GREAT CAVERN

THE GREAT CAVERN WAS IN CHAOS AS SIVARAUS ERUPTED IN CIVIL WAR.

They're trapped, Matron! Janel Ja'Prohn reported through her message spell. *Anyone who's gone into the Sanctuary isn't coming out.*

Any teams manage to kill the Priestess' sons? her commander asked.

Half sprouted wings when they clashed, Matron, then the beasts bolted outside. Reports say their Priestesses couldn't control them.

Bad news.

What about the Drider Keeper?

Wolina hasn't been sighted, but her Driders have engaged our army.

Matron Tala D'Shauranti gripped the hilt of her sword. Fadele's Sisters had just engaged as well. Her forces had enemy flankers incoming on three sides.

Braqth fuck a pickax sideways. I must warn the Blade Singers about the half-bloods but I'm not in range. I must draw back, Janel.

Wait! Tell us what we are to do, Commander!

Tala ground her teeth. *If Taneous won't help us inside the Palace, we must leave him there and meet up with my sire. We take down as many as we can on our way out. No tactics barred.*

6

Fadele felt when the battle turned desperate.

Yes. Seethe and quiver, you traitors.

The time for bluffing, damage control, deliberation, and strategy … all of it long past. The rebel Houses were in full retreat now with hybrid spiders and demons chasing after them, pouncing, stunning, poisoning, and paralyzing.

⋆Take all you can alive, Fadele,⋆ the Valsharess instructed.

Though she acknowledged her Queen, the Prime Sister watched, entranced, as a Blade Singer was picked up by a winged Priestess's son. The bestial, white-maned Sathoet took her to a ledge far above the cavern floor where the feral half-breed could pin her and rut in relative safety from the fighting.

Did she count as "captured," then?

Heh. She's certainly 'taken.'

Those leathers must be torn to shreds. Maybe there were claw marks all over her ass as well. Legs thrashed beguilingly while the dark and muscular demonblood thrust savagely between them.

Too soon, Fadele was forced to look away to focus on the battle at hand. *Bah. Lucky prick.*

The Blade Singers might have the most potent *traditional* magic of Sivaraus, but Fadele and her Sisters had the Abyss, their numbers, and all their fun, little surprises on their side.

Every traitor she captured alive would wish that they had fallen dead on the field.

I'll see to it.

The moment the Grandmaster's Daughter fell onto the stone, it signaled disaster for House D'Shauranti.

Tala knelt in a pool of her own blood, holding in her intestines as the

Drider Keeper prepared to strike again.

"Ssshow usss where he isss!" the contorted spider-elf hissed, manic eyes yellow and milky. Sharp, segmented fingers seized the sides of the rebel leader's head, as if she intended to rip the information from out of her skull after it cracked. "Where hasss Y'shir taken the othersss!"

"Leave him in peace, Wolina," Tala gasped, calling on the last of her reserves to cast a spell that would kill her for sure.

Hopefully she'd take the Drider Mistress with her.

Blade Singers, cover the escape! Stand a hard line!

Then their leader was gone, and the entire House of Blade Singers would never meet up with their fabled Grandsire.

Chapter 2

1700 S.E., Sivaraus – A century later

"We should destroy those records," the Prime Sister said.

"Absolutely not, Fadele!" protested the High Priestess, staring into the eyes of the hardened fighter. "You may like to sweep up evidence of your failures, but there is far more worth in these records than there is in your pride!"

Fadele narrowed her eyes at Panija but kept her face like stone. The Prime's eyes, like scratched ruby, shifted away as she bowed her head to her Queen.

"Your Highness," Fadele began. "If it is too late to find the traitors, then these scrolls only serve to confuse and mislead future Priestesses and Elders. If your Grace does not want the city to remember, we best not keep reminders lying about."

The Prime always spoke straightforward and plain as if there should be no doubt which was the clearest path. Always in favor of the web, however, the High Priestess of Braqth wanted the path to their future as murky as possible.

"Again, no," said Panija. "The traitor Houses were all broken and rounded up, yes, but they still possessed the largest concentration of mages in their bloodlines —"

"We noticed," the Prime said with cool derision. "My caits faced that with your sons a century ago, while you and your incense sisters conveniently watched from a balcony. The Blade Singers turning against us was the only reason they managed to rise and challenge our Queen in the first place."

"Too many of those elite are dead or lost to us, now," the Priestess continued with passion in the face of her rigid adversary. "We need these records still, for a time at least, so we can look more closely at those who remain."

"Why?"

"To be sure we don't snip off the strongest magic we can salvage from our heritage, Prime Sister. That is *my* duty, if not yours. Out of the mages come our future generation of Braqth's Priestesses. None of *your* crop of passably magic-sensitive warriors can fill that vital role, therefore you have no say."

Fadele bristled. "I dare claim you haven't managed a pile of shit for all this time we've been hunting them in the Deepearth, Priestess, while you all sit cozy in your worship rooms."

"Had I known about these records earlier, I would have found them *for* you!"

"A load of tripe, Priestess."

"Oh? Shall I explain to one who can barely read?"

The Prime reined back her expression just before she might have raised her first, again looking to the Valsharess. "My Queen?"

Ishuna did not answer immediately. She sat at the table, lightly tracing fingers over the tattered scrolls so recently pulled from her personal library by her own hand. Although she dismissed the bickering, the Queen within her still listened to the arguments.

Yes, her High Priestess hadn't known about these scrolls. Panija had her own set within the library in the Sanctuary, open to the Valsharess anytime She wished to step in. Ishuna did so on a regular basis, so She knew precisely which differences Panija had spied just now.

The rebellion was now a century past, and Ishuna had awoken from her dreamwalk into the deepest pathways beyond the Great Cavern. An enormous black wing had risen and blocked her Sight and her way.

Ishuna knew they had to give up the search. This had been the sign she sought, and it had to come full circle.

Try as she had for all these decades, the break in their population could neither be prevented nor recovered. The Grandmaster Y'shir had taken the secrets of Blade Song with him when he'd joined House Ja'Prohn in the war. It was quite clear why he'd delayed taking an apprentice in the century leading up to that battle.

The Queen's sole consolation was knowing that House Ja'Prohn and their allies would never make it back to the Surface as they hoped. They would not upset the balance; their return would not occur to tempt the deathless servant who had once been among her family.

The Deepearth would never let them go.

Xala, Ishuna thought, considering family long past. *Glad we are that you did not live to see the day your House cut us so deeply. Only they could have caused a successful break from the path.*

Now the Queen must consider the formal records of Sivaraus and what to teach the newest crop of Priestesses, Red Sisters, and Nobles. Their numbers were finally recovering from heavy losses, and a lot of children were coming of age at once in another few decades. Stories would be handed down by the survivors of the war, but those would fade with time and a little help from Braqth.

The largest House D'Shauranti had been splintered and held to the bottom of their society, now beneath all others. They suffered the blame from the people of Sivaraus for treason, for preventing the swift recapture of the deserters. By order of the Valsharess, the Sisterhood and Sanctuary worked together to make sure this "prisoner House" wasn't destroyed and overtaken in a coup.

"Someone must always be on the bottom," the Valsharess had told her closest advisors shortly after the bloodshed. "We shall continue to choose which House that will be. This shall not change unless We wish it. We shall also choose from among them the next Drider Mistress to replace Wolina."

Ishuna had ignored the Prime's question at the time. Her most loyal warrior had just avoided questioning her outright, wondering why the

Queen didn't seem to care which Matron headed the first House of Sivaraus, only the last.

Because none compare with Ja'Prohn or D'Shauranti.

These Houses were each her own; the two largest with the most influence, which had always produced the next Queen of the Red Desert.

Yet their history was almost gone from Sivaraus and the Deepearth.

D'Shauranti had lost the Blade Song Master, Y'shir Matalai'ko, and their Matron, his Daughter, Tala. They'd lost all their status, resources, trade agreements. Noble children and common fighters alike had died in battle. For this last century, they had been living in slum, waiting for word of those from Ja'Prohn who'd escaped.

Now, Ishuna knew Y'shir was gone for good; he and his traitors would never reach the Surface again. She must decide how to salvage what She could, her way.

"House D'Shauranti must be split up," Ishuna murmured. "As they have failed to train a new Blade Song apprentice, this House has no need for fighter-mages in their Noble line or among their House Guard. D'Shauranti shall become two Houses: warrior *or* mage. We shall keep the former weak while bolstering and annexing the latter."

The Prime nodded her chin, cold eyes contemplating further abductions and imprisonments as their means of control. The High Priestess tapped her fingertips together, just as swiftly considering methods of persuasion and intrigue in the Palace and Sanctuary.

Panija began their plan. "Allow the Priesthood to bring any D'Shauranti sorceresses to Court for an extended time, Valsharess. We can slowly change their thinking. We must remove the sons with mage potential as well."

"Indeed. We have an idea for this. We shall create a tower to train them for our purposes, away from their families."

"The Sisterhood can help with this, Valsharess," Fadele spoke up, straightening her back and crossing her arms. "Though I'd suggest the change must be among *all* Noble buas of every House, or they will see the pattern against House D'Shauranti. More will cling to the stories that way."

Ishuna nodded once, imagining the Prime Sister quite effectively collecting the magical sons and daughters of the Nobles.

She always resented Y'shir's methods. She will enjoy it.

Perhaps the time had come for this change as well: to separate the bua from the cait even more. They would only distract the best Davrin which remained to keep back the threats of the Deepearth.

Separation would prevent further confusion in choosing between their Queen-Mother and those they mounted. Eager and selfish as males were for female attention, they must not turn mothers against mothers or sisters against sisters again.

Or we will not survive down here.

The Davrin could not afford another war with such loss among themselves, and Ishuna had not missed the explicit competition over Taneous Ja'Prohn as it all came down

Panija smiled at Fadele for once. "Over time, one House will be martial only, and all their best mages will be under our Queen's direct control."

"So, the 'mage' House is just temporary?" the Prime asked with a smirk. "Sooner or later it's got to disappear."

"Agreed," the Priestess said.

Quite a rarity to hear that word between them.

Regardless, Ishuna saw the plan coming together. She already knew which wizard would become the Headmaster to this new crop of children: the sole defector from House Ja'Prohn, Taneous. Her Royal Consort would inherit the surprise bua mages which might show up in the bottom House, now destined to be nothing but fighters and mundane healers.

The Valsharess pulled out a fresh sheet of parchment at her desk, drawing the standing advisors' full attention. She wrote with an elegant script, beginning with one name at the top on the left-hand side.

House D'Shea.

Ishuna considered the other name. It came to her so abruptly, she wrote it down on the right side without second-guessing it.

House Aurenthin. Yes.

The ancient dunes hidden in plain sight.

"We shall keep both sets of these records, Fadele," Ishuna commanded, to be clear with her stubborn Prime.

"Yes, Valsharess."

No hesitation or bitterness?

That was good. The Prime Sister should be the example of what they could accomplish without manipulative males dragging them down.

Again.

"Come closer, both of you, and let us sort this out."

With a few strokes of her fiberstalk quill, Ishuna created a new genealogy from which they would work for the future stability of Sivaraus and all its connections beyond the Great Cavern.

CHAPTER 3
1722 S.E., SIVARAUS

FADELE'S HEART POUNDED FROM THE THRILL OF THE CATCH AS SHE WRESTLED the young, Noble fighter into a hold she couldn't break. The Prime loved the way the other female's leather-clad backside rubbed and writhed against her mound as they struggled, soured only by the thought that the youth wasn't afraid *enough.*

Not yet.

Yet if some pathetic male's pole was sliding up in between your cheeks right now, sweetmeat, you'd be livid with fear and indignation.

Fadele had been chasing this slit for most of the cycle through the borderlands, aided by a borrowed Sathoet herding her where the recruit couldn't stray too far from the safety of the Great Cavern. The Prime was satisfied this recruit had the speed and toughness to be part of the Sisterhood, but now she wanted to test how the cait handled humility.

Still, the eldest Red Sister hated having to use the Priestess's sons to *really* break caits down and see what they were made of.

The youth was tempted to cry out as the Sathoet appeared and the two of them stripped her of her pants. She wanted to scream, but she didn't. She stayed silent in the wilderness of the Deepearth.

Noting that as a mark in her favor, Fadele could enjoy every expression of horror and denial on the young face as she held their new Sisterhood toy by the front end, arms and torso in a lock, that sweet mouth close enough to her crotch to fuel her desire as the Sathoet took care of the bottom end.

"No … !" the young female whispered, trying to look behind her but she couldn't see past the Prime's muscled thighs. "Please, Prime, stop him! I submit!"

You bet your netherhole, you will, Aurenthin slit.

The recruit's face grimaced and her mouth opened in a silent scream as the demonic male trust into her cunt first, but Fadele knew that was only to get it wet with a handful of thrusts.

With a nod from herself, the demonblood held the new novice down and slowly, humiliatingly speared her purple star with his pointed cock, drawing out the time she felt her netherhole swallowing all that length. The Sathoet quivered with the joy to press his bushy white crotch-beard flush against her sweet ass. The impaled recruit was so tense, Fadele imagined how stretched and vulnerable she felt right then.

The Sathoet waited for the Prime's signal like a good bua before he drew back and stuffed his cock up inside the Aurenthin fighter again. Soon, he sped up, reaming that tight hole until he rutted like the brute he was.

Watching the cait's face, studying every change and tick and eye-widening surge of sensation, hearing her whimper or choke on a gasp, the Prime trembled in arousal yet burned with intense envy of the Sathoet himself.

The Priestesses and Nobles might be satisfied directing buas to humiliate the competition on occasion, but the Sisterhood should have something *more.* A Red Sister should have something no one else in Sivaraus had, something which should terrify *everyone* no matter their station.

Even a Priestess has a netherhole.

Fadele was bored with holding her would-be rivals down as they got fucked by someone else, but she still wouldn't wear those stupid-looking contraptions some caits wore for their mistress.

Why should someone of her station tie on a fake cock she could neither feel nor control?

The Prime wanted to *be* the one fucking her caits. She wanted them to feel *her* mounting and claiming them for her Cloister. She wanted them to have no doubt who they truly feared.

She also wanted to feel those elites' holes spasm and tighten around her as they yielded to her.

Most importantly, she wanted to climax from it.

"Prime … !" the recruit pleaded as the Sathoet snorted and huffed.

He was about to soil her back passage with his messy spurts.

"Oh, P-Prime!"

That's it. That's what you should be saying now.

The only thing missing from that precious, breathless squeal was Fadele's rush of pleasure from using her gaping hole. It just wasn't enough.

This would *never* be enough!

The Prime panted, dry-humping the younger female, nearly coming but only fucking *nearly*. She'd force the slit to suck her cunt later once they were back at the Cloister, but she wouldn't get all tangled up in her leathers out here.

Braqth Web damn it all.

As the Sathoet growled low and his cock unloaded its slime deep inside her recruit's asshole, Fadele had an idea.

I'll talk to Taneous in the Wizard's Tower.

Fadele had given him enough quality young bloods of his own over the last century. More than enough.

He would repay her with a favor.

CHAPTER 4

1903 S.E., THE PALACE OF SIVARAUS

Here, sorceress, let us drink.

One time out of ten, the simplest of cantrips could work against the strongest mages. It was one of those tricks which beginner mages played on each other all the time and soon grew out of.

This *should* be far too obvious for any seasoned wizard or sorceress to fall for, yet the Headmaster of the Tower still used it on occasion. Especially when his guests expected something more complex and powerful on his home turf.

That moment of dismissal was all he needed.

Taneous grinned as the attractive cait followed his lead and tilted back her head, holding the tiny cup to her lips. The fluid poured between her full lips, and she swallowed.

Now if only she doesn't —

Jelani's eyes widened as she realized what she'd done. She turned from him, putting a finger down her throat to force a retching.

Taneous sprang forward, gripped her wrist to pull it from her mouth, and clutched her to him, keeping her upright. He kissed her temple, pressed his aura out upon her, searching to entwine them.

Now he could draw the more complex spell and begin the binding.

Calm, sorceress, be calm. This is decreed. It will be better if you don't fight

18

me. You shall remember that you accepted my gift. You are ready. Remember, you are ready. ★

She grew lax, unable to hold herself up, and Taneous placed her belly-down and bent over the table in his greeting room. She groaned, pawed drunkenly at something, anything within reach, but he hurriedly pushed the scrolls they'd been studying together out of her grasp. Those wouldn't help her stand up again anyway; nothing would.

Not for the next few marks at least.

Absently he rubbed at the silver ring on his finger with his thumb, willing his Queen to become aware of him.

I am ready as well.

Within moments, the Valsharess and the High Priestess arrived inside his jump circle within his tower room. His superiors stepped out from behind the wall with a perfunctory sign greeting to the scholar, though their eyes landed on Jelani D'Shea and back on him.

He waited, keeping his eyes down and his hands lightly on the warm back of the enchanted.

"You need more from this than my seed in the right place, my Queen?" he asked, already knowing the answer. He asked for the High Priestess's benefit.

"Yes, We do. You recall how to overcome Jelani's aura, Headmaster?"

Taneous looked down at the sorceress whom the Valsharess had chosen, admiring her shape and her bottom through her gown. He held her steady to keep her from sliding off the table when her legs finally gave out.

Jelani relaxed utterly, and Taneous could feel a bit of her drugged blur himself as he focused on the sound of her heart and the subtle waves of her aura. She'd feel something of what he felt as well, which would be pleasurable, but she wouldn't remember much, if anything at all.

"With her unconscious, it will not be difficult, my Queen. There will hardly be any resistance."

"You have one try, Headmaster," High Priestess Panija said with a hint of derision. "Let us hope you are potent enough so far from Braqth's altar."

"I shall succeed, High Priestess. I wager the Spider Queen never needed to provide instructions on how to procreate."

"You border on insolence, Headmaster."

Of course he did. What he was about to demonstrate was something an Abyssal Priestess could never do.

The Valsharess lifted Her hand, silencing them both, as She stepped forward to stand at Jelani's lolling head, making eye contact with Taneous. He stared once again at those sandy-yellow eyes and felt bumps rush along his skin.

The things She has Seen. For so many centuries.

His Queen took hold of the sorceress with whom he was supposed to breed, silently giving Her final blessing as She made sure the sedated sorceress wouldn't fall. She touched his aura, *tugged* on it, pulling him closer to Her; She encouraged him to kneel and lift the fine silk gown.

Almost as if it were Her own.

He dared to think it.

Taneous exposed Jelani's equally smooth and tiny smallclothes of the style at Court. He admired how they echoed and accentuated her curves, so stark white against her flawless, dark skin.

"Pull them down," his Queen instructed softly.

Hearing that command and the subtle undercurrent caused his cock to harden when he least expected it. Until that moment, he'd anticipated stroking himself for a while before being ready.

Now the Headmaster eagerly slipped the underclothing off Jelani's hips and let them fall to her ankles, smoothing his hands up her legs to settle her skirt above her waist. Finally, he nuzzled his nose and mouth against her pouty netherlips and inhaled her musk.

Jelani wasn't completely dry; she had come here under the impression that she might have the opportunity to mount the Royal Consort. Apparently, the young sorceress had looked forward to having him.

By Royal decree, he would mount her instead, and these two elders would bear witness that he used the right hole and that *he* was the sire. No delaying or forcing multiple engagements by practicing anything other than the breeding position, either. No opportunities for Jelani to mount someone else.

This would be quick.

Taneous flicked his tongue out and tasted her, sucking to help moisten her a bit more. He heard a muddled moan from Jelani, but she didn't move. He half-expected either the Valsharess or Panija to tell him to hurry but soon realized they studied his aura as it mingled with the unconscious Daughter of House D'Shea.

The Valsharess would make certain he enhanced her fertility correctly while the High Priestess observed how it should be done. Panija was too young to remember how it had once been with Davrin.

With a last kiss on Jelani's wet labia, Taneous stood up and pulled his robes over his head, setting the heavy material aside at the leg of the table. He kicked off his sandals, standing naked in front of Panija for the first time. Her crimson eyes raked over him with a covetousness she dared never show the Valsharess directly.

With a private, mental smirk for the Priestess and a last, respectful nod to his Queen, the Headmaster stepped up behind the young sorceress and pried the cleft of her bottom open with one hand, guiding his erection into place with the other. He paused, letting Panija get a good look before pushing.

One of them gasped softly, and it wasn't his Valsharess.

Taneous nudged partway in, pulled out a bit, then finally sunk deeply in, seating himself inside the unconscious cait. Her body clutched him in reflex, an unintelligible sound escaping her throat as her head flopped to one side.

The Headmaster had only to look up and lock eyes with his captivating Queen before he was thrusting hard and deep into Jelani's breeding hole. All the while, he stared at Her beautiful, exotic face. He'd begin and finish in the same place; his seed and magic were potent, he knew.

All that mattered now was what he and his Queen did *together* with Jelani's aura.

They opened the cait's aura slowly so as not to tear her, then Taneous merged with the younger, ready to impregnate another D'Shea in one coupling using all magic at their disposal.

He tried not to break her while they made an equally magical child for the Valsharess. Whether Jelani willed this or not didn't matter; the Priesthood and the Valsharess would watch her after she caught. They would take care of her as the sorceress D'Shea would eventually give birth to his replacement.

Unless it was a cait.

Then Taneous would be tasked to try again.

CHAPTER 5

2079 S.E., HOUSE AURENTHIN, SIVARAUS

"So, I hear House Chenir won over House Sil'tren," Jalen Aurenthin said as she walked with her older sister, Treya, by the grubby Pyte slaves digging up their mushroom patch.

"So what?" Treya replied. "The numbers change, what, seven levels above ours? Nine? And we stay the same? *Peh.*"

"Well," Jalen responded, uncertain. "I thought at least one of us should be up on current politics."

"Why? If we aren't fighting in the other House's army, and the Valsharess isn't pulling Her own to decide the bickering for them, why should we care?"

The younger sister bit her bottom lip, trying to muster the courage to say why she should.

She couldn't. *Not yet.*

"I also heard the Sisterhood took every bua from Matron Kilgari," Jalen said instead. "They say she was hiding two mage sons behind her Second Daughter at her estate, and the Valsharess punished her by claiming all her sons entirely. The two mages went to Headmaster Raneous, of course."

Treya rolled her eyes. "Again, so? We don't have much to do with mages anyway. Can never trust 'em, those mud-nosed, thieving worms."

Jalen's body flushed with confused fear, and she waited for her older sister to change the subject again.

Just tell her. Tell her you can make fire just pointing and thinking about it!

No one else in her family could do it. Jalen had no tutor as the other Noble Houses did. What was she going to do?

Sooner or later, I'll make a mistake ...

Jalen wandered a bit from Treya while she counted the Pytes' mushrooms, for she smelled something odd. Like a humidifier spore. Peering carefully into a nearby crevice, she found the source.

Something rare, for our healer's potions. Mother will be pleased.

She leaned in, and a strong, gloved hand landed on her shoulder as someone stepped out of the shadows beside her. Then, another dark form stepped out in front of her from the crevice. She nearly screamed, but hands smothered her mouth and grabbed her, pulling her out of sight from her sister.

Jalen struggled and tried to call for help, but three bodies including hers filled the crevice with little extra space. They held the young Davrin tightly, pressed her stomach-first into the stone wall while crowding against her. She smelled the sweaty leather of her captors and felt the cool metal of a blade at her throat.

"Surprise, cutie," another cait whispered in her ear.

Jalen flushed in pure fear to realize who they must be while the Red Sister slowly inhaled the scent at her neck. With a hum, the warrior ground something oddly firm into her buttocks before whispering again.

"So ... have you told anyone yet?"

"Think carefully," the other Red Sister whispered, reaching to clutch Jalen's front, shoving a strong hand between her thighs.

Jalen whimpered, and her hand shook as she signed, ★Told anyone what?★

"About that little spell you stumbled on," the Red Sister behind her said. "Told anyone at all?"

Her heart slammed into her ribcage, and she knew the other two caits could hear it. She signed with utter truth, ★No! No one!★

"Think she's lying?"

"We'll find out sooner or later. Just depends on if she wants more family members to disappear or less. Here, lift her dress, get me wet."

The hard ridge lifted from between her buttocks, and the more submissive Red Sister acted as ordered, pulling Jalen's gown up to expose her legs and backside to the air before kneeling to do something to the other Red Sister.

Jalen could imagine the one tonguing the leader's crotch from sound alone, but she didn't understand what that might accomplish. Everything happened too quickly for her to grasp it.

"Whatcha think, Jalen? Anyone around who could gossip to others about you being a mage?"

Something hard, smooth, and very wet slipped between her thighs, nudging into her slit. Jalen squirmed, making noise against the hand still covering her mouth. She barely had time to understand the thing was a fake phallus, and the Red Sister intended to fuck her with it.

A sharp, pinching pain forced a loud squeal into her throat before she could stop it. Her sex burned as the Red Sister grunted and thrust into her. They all smelled a hint of blood, though the dagger at her throat hadn't nicked her. Jalen grunted at the uncomfortable rod prodding her guts; it was slicker now though not because the young mage was aroused.

"Fuck me sideways," the kneeling Red Sister murmured. "I don't think she's fucked before, Hanna."

"First time for everything. Virgins don't last long around here anyway. But let's get back to my question, cutie."

Jalen stared at the stone, seeing nothing. She couldn't even remember the Red Sister's question. She felt a punishing thrust trying to force her to remember.

"Well? Anyone who can gossip at House Aurenthin about you doing magic? If there are, we'll find them. If they tell anyone else, we'll come for them, too. We'll enjoy them like this before we kill them, Jaeln, so you better tell us the truth."

She shook her head, shaking, in shock, but at least able to sign, *No one! No one!*

"Good enough," the Red Sister grunted, seeming to feel true pleasure in what she was doing. She fucked her captive like a bua would, Jalen understood that much easily enough, but with no respect whatsoever; the Red Sister was just using her hole.

The warrior even seemed to reach a climax somehow, pulling out quickly enough to allow her Sister to have a turn using a fake phallus, too. Jalen groaned in dismay, and they pulled her hair harshly before a strangely warm and fresh cock entered her sore hole.

"Shut up, mage. No one asked you."

"You're in the wrong House, so we're going to take you somewhere you can't cause trouble."

I don't understand ... she thought, enduring the second rut as her fingertips seemed to go numb from fear. *What trouble?*

What would become of her? What had she done other than be born?

Chapter 6
2150 S.E., Sivaraus

It is time. At last.

Beliza D'Shea was ready to die, but she wouldn't die at Court like her mothers and grandmothers before her. Once she had decided these two things, the prospect of entering the wilderness had dropped its oppressive, looming curtain, and she had chosen the last act of rebellion she would ever attempt.

She did not even need to succeed. The fear of failure had prevented her from acting too many times already. The fear of suffering, as well.

Ah, but the fear is always worse than the suffering itself.

Someone had told her this in Reverie, and she believed him. Someone wise, older than herself, and she had made it past four hundred.

No small feat within the Valsharess's official House at Court.

Her Mother hadn't lived this long. Neither had her Grandmother.

Perhaps her elders hadn't made as many concessions as she had, as far as she remembered. With no land to call their own and no single Matron to lead them, the "Sorceress House" still possessed a lot of status within the Palace itself. The Daughters of D'Shea were not unlike the Headmaster of the Tower — in fact, all their sons ended up there — though still well below the Priesthood and Sisterhood.

House D'Shea was small but potent, often acting as the mediator or a third objective view in disputes between the landed Houses if they didn't erupt into a coup. They were advisors to the Queen with a long but fuzzy history of being feared and shunned by the other Noble Houses for reasons no one seemed to remember anymore.

Keep your allies close and your adversaries closer.

The only one in Sivaraus to who seemed unconcerned with this ubiquitous bit of advice was the Valsharess Herself. Untouchable, untroubled by the slum or the fringe, about whom were gossiped in looking for ways to cause civil unrest.

With the massive power of the Sisterhood and the Priesthood standing in the way and enforcing Her Will, with the Wizard's Tower and the Sorceress House on auxiliary support, not even an alliance of the top three Noble Houses could challenge the Queen, let alone some dirty underground black market.

Likewise, the Noble houses desperately wanted to keep what they had, so they willingly snitched on each other, performing most of the grunt work in maintaining the Queen's order.

"The fringe makes a good, continuous source of slaves and sacrifices," High Priestess Kian had drawled in her personal quarters within the Sanctuary. "Captured by their own actions and broken in the dungeons before being made useful. The black market is nothing more."

The escaping sorceress would depend on these "fringe" Davrin to leave Sivaraus behind. She must believe some of them could live without the Valsharess, for she discovered recently why keeping adversaries closer had indeed concerned the Valsharess most of all.

A few marks later, Beliza D'Shea stood within a jump circle well outside of the Palace, one built in secret over the last few spans by her instruction. It was miraculously well-hidden. Although her heart pounded in anticipation of a Red Sister stepping out of the shadows with a smirk, this didn't happen.

Jaush of House Aurenthin was there instead.

★You made it,★ he signed, adding his winsome youth's smile.

He had brought her everything she needed to know to try this; in his meticulous collection of details told her where to aim. His head was still attached to his shoulders. No enforcer held him at knifepoint.

Jaush was proof that Beliza still remained ahead of the schemes within the Palace.

Help me destroy the circle, she signed without a formal acknowledgment, safely neutralizing the most dangerous rune first.

Her much younger bua took no insult as he messed up all her careful work without a firm idea of what he was doing.

There.

The Sisterhood could not follow her this way. Let them work a little harder to reclaim her hide.

This way, Jaush signed, impressively silent as he led her out from among the debris. *Let's get you changed. And remember to breathe, sorceress.*

Beliza waited for that last-moment betrayal, expecting it, and ready to embrace it should it come. Jaush would do what he needed to live and try to escape again into the wilderness. Although, if the Red Sisters had turned him against her, then there was little chance he would live much longer than her.

Four marks later, the sorceress walked into new territory using her own two feet, still free. The slum barely paid her any attention, for her clothes were smelly, ratty, and drab like theirs.

She kept her magical aura viciously suppressed while Jaush contacted many others on the way, signing his way past them or calling on a few favors of his own. He put up a confident front for her, though she could tell he was alert for possible trouble.

The path gave way to wilder space, rough and dark, lacking in sentient auras and significant upkeep. Beliza began to believe that Jaush hadn't betrayed her into the hands of her keepers, and Jaush himself wasn't followed by his contacts.

After six marks, her back and legs felt gloriously tired from climbing boulders and crouching through low passages. The dark anticipation clutching her chest gave way to something better but just as tight and frightening. It made her eyes water.

Sorceress? Jaush asked when he noticed. *Do you need a rest?*

★I think so,★ she admitted. ★Where is a safe place?★

He smirked. ★None out here, but we can hide, cover our tracks, and hope nothing finds us. If it does, we can fight it off, get eaten, or be captured.★

She nodded. What else could she expect as a docile brood stock wandering out of her stable? Every cycle would be unpredictable and unrecognizable from here on out. She may have few cycles left in any case. That had been acceptable, or she would never have tried this.

★Jaush,★ she gestured for his attention after they had found a place to rest. ★I must tell you now, I must tell someone. House D'Shea is a false one. It is made up of mages stripped out of other lineages.★

He understood her but the statement didn't excite him. Baffled, he shook his head. ★Such intrigue isn't useful to me, sorceress, and 'secret' or no, it makes sense. The Valsharess draws upon other lineages to create the Sisterhood and the Priesthood and the Tower, does She not? Not to mention Her army. What's one more organization groomed to be loyal to Her?★

★I believe your House Aurenthin was the first one She culled for mages to make House D'Shea,★ she replied bluntly. ★That is as far back as I have been able to track our name. I believe we arose out of the lowest House. Yours.★

He frowned. ★Okay?★

She exhaled silently. ★Think! If it began with your House, then Aurenthin used to be powerful! You were intentionally made powerless, the magic removed, and all your tutors relocated elsewhere. House Aurenthin was a threat to the Queen.★

Jaush grinned with a youth's charm. ★That makes a certain amount of sense. So are you saying you and I are related?★

★Distantly,★ she signed, her lips pursed. ★Long enough ago to be strangers now.★

His eyes dropped over her, appreciative and insolent. ★I consider that a good thing.★

Beliza felt her body flush in irritation and an inconvenient arousal. This one, this *bua*, had no mage's aura to speak of, though he was still a trueborn Davrin. He possessed the expected sensitivity to magic, the ability to "call" magical items to answer his will, if done correctly, but not much more.

He was oddly fascinating to her instead of contemptable because he had managed to fool so many Priestesses with enough wit and resources not reliant on magic. He had proved without a doubt that the powerful Sanctuary underestimated those "beneath" their notice.

Beliza had never spent much time around any Davrin but mages before meeting this serving bua by chance. In theory, it was chance. Or luck. She had never been able to tell the one from the other.

★So what were you looking for during your time in the Sanctuary?★ she asked him, not for the first time.

Jaush shrugged. ★I found it. Moot now. Where do you want me to take you, sorceress?★

Her palms were sweating; she rubbed them on her scent-masked pants before signing her answer. ★Deeper this direction. I found records of drakes with intelligence.★

★Drakes?★ he repeated with a wry, disbelieving smirk. ★You risked everything to get out of the Sanctuary, out of Sivaraus, with nowhere to go except to sit and taste what real freedom is in a rock-nest. And first you want to look for those thieving, jabbering lizards?★

Beliza's temper flared, and she lunged for Jaush in the tiny space, pushing him up against the stone and cupping his crotch to get his attention.

At once, she had it. He met her eyes, wide, surprised, and delighted. His cock swiftly stiffened in her palm. Whatever spice and nuance she'd enjoyed in mounting a deplorably low bua like Jaush, Beliza had become accustomed to the taste of it. He was *entirely* her choice, and she was his.

No one else.

"Yes, I seek those 'thieving, jabbering lizards,' " she whispered without voice, neither of them blinking. "And I see you know more about them than I do."

"*Mmn,*" he cooed, his prick pulsing once as he glanced once more out into the wilderness. "Maybe."

"Any more than you've said? They steal things and they chatter?"

"Little hoarders, all of them, sorceress," Jaush whispered, unable to keep from smiling as she stroked him with a firm grip. "They understand taunting laughter."

Beliza nodded and with one hand started pushing her pants down her hips, first one side then the other. His eyes dropped to her well-trimmed crotch, and he inhaled slowly catch a whiff as she opened her thighs. He was such a slum animal.

"Do they live solitary or in social groups?" she whispered, turning around to place her back to him and sit in his lap.

Her pants were around her knees and the bare, smooth skin of her backside replaced her hand in rubbing through his trousers. Jaush encircled her waist with an arm and held her close and steady, bracing himself as he lifted her briefly to pull his bottoms over his ass. She helped him get them down just far enough.

Finally, they relaxed as he held her with both arms, sniffing and nuzzling the back of her neck while she slowly shifted her hips. His erection was trapped between her soft thighs as she rubbed her own moist slit along his pole.

"Well?" she asked, teasing him as she prevented an attempt to worm his way inside her.

"Huh?" He slurped in drool.

She smirked. "Drakes. Solitary or groups?"

He inhaled as she writhed. "Both. Depends on the drake."

"What have you seen most often?"

"Groups. A parent with young, or a grown pair or three."

Beliza figured her scent wafting like this for long was a bad idea out here, so she reached down to push the head of the Aurenthin male's prick into her cleft. Boldly, he claimed more depth the moment he felt her body surrounding him, swallowing his groan as he probed deeper.

They must be as quiet as possible, but Beliza would allow this lowest, distantly related and barely Noble bua to hump himself to climax and spurt inside her. *Far from the first time.*

She wanted to see and smell the white cream dripping down her dark thighs. The taboo of it stiffened her nipples like nothing ever had for centuries in that luxurious Palace prison. The sorceress also teased herself with the mystery of Jaush's origin, about which he knew nothing himself.

What had House Aurenthin and House D'Shea once been together to wind up like this?

Asking this question while feeling his phallus squeezed tight inside flushed her sex with pleasure as easily as the thought of being "soiled" by an unworthy male. One *not* chosen by the Valsharess.

Ha!

He couldn't be so unworthy if he was what the Valsharess had been trying so earnestly to keep apart from the invented Sorceress House.

JAUSH HAD NOT SPOKEN FALSELY ABOUT THE DRAKES.

Beliza had received a few glimpses before they retreated and experienced two attempts to steal food and weapons. They indeed knew how to laugh but only did so when they were seen, caught in the act dragging away something belonging to the Davrin. They swiftly disappeared, as if by magic, melting into the silent shadows.

You asked to see some, sorceress, Jaush signed with amusement. *Now what?*

Beliza had no answer, really. She still had no plans for her own future — a first in her entire existence — and she hadn't planned for it to be long. Jaush seemed to carry a degree of luck around with him but how long before it would run out and something trapped them?

This was what Beliza waited for.

Do you wish to return to Sivaraus, Jaush? she asked him, the flow of her hands neutral in tone.

He noticed and eyed her with curiosity and suspicion. *I could take it or leave it. Why?*

I do not expect to make a full life out here, she signed. *I haven't the experience, I know this, though I plan to make a good showing with the magic I command. I will die free and no Tragar or scavenger party will take me alive. You may return to the city any time. You need not stay or take the same risks with me.*

The young bua eyed her with growing amusement. What did he find so funny?

The upper Houses love their spectacle, don't they? he said, shaking his head.

She wanted to strike him though he kept signing.

Believe, sorceress, that I'm enjoying this adventure. I've never wandered the Deepearth with no purpose before, certainly not with one who makes the important parts so easy: cleaning water, calling fire, mending clothing, boots, and tools. You don't complain much about the blisters and the work for a Palace Noble. If you've got no plans, let's keep going. That's good enough for me.

Beliza couldn't decide if she should be insulted or grateful.

Later, given how wet she was when his turgid prick once again slid in between her thighs, she decided it didn't matter.

THE TWO DAVRIN ELVES LASTED LONGER IN THEIR AIMLESS WANDERING THAN anyone back home would have wagered.

That's because, Jaush signed, *our exploration is 'aimless,' not 'clueless.'*

Her bua estimated they had been outside Sivaraus for about half a turn, and they had each suffered their share of attacks, injuries, and close calls. None had yet ended their life or seen them enslaved by another race. For as long as they did not become complacent and outnumbered, or fight between themselves, the couple remained free to travel the Deepearth as they saw fit.

The ex-subjects of the Valsharess moved with appropriate alertness through one territory after another. Of all other creatures challenging them for space and resources, the darkest colored drakes were the only ones who seemed to enjoy tracking Jaush and Beliza over long distances without always engaging them. At least five were individuals Jaush recognized from among the first group they'd bothered much closer to Sivaraus.

★You tried communicating with them,★ Jaush suggested one evening. ★Maybe that spell was wrong. Maybe you promised something without realizing it.★

Beliza only sighed to herself, as baffled as he was by the drakes' behavior.

They had seen a few lighter-colored groups of drakes as well, which were more territorial and hostile — and less intelligent. They would disengage entirely once Beliza and Jaush left them uncontested ownership of the area. The dark drakes seemed to wander between areas as much as the two fugitives, and they were many times more curious than their light-scaled cousins.

What seemed more odd was that these specific, winged lizards had managed to filch enough food from the Davrin to annoy them, but the beasts never took all of it. They seemed to consciously avoid single-minded gluttony or any actions which would leave the travelers starving, nor did their taunting led to anything disastrous.

Regardless, the two Davrin never rested in Reverie at the same time, and if they'd ever been tempted to do so, the lingering, playful drakes were ample reason to resist.

★I've tried engaging them again,★ she said. ★They always vanish.★

★You're not exaggerating,★ Jaush commented. ★I am certain they transport themselves somehow. There one moment, and then they are gone.★

The sorceress narrowed her eyes at him. She had been privately thinking the same thing for some time now, even as she sensed no explicit magic being used. Interesting that even non-mages could tell with enough repetition and observation.

★Interesting ability,★ Jaush added.

★Understatement,★ she signed with a smirk.

The Davrin would never hear the drakes coming if that was their goal. The test of simple reflexes would determine the outcome should a drake appear beside or atop a Dark Elf, whether it could dodge a blade through the wing or an explosive burn to the face.

Thus far, the beasts had not tested that.

Spans later, long enough that even Jaush had lost count, they unintentionally got too close to a new race with tentacles attached to their faces. Only then did one of the drakes do something other than stalk, spy, and steal.

"*Jaush ... !*" Beliza cried when something she could neither see nor sense struck him down.

He'd fallen clutching his head, and three gaunt, purple-skinned mages drifted eerily toward her next. She couldn't move!

Staring at their clawed hands, their huge, lantern-like eyes, feeling something on the edge of her thoughts, Beliza imagined the same feeling as a Priestess's enchanted blade hovering at the throat of an altar-sacrifice.

This was it, then. They wouldn't escape the Deepearth's dangers this time.

What torture do these Abyss-spawn have in store for us ... ?

Air sucked upon itself right beside her. The following burst was tremendously loud as an unseen force thumping against her like a solid wall. She stumbled, falling next to Jaush to cover him with her body. She didn't know why she did that except to have one last whiff of his scent.

"Fire!" a small voice squawked in Davrin. "Mage fire!"

Beliza gaped upon lifting her head. The little black drake filled a stretch of skin beneath its chin to its taut capacity then released it in one blast, knocking the bulbous-eyed creatures back before they had sat up again.

All three of the other tentacle-faces were down.

The sorceress was galvanized into action and scrambled up to cast her most powerful fire spell, pouring every drop of her will into it.

"*Furamil ioshen!*"

The fireball engulfed them, caught them up in its belly, set them on ablaze to make their moist skin crackle. She maintained its radiance and intensity. She had to make sure they were *dead*, even if she must hold her breath against the stench. What terrible sound they made without mouths!

Oh, Braqth, what are they?!

The drake nosed Jaush persistently with the small horn on its snout, repeatedly jabbing to force the Davrin to groan in protest.

"Go," the drake muttered. "Go. Must go!"

Trembling, Beliza knew the beast was right. Those three can't have been alone. They would be tracked with so much light, heat, and stench to trail back to its source. She grabbed an outstretched arm to pull Jaush up to sit, working to lay him across her shoulders the way he had taught her.

Almost a turn ago, with her soft life within the Palace Court, she would not have been able to do this. Beliza was much stronger now from living in the wilderness. She looked for and made eye contact with the drake, something the beast apparently waited for, and Beliza could swear she recognized that perky, concerned expression.

"This way."

The drake scuttled in one direction, spreading its wings to take off down one of the smaller tunnels. Beliza whispered a small enchantment for added endurance to sprint after it at a good clip. She didn't have time to second-guess or wonder why the beast had revealed itself only in dire circumstances.

Maybe she would be led straight into a tentacle trap, but that seemed a terribly long and convoluted plot for a curious thief who just helped her roast three of the monsters alive.

Eventually, Beliza's spell wore off and she stumbled, forced to set Jaush down before she dropped his head onto the stone. She gasped for air, trembled with exhaustion and fear, and wished her companion was awake to find them a good place to hide.

"Here," the drake whispered, showing her a hidden crevice which took them off even this ragged path.

Hooking her arms beneath Jaush's pits, the sorceress clutched him to her while standing almost straight up. She dragged him with her into the tight passage, fretting about the heel marks left behind in the fine dirt. As if in response, the drake slithered over and started mussing them up with belly, tail, and wings, leaving any mark indistinct.

Amazing ... what are you doing, little beast ... .?

Helping. What does it look like?

The sorceress bit back a gasp at the unexpected response. She had thought herself alone in her head. Was this some ill aftereffect of the mind attack on her mind?

No time to wonder, the drake reprimanded. *No stopping. Protect mate and young.*

Mate? ... wait ... 'young'?!

Her stomach chilled as familiar signs which she had been ignoring reared up in her mind.

Oh, fuck me ...

The drake nodded, showing teeth in a grin. *Watched plenty enough to recognize breeding, mistress.*

EVENTUALLY, JAUSH'S CRUSHING HEADACHE RECEDED, AND THEY HAD STARTED moving again. He needed a long time beyond that to be convinced they weren't being tracked.

So ... . Jaush signed hesitantly, eyeing the drake scouting ahead. *It's female?*

Beliza nodded. *She is.*

And she talks to you now.

Correct.

Does she have a name?

Beliza's lips tugged on a smile. *Not one I can pronounce even in sign. We have agreed on 'Ilka.'*

Ilka. Why is she here? Where did she come from?

You recall that group of five that's been trailing us? The siring male led them, to teach them how to survive before they go off on their own.

So, she's young. Jaush looked around the darkness. *Are the others still following us?*

Probably. Ilka came out to help after you were struck down.

Why?

I don't know exactly. She's said she heard me louder than the others when I tried that communication spell, though I thought it failed. Over the quad-spans 'listening,' she has absorbed our language, and we can share thoughts.

Jaush's mouth twisted. *That's not possible … *

Isn't it? she challenged. *It's magic, and I've done things I wasn't expecting before.*

Her bua frowned but remained silent for a while, thinking. Jaush had spent more time thinking after living with her for a turn, especially with her willingness to answer his questions without belittlement or impatience. Beliza encouraged it, and they had worked out their problems better this way.

Why did the those purple things attack me first? he asked. *You are the mage. Everyone knows to take out the mage first.*

Maybe they didn't know, she signed. *I've never even heard of such creatures before, and you haven't either. You were the only one with obvious weapons out. Maybe they assumed you were the threat, and that was their mistake.*

Lucky us, he commented. *But you hadn't been suppressing your aura when they surprised us. They should have seen it.*

She shrugged. *They didn't.*

Some 'mages.'

It's just a term, Beliza protested. *I don't know what they are, but all three could attack like the Tragar mind mage, only more so.*

Jaush shook his head. *We've avoided all Tragar Dwarves. They're dangerous but don't like to go far out of their territory.*

I know. But according to witness reports I read, some of them can move or throw objects with their will alone, and it's not magic as far as the wizards have been able to determine. They can overcome the will of another, like some of our mind-bending spells.

But it's not magic, Jaush repeated. *So they aren't mages and they couldn't see your aura.*

She shrugged helplessly. *I never studied the grey dwarves deeply.

There was probably more to know, the Queen's been archiving the area around us for centuries.★

★Doesn't do us good now.★ His eyes hadn't stopped scanning for danger, his ears alert for changes that weren't part of Ilka's gliding or perching. ★So I guess it's the three of us? Ilka is staying?★

Beliza nodded but then turned away and bit her lower lip. She still hadn't told Jaush that she had caught again. She had been foolish many times, yielding in the heat and throes of lust, but—

It wasn't supposed to happen again this soon!

She had *reason* for timing her escape from Sivaraus the way she had!

Nonetheless, when her young bua sought to pleasure her once again, Beliza didn't turn him down. It wasn't as if more cream in her cunt would somehow make her more pregnant.

QUAD-SPANS LATER, WHEN BELIZA WOULD HAVE REAL TROUBLE KEEPING HER appetite and sore breasts secret from Jaush, they found a wild cave garden.

"Garden" was only a term, as no sentient being had designed or tended it, but was one of those rare places in the Deepearth with an abnormally high concentration of lichen, moss, fungi, and various rare plants. Their accompanying worms, insects, and larger animals were the actual tenders of the garden.

Such places didn't tend to last long before something discovered it and stripped it of all its resources. The remoteness of these hidden spots was the only reason they existed at all.

Beliza's first thought was whether she could identify something that might cause her to miscarry. Any number of them could be poisonous enough to do the job, but knowing which toxin wouldn't outright kill her while still putting her body under enough strain to expel the passenger in her womb? Without any resources or prior knowledge on such things ...

Yeah, good luck with that, as Jaush would say.

Recovering afterward was no small feat, either, depending on Jaush and Ilka for too long and leaving them all vulnerable. Poisoning herself now might be worse than simply carrying on, but sooner or later the balance could shift.

Beliza was becoming more and more afraid, despite her iron resolve not to show it.

Just tell him, Ilka said for the fourth time that cycle. *You can't hide much longer, and would need a potion maker to safely reject breeding now, yes?*

That was true. Given Beliza's purpose at the Palace, despite all distractions until recently, she knew the Valsharess and Her Priestesses held a vested interest in keeping such knowledge or contacts out of her reach.

No one in the bloodline of House D'Shea had learned how to make those potions. Because of this, Beliza didn't know what she could do except to suffer, starve, and eventually miscarry anyway in the wilderness.

Would slow and inevitable be better or worse than quick and harsh? Without knowing if she would survive either way, it was a terrifying decision to make, and she hadn't been able to choose yet.

The voice in her dream had been right. The fear of suffering was the worst, but she couldn't see how she would avoid it. Ilka was right as well; Jaush would know soon. He was observant; he had already commented on how hot her breasts felt to him the last time they'd coupled.

It's not fair, she thought. *I was supposed to have ten turns, an entire decade, before chancing to catch again. This wasn't even a turn. What did they do to me?*

Feel pity, mistress, Ilka acknowledged. *But don't drown in it.*

Beliza sighed. The drake was an astute but annoyingly blunt "second voice" to her own practical thoughts. *Very well. I will tell him.*

Maybe talking would help, though Beliza didn't figure it would summon the amount of food she'd need if they went on like this.

Remember, you'd been ready to die when you left the Palace, Ilka said. *This is still the case, yes?*

Beliza blinked, her mind sweeping over the many adventures she'd had already, all those experiences she had witnessed and from which she had learned. The conversations with her companion, authentic because no one was watching her and because he hadn't been beaten until he tried not to think.

And now adding this extraordinary connection with a small, magical creature?

No, she answered with a touch of anger at her own attitude. *I'm not ready to die.*

Ilka grinned, showing teeth again. *Good.*

That eve, they set camp near the garden though not within it. Welcome as it was over barren rock, neither Davrin nor drake would rest among potentially venomous insects or small creatures, nor breathe in the vapors and spores of unknown plants and fungi.

After eating, when Beliza and Jaush were awake before trading watch duty, they often conversed while sipping magically purified water, and went over recent mistakes or observations. Rarely did their plans lead them forward more than a cycle or two unless they were near a settlement which may or may not trade with them.

Beliza reflected on a rather large mistake before saying anything, wondering if she could have resisted the temptation for pleasure out here alone.

Except for one Davrin bua over two centuries younger than me.

Maybe she should have been extra careful and only taken him in her non-breeding orifices …

So, Jaush signaled, catching her attention, *you seem like you have something to say.*

Beliza looked at his face, his body language. He was wary. He wouldn't be able to help that; even still young, he knew an unhappy matron was something he could not ignore and maintain his well-being. She smirked, which turned into a grimace when she thought about how her peers would have had the luxury to shift blame onto the male.

How readily another might distract herself and others from the embarrassment of her poor judgment by entertaining them with the shaming and suffering of a powerless bua. She felt a little sick from what she'd seen at Court on things like this.

Back in Sivaraus, Jaush would be in mortal danger for my own stupidity.

But that was only one of many reasons she had left.

Beliza took a deep breath and looked at Ilka, who was perched with wings drawn down tight, watching them unblinking. The very tip of her tail flicked back and forth in front of her forepaws.

The drake didn't seek to be entertained by this, unlike the sorceress's peers back home. The magical creature only waited for Beliza to follow through on her convictions, whatever they may be.

The runaway from House D'Shea looked at her Aurenthin bua's worried eyes. She signed simply, *I'm pregnant.*

Slow shock caused him to go still and expressionless, and she gave him time to fully absorb the statement since she had no idea where to go next anyway. She watched his heat sign change in the pitch dark, like those times he'd been under threat, when he had to choose whether to fight or flee. Fortunately, he did neither.

He asked her, *And ... I'm the sire?*

Beliza's mouth quivered as an inconvenient burble of laughter lodged in her throat. *Certain things buas do not assume about the matrons, do they? Even lengths from nowhere.*

Ilka snickered.

No, the sorceress signed with irony, *I've been sneaking away to a secret lust-nest every eve as you've been resting, Jaush, leaving you unguarded so I could get my belly stuffed by someone else.*

He just stared at her.

Yes! Of course you're the sire! she signed with frustrated release of overwhelming tension.

Jaush was still tense but decided to smile. *You're getting better at sarcasm, D'Shea.*

An unnecessarily exaggerated bad habit I learned from you, she accused.

She could see his teeth as he grinned in the dark, though their communication paused. He was only beginning the same paths of thought she had already worn into ruts inside her own mind.

You'll need more food, he signed.

A lot more, she emphasized, *over the next half turn. My need will lessen for a time after the one turn mark but then will increase again as I near birthing. If we make it that far.★

Jaush pursed his lips. ★You are familiar. Have you had a child … ?★

Beliza nodded, a hard spot centering in her throat as she swallowed. ★Several. I just weaned my last before I ran away with you. I left my four-turn-old Daughter with the Priestesses back at the Sanctuary. But that is what they wanted anyway … ★

Her hands stilled, and she felt more pain spread from her throat down to her chest, making it hard to breathe quietly or steadily. She had purposefully *not* thought about her little Claret D'Shea or her older siblings since her escape.

★I didn't … um … question,★ Jaush stammered, ★I'm sorry, Beliza, though I know that doesn't help us now. Unless you … um … already decided to, uh, expel … ?★

She shook her head as she slumped. ★I don't know how to do it safely, Jaush.★

He blinked, clearly surprised. ★But all matrons choose whether and when to carry. You *must* know.★

They stared at each other for several heartbeats in utter stillness. Her worried expression turned into a dark frown.

★Not House D'Shea, Jaush,★ she signed bitterly. ★The Valsharess and Her Priesthood decides that for us. I told you once that the mages had been stripped from your House, yes? And House D'Shea was artificial.★

He nodded, paying more attention now than he had when she'd first mentioned this.

★We breed how and when *they* decide,★ she said. ★They're making a concentrated mage line, though I am not certain of the purpose beyond, as you said, another organized group loyal to the Queen. I know that this … common knowledge of making every child born a *desired* child is … is not so common among some of us. I have already had four children, all of them under compulsion, not my conscious decision. None of them were sired by males I would have ever chosen for myself.★

Except you.

Her eyes blurred when she thought that. After a blink, her cheeks were wet with tears. *Perfect, such dignity. Braqth damn it all!*

Ilka snuffled softly and slinked over to curl up in her lap; it helped as the sorceress cuddled the drake close to her.

"I wasn't supposed to catch this early after weaning," Beliza whispered. "I-I'm sorry, I thought we were safe for several turns at least, maybe a decade … but … even now I won't go back. *I won't*, though I will likely starve. Still, we should consider turning around before the hunger grows too much. You could return to Sivaraus rather than be left out here alone."

Jaush shook his head at first, but she leaned forward and signed urgently.

*You know how much work it is to keep us both fed! You can't take this on alone out here, Jaush, and I will not be as helpful given enough time! As much as the Davrin hate and fight among each other, we *need* each other when it comes to breeding! There's a reason we leave other matrons alone when they are close to giving birth! It is our one weakness, the easiest thing to exploit but to the detriment of us all!*

*But — *

Her temper snapped at any suggestion that it wasn't as bad as it seemed.

Jaush, do you honestly expect the Deepearth to leave me alone and untouched while I flounder and bleed like a landed fish? Whether I weaken from hunger so much as to miscarry or bear a full-grown infant, I will die out here! And it was my own foolish lust for a bua like you that did it!

CHAPTER 7

2151 S.E., THE DEEPEARTH WILDERNESS

BELIZA PROBABLY WOULDN'T BE RESTING IF NOT FOR ILKA. THE TWO SNUGGLED together for warmth and, occasionally, the drake's eye would crack open to make sure Jaush was still there.

I'm not sneaking off, if that's what you're assuming, he thought in a challenge to the sorceress's beast, even if Ilka couldn't hear his thoughts as she could those of her mistress.

Jaush took first watch after Beliza's flood of doom and dismay had battered him for over a mark, yet most of the accusations he'd been expecting to read or hear from his traveling companion hadn't been signed or whispered.

Beliza blamed only herself for this turn in their fortune, despite that it took two to breed. He remembered quite often picturing his seed washing over her high-status womb repeatedly as she urged him on. The taboo was such a damned high in its moment, though he hadn't thought hard about the consequences until now. He had figured she knew what she was doing.

Apparently, so had she.

They'd been satisfied with him obeying her and indulging her while he indulged himself.

What mattered to him most, however, was that Beliza hadn't turned to petty contempt of him to distract from her true worries. She had not hurled insults to make him feel small and valueless as the fear had overtaken her.

The genuineness he'd always liked about her remained, even now.

Truthfully, this was why he was still with her. He had seen her at her worst, and her "worst" wasn't any more than those females at House Aurenthin. The caits and matron of his blood were the reason he was even free to walk out and about as he did. He knew he was lucky to have the Mother he'd had.

If what had been done to Beliza D'Shea at the Sanctuary was true, if what little she had just told him of her past had happened, then the sorceress had been tortured far more than him. The Priestesses conditioned her to take the burdens until it was too much, until she collapsed from them.

No wonder she still clings to Noble spectacle, he thought, keeping his senses open but letting his mind work their problem a bit.

The three of them were far from dead, and a possibly solution seemed fairly simple to him.

Trade for the right potion, if possible. Obtain food, whatever it takes. Always seek better shelter.

Jaush needed to look seriously at all options and every opportunity which could save his companion's life, one way or another. Yes, they couldn't continue exactly as they had been, as fun and exciting as it was, but there was more than one way to survive in the Deepearth.

As odd as it felt knowing he had helped to quicken an unborn within her womb, his first as far as he knew, Jaush must put Beliza above any of them. She was the one most in danger and she knew it, or she wouldn't be showing such fear right now, like an animal caught in a trap.

Matrons couldn't help but know their vulnerabilities more keenly than any bua, he'd always thought. They had so many responsibilities building a place where children could be born and thrive. Beliza would need him to take on some of those worries for her; she had no one else.

If I can find a way to lift the burden, or share it, I will.

Pretty straightforward. She just had to allow him to try.

This eve wasn't the time to push, though. Let her sleep on it, a few times if necessary, and he would keep his senses open.

As he always had.

BELIZA'S PESSIMISM TRIED JAUSH'S PATIENCE MORE THAN ONCE IN THE FOLLOW-ing spans. It even sabotaged one opportunity he had thought he'd seen, approaching a tribe of Yutogul near a large lake they'd found. Her open distrust had made all Jaush's efforts unsalvageable with the overall friendly race, and he had needed to shift his tactics.

Soon after they left the lake, instead of trading knowledge of the plants he'd collected from the garden, Jaush stole food from a group of Ketro with Ilka's help, because there was no way a Ketro would knowingly trade untainted food with a Davrin.

Beliza had been angry at him for "risking" it and refused to eat.

You must let me try to help! he tried to explain.

Knowledge of those plants won't do either of us any good!

Funny thing for a mage to say.

No, funny thing for a healer to say, of which you and I most certainly are not!

Jaush threw up his hands, waiting for her spiking appetite to change her mind. He also took some time to think over the last several spans during his next watch.

She's afraid of losing me, he realized as he tried to see through his bafflement in her behavior. *Now more than ever before.*

If she had to die, then let someone else of her own choosing live on. A mother's instinct, they called it, but it could apply to others. Beliza saw no way she or her unborn would live despite his encouragement, but she wanted *him* to survive through her own "decision" of sending him back to Sivaraus, which he'd been resisting.

Neither of them was taking the other's encouragement much to heart, but there was little reason for him to get upset with her blocking him every half-step. Mother would be telling him now that he was sliding into the power struggles and distractions, not seeing the obvious above him.

Right. I know what drives you, Beliza. Time to play again.

Jaush patiently coaxed his sorceress into a game of chance he'd taught her for entertainment, especially to trade sexual favors. Beliza's libido and interest lessened while her appetite grew, but at least the spark of fond nostalgia worked in his favor, and he'd found some of her favorite mushrooms to barter with.

She won the first few games and was nibbling contentedly on meaty-sweet brown flesh while scratching Ilka beneath her wings. She sat at ease, waiting for his next barter.

Now pick a direction to walk, he suggested.

She nodded. *I win this one, we head back toward that garden for a few cycles.*

Jaush smiled at her obvious motive. *Brings me closer to Sivaraus.* *Agreed. And if I win, you don't interfere on my next opportunity to trade for knowledge about the pressed plants from that same garden.*

She stiffened indignantly. *You … *

He shrugged innocently. *It's even. The knowledge won't do us any good, remember? What do you care, sorceress?*

Fine, she agreed sulkily.

Then she cursed aloud when his luck returned, and he won that round.

THAT NEXT OPPORTUNITY TOOK MORE TIME THAN JAUSH HAD WANTED. THE longer it took, the more Beliza fretted about the distance they traveled from Sivaraus and the hungrier she grew.

Not only that, but he was beginning to see what four forced births in captivity did to a matron's mind when she could never take her mind off the fifth.

"B-Braqth's agents are after me!" she whispered one eve after she'd woken from Reverie, badly disoriented and feverish. "They must know!

The Valsharess probably had a Vision ... they'll not let me bleed it out! They'll make me keep it and tear him away and make me forget again ... !"

"Shh, Beliza. Shh. I'm here." The young Aurenthin cradled her for most of the next mark, holding her tightly. *Come on, I have something for you to eat. You're with me. You're far, far from the Priestesses. They can't reach you here."

Jaush regretted taking this so lightly at the start. Court spectacle or not, this kind of stress had taken its toll on the powerful sorceress. The brief period he'd spent with Beliza, he thought he knew her ...

But the part I know is the side of her not thinking about the Priestesses of Braqth.

Jaush felt the creeping doubt of concern that maybe she was right. Maybe he couldn't help at all. She said she wouldn't go back, so she still expected to die from lack of resources.

"Ilka," he whispered, beckoning for the drake to come closer while they were foraging. "She doesn't really want to die, does she?"

The drake wasn't her usual confident, playful self either, keeping constant alert and even hunting for herself less than she had been. The fact that she nuzzled Jaush's palm with her horned nose told him she was worried.

"Strange place," the shadow drake said. "Giving bad dreams."

Jaush looked around him. He didn't think it felt any stranger than most of the Deepearth. "So they're not real? It's just in her head?"

Ilka shook her head. "Is real. Is warning. Sense magic."

"So we should move out as soon as possible?"

Ilka's glossy, black eyes looked around them unblinking. "Will make no difference."

"Why?"

When she didn't answer, he thought to ask another question. "What will happen to you if ... the ... if she gives up?"

Ilka just whined and wouldn't answer that either, throwing her head toward their camp still in sight. Then she flew back to her mistress.

Jaush harvested more mushrooms and lichen to add to the blueblood soup while thinking this over. Some strange magic was giving Beliza bad dreams? And Ilka said it would make no difference if he moved them out or not.

What, then? What can I do?

Nothing, really, except keep his mind open to that next opportunity. What would his Mother say now?

If there's magic, there must be a mage.

Yes, but a mage powerful enough to unnerve his own sorceress in Reverie? Maybe he should skip over this one and take the next opportunity.

You do that, and you're no son of mine, he heard his Mother say at the back of his thoughts.

Jaush sighed to himself.

Since when did any of House Aurenthin let themselves be intimidated by another's dreams?

Especially a mage.

JAUSH WAS AWAKE TO SEE THE FIGURE COMING DOWN THE TUNNEL. IMMEDI-ately, he slipped into his carefully chosen and defensible position within the jagged stone. Beliza was only accessible by moving a large, camouflaged boulder which covered a short passage to a tiny waterfall.

This wouldn't have worked if she'd been awake. Ilka had helped him time it, but only with the understanding that she would perch and witness.

"You disappear, opportunity seeker," the drake had grumbled, "and Mistress will know why and how."

"Fine. Though you could be more useful than that."

Tattling beast.

The figure coming now was bipedal, top-heavy, and bulky, possessing a long stride graceful and hypnotic. It had a tail, Jaush was sure, but he couldn't make out much of the figure otherwise.

Was this the mage? Or at least the magical creature causing dreams? Would it speak? *Could* it?

Jaush hadn't decided upon a hail and wasn't convinced he'd been spotted. He contemplated letting the creature pass by first, maybe following it if it still seemed like a good idea to make contact ... ?

It stopped parallel to his hiding place, tail waving smoothly, and only very long practice kept Jaush's heart steady and inaudible when he recognized in its profile that the extra bulk was a pair of large, black wings.

Shit.

If Ilka had been larger — no, enormous — and if she stood on two legs, Beliza's shadow drake might look something like this.

The mage tilted his jaw toward Jaush, a readable, wry smile on his very toothy mouth. "A bit far from your Great Cavern, aren't you, Queen's Elf?"

Jaush blinked hearing the low, rumbling voice. *Good guess.*

"It's not a guess," the drake-mage said calmly, as if he'd heard. "And you have no idea, do you? Come out where I can see you."

The Davrin looked around for Ilka. She had vanished into some shadow. *Great.* Sighing, he slowly stood up, expecting to have a spell thrown at him. He was prepared.

"Yes, you have a nice ring of protection on your left hand. Just come down. You want to talk, not fight or steal."

Jaush checked himself just before he obeyed without thought.

Wait ...

"Are you reading my mind?"

"You are thinking out loud," the huge Drake said as if he was bored. "There is a difference. And if not for the fact that you come from the wrong direction and you've brought a shadow drake with you, you wouldn't be interesting enough to spend these few moments talking. So stop wasting my time."

"Well, you're as arrogant as all mages, at least," Jaush grumbled, climbing down to the other, who chuckling a bit.

"Are you lumping me in with your Queen?"

The Davrin bua shrugged after stepping on the floor of the tunnel. "If it suits. Never had much use for mages who hoard knowledge and only use magic to serve themselves."

"Rrrrrr ... I see you're not even close to realizing a few things."

Maybe, but Jaush did at least realize just how *tall* the creature was and not only that but blatantly male as well. Sharp teeth revealed as he pulled his lips back were more than enough to bite him in two.

The drake-mage also looked irritated, his eyes somehow appearing metallic even with Dark Sight, and his tail coiled with agitation. Jaush sort of wondered what kind of aura Beliza or Ilka would see; he almost felt something unseen pressing out at him.

Maybe Beliza should have interfered this time.

Ohhh well, he sighed. *We knew this couldn't last forever anyway.*

"Who is 'we,' " the Great Drake asked, demanding and curious.

"Stop that," Jaush replied and heard a mean chortle.

"You have no defenses, bua. I'd never expected a grown Baenar to be so wide open. Now ... *Tell Me Who Else Is With You.*"

This time, Jaush could have sworn that invisible pressure had reached around his throat and squeezed out his words before he even had a chance to think on them.

"My traveling companion, Beliza," he blurted. "She's a mage, and she's pregnant, and very hungry. I seek a way to help her make it through this alive, with or without the baby"

The metallic eyes stared right through him, though the tail calmed down some as the Great Drake considered what Jaush now kicked himself for saying. At least the open irritation had lessened, although the young Davrin didn't think the Drake was going to barter. He didn't need to.

Only now did Jaush question his sanity engaging with one who had absolutely no concern for the presence of Davrin in his territory.

"Hm," the Drake grunted. "How refreshing. Let us bring Beliza and her familiar out to join the conversation, shall we?"

Oh, fuck.

"Wait!"

The Drake already leaped over his head, climbing straight toward the boulder hiding the secret passage. Jaush launched himself partway up the rock wall and grabbed the end of the reptilian tail. This proved another mistake as the young Davrin was tossed to the side with stunning ease and smacked against the rock as if he was the size of a fly.

Owww ...

The next moment, he heard Beliza screaming in terrified rage.

CHAPTER 8

THE HUGE, CLAWED HAND REACHED STRAIGHT THROUGH HER BLAST OF FIRE, unperturbed by searing heat as it seized her boot by her ankle.

This was straight out of her nightmares! Right up to the detail that her spell quickly used up all the air in her crawl space. She couldn't breathe; suffocating; she couldn't scream.

Ilka followed her ill-conceived spell with a welcome blast of air in the opposite direction, preventing her mistress from passing out unconscious, which at least gave her the time to realize that she wasn't asleep.

This was real, and the fire hadn't singed a single scale.

"Let me go!" she cried in full panic as the irresistible grip dragged her out of the smaller passage and into the larger tunnel. "JAUSH!"

She wasn't sure why she cried his name. Exactly what would her young, non-magical bua really do for her? Maybe he was in hiding and she'd just given him away.

Stupid, stupid! Oh, Goddess, let it be quick …

"There you are," a deep, rumbling voice crooned. He was rank with magic. "This is much closer to what I expected to meet from the Queen's City. I'm sure you both have an interesting story."

One arm trapped Beliza against him like an iron band, her feet dangling well above the ground. Ilka was growling loudly, slipping around to different vantage points to spit and snarl. Despite her size and clear terror, she was threatening the black beast who held her mistress.

Her captor observed this for several moments. At best, he was curious and amused.

"It is genuine," he commented, turning his hot, sour breath toward her. "Your bond with the drake is not a forced compulsion, is it, Baenar mage?"

Beliza couldn't stop trembling and hadn't the courage to look this creature in the eyes. He was so powerful; his aura was simply punishing. In her weakened state, it felt like he was kicking her only after she discovered she couldn't pick herself back up off the ground.

"Just kill me," she whispered miserably.

"Mm, no, I won't be doing that yet. Now where is your lover … ? Ah! There you are." He turned, the slow swing making her nauseated. "Nothing broken, bua? Good. Do try to keep up. You don't want to get lost alone out here. The very worst you can imagine is not far, and they would love to discover you."

JAUSH RAN AFTER THE DRAKE WHO CARRIED BELIZA AS IF SHE WEIGHED NO MORE than a toddler. Ilka flew after them as well, whining and squawking and generally making more noise than he'd ever heard her make before.

His sorceress trembled and shook like a helpless child, trying to free her arms as if she would reach out for her animal companion. Jaush hoped the Drake-mage wasn't hurting her in ways he couldn't see. There wasn't much he could do if this was the case, but he couldn't help uselessly wishing for less suffering for her.

Especially when it was marked so clearly on her face.

Beliza …

A few times it seemed like the Drake was trying to lose him, or test him, despite telling him to keep up. The bipedal beast would pass from sight for a time after rounding a bend or speed up without seeming to move his legs any faster. Jaush could only rely on his senses, endurance and Ilka to follow them.

He could only keep going.

At one point, Jaush thought for certain he'd lost them, even Beliza's familiar. He turned around and around, seeing only stone, hearing no clucking, or puffing from the small shadow drake.

Then he heard the Great Drake sigh, and a huge hand clapped on his shoulder, gripping then pulling him backward. The young male stumbled, and he felt he had fallen into a wall of tepid water which was standing calm and vertical. Bumps broke out along his whole body but not a drop of wetness besides his own sweat clung to him on the other side.

"Impressive, Jaush. Such stubbornness with such non-aggressive intention. A rarity down here."

Jaush caught his breath as his muscles quaked and suffered spasms. He might have been running for most of the cycle without a break.

Where am I … ?

Ilka's rattling purr when she vibrated her throat pouch drew his attention, and he found the drake nuzzling an unconscious Beliza. At least his sorceress was breathing, and …

Lying on a bed of gold coins.

The Great Drake called a soft glow to certain items around the cave. After rubbing his eyes against the light, Jaush gaped around him, noting the spread of metals in all forms: coins, jewelry, swords, armor, plates, chests, cups, statues. Innumerable shining gems of all colors added to the wealth. The black outline of the treasure's owner amid the shimmer made him stand out all the more.

"Do not attempt to take a single piece, no matter how small," the Drake said. "I will know if you do, Baenar."

Jaush believed him, and he had been living a long time without long-term ownership of coins. "I won't. I don't need them."

"Good."

They certainly weren't worth the dark mage's anger. Jaush wasn't surprised when he "felt" satisfaction and approval coming from the mind-reading beast.

"What are you calling us?" Jaush asked. "Baenar?"

"My Word for you. The Dark Elves. And making quite a Name for yourselves, too. Most of the Deepearth whispers your horrors now, rivaling the Elder Minds with the various realms of magic you now command."

Jaush felt clueless to anything past Elves.

"Not you in particular," the Drake continued, stepping to relax sitting upon a metal chest. "You are oddly mundane and lack the conniving habits of your 'betters.' I'm not sure of what you remind me."

Enough …

"Beliza," Jaush said bluntly. "Is she alright?"

The black, golden-eyed creature tilted his head. "The shadow drake would be keening much more loudly if she wasn't."

"Alright. Do you have untainted food you would barter away, Great Drake?"

Jaush could at least read that he liked the honorific well enough and wasn't insulted with the directness.

"I could get some," he mused. "How much food do we speak?"

Jaush considered. "I … um …"

What good would a few spans' rations do when Beliza's belly would swell for over a turn yet?

"What about knowledge of medicinal plants and fungus in this area?" he asked. "Do you have that?"

An eyebrow arched. "Of course."

"Something that would allow a Baenar matron to purge an unwanted pregnancy and be well again afterward?"

"Yes." The Drake tilted his head. "Although I would want to know more of where you come from before I'd give you that."

"You know where we come from."

"And I want to know why *you*, specifically, ran away with *her*."

Jaush shrugged, uncomfortable with the penetrating gaze. "You'd have to ask her. It was her idea."

"What about Ill'irkya'e?"

Ilka's head shot up when she heard that, her red eyes wide open and wings partly splayed out. Her tail lashed side-to-side, and she trembled with a ruffle of her throat.

Jaush guessed that was her real name. "I … sh-she followed us."

The Drake harrumphed and looked at Beliza and her little companion with a smile. "I think we can barter something, young one. Thank you for not wasting my time."

Hunger awoke Beliza first, and Jaush watched her initial tense inter-actions with their host, as well as took an accusatory glance saying, *What have you done?*

The younger Davrin went back and forth whether his companion had actual knowledge of their host or just sensed the enlarged shadow of it as she tried to bluff with educated guesses. Possessing strong magic wasn't an advantage if another had even stronger.

Beliza seemed to be grasping for control of the exchange which the Great Drake dangled in front of her like a toy on a string. The harder she tried to get out in front of him or simply catch up, the more the beast seemed to be enjoying it.

This was so obvious to Jaush, he wondered how long he would have to wait before they got tired of fencing wit, or before the Drake won and something else happened? If Beliza didn't mind entertaining him so, then fine power to her.

The real question for Jaush, should he be worried? Maybe he was too ignorant to know when to be afraid. The Great Drake had certainly hinted at that more than once. But then, if he was ignorant, why waste the energy if he couldn't know more than he saw?

The bua saw a hoarding, solitary, mage-creature who held more inter-est in the sorceress and her shadow drake than in someone from Sivaraus's lowest House. Yes, they were probably in trouble and Jaush himself would have to watch out for being eaten if he didn't have much value otherwise.

But the Great Drake had also implied he was willing to barter with him. If that was a lie and an attack came as an ambush as well, Jaush might not even be aware of it so …

I won't worry about it. Whatever happens, happens.

Jaush laid back on the piles of gold, thinking if they hadn't been flat, smooth, and in tiny bits, they wouldn't be comfortable. As it was, they weren't bad. *Better than bare stone.*

His Mother would be proud. Magic begged for all the attention as always, yet his heart was beating along steady, strong, and peaceful.

"Bored with our talk already, Jaush?" the Drake asked with clear amusement.

"Huh?"

"Or just determined not to be afraid?"

The bua frowned a bit. Then closed his eyes.

"Jaush!" Beliza whispered with reproach.

"Let me know when you're done," he muttered with a bit of resentment at her tone.

Enormous paws slammed onto the coins on either side of him. Teeth snapped so close that it took a bit of skin off the tip of his nose and the Davrin jumped, pulling a boot blade, and stabbing it up at the throat of the target before he could stop himself.

Beliza screamed a denial.

Then Jaush blinked, and the beast began with a chuckle.

The blade didn't even scratch the tough hide, and their host's laugh grew so loud that it hurt his ears. That breath wasn't fragrant in a good way, either. Jaush exhaled; his heart had sped up but the flush of energy was settling already.

"Sorry," the bua apologized, dropping the blade. "Bad form for a guest, I know that."

The Drake's guffaw was loud. And genuine.

"Not bad, young fighter," said the Great Drake, looming over him in a four-legged hunch. He shifted shoulders and hips, kneading his coins with his paws and dragging large, engorged genitals over Jaush's thighs and causing the young Davrin to look down at the source of heat seeping through his clothing.

Oh.

"What do you think?" the Drake teased.

"Impressive," Jaush replied, not acknowledging the need to panic. "Did you shapeshift that fast, from two legs to four?"

"I did. I may take any form I wish."

"Bet that's useful."

"I have always thought so."

"So we haven't seen your real form, Great Drake?"

"No, you have not. You do not likely want to."

"Oh. Agreed."

Jaush trusted his instinct and stopped talking then, relaxing, and letting the Drake nudge and prod him with that dark, pointed erection while he lay upon his back on the coins. He didn't shy away and even provided a good platform for dry humping as the Drake's prick grew stiffer with the stimulation.

Beliza was holding her breath, he thought; she and Ilka were utterly silent.

"You would not try to stop me, would you?" the beast cooed.

"Stop what?" Jaush reached down and lightly caressed smooth, scalding phallus. Not scaly like the rest of him, and it was large. "You said we could barter. I don't have jewels or coins to add to your pile, do you think I hadn't considered this? I have before. There are worse things than stroking off another's cock, Great Drake."

A few white spines raised up along his captor-host's back as wings unfolded a bit, his tail swiping side-to-side with increased aggression and arousal.

"But what if I refused barter? You cannot stop me, Jaush, you do not have the strength or the magic. You cannot leave here unless I will it. I can simply take my pleasure and there's nothing you can do to escape it."

The bua sighed with a frown, dropping his hand. The Great Drake seemed disappointed.

"Then just do it and stop wasting my time, as I agreed not to waste yours," he said. "You would rather have sex slaves than barter? Fine. So you lied. I imagine it'll be fun for a while and then you'll get bored having us hobbling around. You'll eat us and start over waiting for 'Baenar' to wander into your territory. Pretty limited options for a highly intelligent mage. I thought you'd do better."

Jaush blinked dry eyes at last, realizing that he'd been staring into those metallic gold eyes for some time now. The Great Drake was smiling.

"Hmm," his host purred, pre-cum still leaking out to stain the Dark Elf's clothing. The fluid stretched in a long, clear string as the Drake finally shifted up and backward a bit to give the younger male space. "Perhaps I was wrong about you being uninteresting, Jaush."

CHAPTER 9

THE DRAKE WANTED TO BARTER, AS IT TURNED OUT. HE FINALLY GAVE THEM A name as well: *Sargt.*

The first trade was a simple one, like a test: One meal for one climax of pleasure.

"Like for like," the Drake said smoothly. "Body for body, mind for mind, knowledge for knowledge. We'll get where you want to go, sorceress and her youth. Just relax for now. There's no rush."

Those rules weren't so rigid yet. This was just a start.

"You prefer to be in this form?"

"You said it was 'impressive.' "

Sargt withheld another laugh, and Jaush exchanged a look with Beliza. She didn't complain given the circumstances, but she must be extremely hungry by now, and Jaush had been sensitive to that need for a while.

"Alright. Like for like, I'll use my hands."

"And mouth. You eat with your hand and mouth, do you not?"

"Fine, but I don't swallow this time."

Sargt grinned impossibly wide. "This time? I like you more and more, mundane. Agreed."

The beast laid down on his side, huge erection jutting beneath his hard, scaled belly, and laid his head down in the coins and jewels to where he could look at Beliza but not touch her. Jaush thought that was telling of something, but he did not know what.

"Begin, if you please, Jaush. I am sure you are both hungry."

The young Davrin kneeled and removed his gloves to get to it, placing both his hands, one atop the other, around the black, fleshy sword. He still had room to fill his mouth with the crown.

"Ohhh, go on," the beast rumbled.

Learning how to please his host wasn't that hard; despite clear arrogance, the Drake was easily satisfied as long as Jaush made an effort, which he did. He'd always given that effort in any challenge he had chosen to take.

The Davrin bua stroked firmly, diving down to suck the head firmly. He concentrated on the salty, musky scents and flavors, on the infinite sounds Sargt seemed to make even beyond the Davrin's own hearing.

"Errm! Yesss … harder."

Jaush was startled near the end. His jumped in surprise, his cry muffled when the Drake's tail whipped eagerly around his thigh. The coils tightened, nudging up beneath his own cock and balls and unwinding before slithering around to tighten up again. Jaush's sudden erection strained his pants.

"Mmm. Nice …"

The Drake's paws stretched and mauled into his coins as his back arched while Beliza watched, fascinated despite herself. Jaush received the impression this kind of attention wasn't frequent or regular for their host, either.

At the end, his emission proved … abundant.

A warning caused Jaush to pull back, a change in the taste of the fluid seeping out of the hole at the tip making his tongue and lips tingle. Jaush spat it out just to be safe, stroking harder with just his hands to pull the Great Drake over the edge.

Sargt rolled and thrashed in his pleasure, his scaly, black tail squeezing Jaush's thigh. He made it difficult to aim the thick multitude of unpredictable spurts shooting farther and at varying intervals compared to a Davrin. He also wouldn't stop writhing and growling.

The Great Drake's spending ended up marking guests, coins, and himself. Only Ilka had the distance to avoid it entirely, though at least Beliza had avoided getting any on her skin.

"*Ohh,* worth a meal for certain," Sargt sighed.

Jaush sought something from his pack to wipe off his face and hands as quickly as he could. "Should I be concerned that it's burning?"

His host chuckled deeply, watching the bua scrub exposed skin which had been splashed with Drake seed. "It will fade. Although you may feel dizzy for a while."

With another deep, satisfied sigh, the creature rolled up onto four legs, curving his medium-length neck to look at him. "An added benefit: nothing will attack you while you have my scent on you."

Jaush arched his brow. "Not of much use if I can't leave."

"But the knowledge is free all the same. Stay and relax while I complete my end of the bargain."

Like Ilka and her family, the Davrin Elves could not tell exactly when or how Sargt had left the cave filled with treasure. There was no tunnel leading out, no hidden passage they could detect; he just seemed to fade through a deep enough shadow, making no sound.

Taking their host at his word for now, Jaush relaxed, able to ignore his own hunger pangs better than his traveling companion could.

"So what do you think he is?" Jaush asked.

Beliza's eyes bugged out as she stared at him with mouth agape. "He is *the* Dragon of the Deepearth! You ... you foolish bua! How can you not know?!"

Jaush exhaled with an annoyed grunt, feeling that dizziness Sargt had predicted. "Lowest House, remember? I barely know how to read, Beliza, and I haven't had access to all the libraries you did. What do you know about the Dragon? Or even Ilka? Sargt knew her real name."

Beliza looked over at her drake, who came to her then, although she was snuffling the scent of the strange male marking her with a less than-pleased gurgle in her throat. The shadow drake flopped her haunches down and against her mistress to lay down in the coins, communicating in a mysterious, mental way which Jaush could never read well except by

Beliza's reactions.

"We only know of the one, no others. He seems to have no true name; everyone calls him something different. Every intelligent race in the Deepearth has stories of him, but he is not seen for centuries at a time and ... uh, I think we forget them until he reappears."

No wonder his companion — his pregnant companion — was so distraught. There was only one of these creatures, and Jaush had just agreed to play pleasure servant for who knew how long.

"He just reappears now and then?"

"Well, the books say the Dragon sleeps in long cycles."

Jaush huffed a laugh. "He's awake now. And horny."

Her tension rose with her immediate concern rushing out. "What if he wants to barter me into this next?"

"Possible, I suppose, but he hasn't dragged his penis over you yet. Maybe he has a preference for males?"

Before she could reply to that, Beliza looked at her drake who had said something else to her. "It can't be that simple, Ilka."

"What?"

The sorceress narrowed her eyes at him. "Ilka says while I'm pregnant, the Dragon won't touch me in that way."

Jaush thought on that and shrugged. "Why couldn't it be that simple? He was painful to you at first, I could tell, and that was just while he carried you."

"His aura," she supplied, "was too intense. Yes, it hurt, and he wanted me to hurt at first, so that I understood who held us. But he's suppressing his aura around me already. It didn't hurt when his tail brushed me just after he released you. He *could* touch me if he wishes."

Jaush grinned a little. "Are you saying you feel left out?"

Her face flushed hot in the dim light, and she scowled. "No! I just ... don't know how far ... Jaush, what are you doing? Why?"

He shrugged. This concept always more complicated for matrons, especially when they were accustomed to living with status. Of course she'd assume it was so for him.

"If Ilka is right, Beliza, then you're safe."

"Only while I'm pregnant!"

"Then stay pregnant until you are sure. I'll do the slut work while we figure out what happens next. It's what we've done before, right? And things like this are expected of Davrin buas."

"Not quite. I didn't even know you'd bartered with other buas this way before! What if he wants to mount you?"

"Um, I think that's inevitable at this point," he said, feeling his own face heat up. "I'm only hoping I can convince him to use a smaller form than what I handled just now."

"Even if it changes you somehow?" she continued, her concern growing. "He's powerful, Jaush, and you already mentioned his seed alone caused you to feel something strange."

He rubbed his forehead. Another thing he couldn't predict, so why worry? "Yes, even if."

"Why agree so easily?!" she demanded.

"Because the end result will be the same or worse if I don't," he replied, more force coming into his voice as he wondered why this was so complicated to her. "And you need to eat and have time to figure out where your head is at!"

The older sorceress closed her mouth, watching him, waiting for him to continue. Another thing he liked about her.

He calmed himself. "*We* made you catch, Bel, when you didn't want to. And I'm sorry. I didn't know what the Priestesses had done to you, I still don't, but I've watched your Reverie and your dreams have gotten worse since you told me."

Her eyes shimmered as she stared at him.

"I've heard you say some strange things when you weren't fully awake," he confessed, "and starving in the wilderness is *not* what I want to see happen to you. I'd rather you have a chance, and a *choice* since you never had one before. It seems like we might have that now. Sargt said he knew ways of ending it safely if you wanted."

"He did?" Beliza blurted.

"Yeah. I'll fuck a Dragon to find out, and to give you time. I'm still out here with you, I haven't run off scared, and I don't have anything else

I'm doing right now."

Beliza swallowed, slumping down against a chest as her eyes watered. "Where in the pit did you come from, Jaush? Why does someone like me deserve help from someone like you?"

"It sounded like you knew more where I came from than I did," he commented with a smile. "A formerly powerful House with no magic left to speak of?"

"And not touched so deeply by the Abyss," she whispered, tears starting to drip as she turned the thought over. "No Priestesses come out of your House, no wizards add to the Tower. Much less influence upon the Matron … your Mother … Wh-what you've described to me of your family, Jaush, it sounds … different. From everything I've seen."

"So do you," he offered. "You were kept in the middle of it all, the Abyss itself, but you seem different to me, Beliza. Over the last turn, you've proven to me that you are. *That's* why you deserve my help. I made my choice when I met you by the secret jump circle, to help you walk without chains." Jaush looked around the Dragon's hoard with no doors. "I'd still like to see you free of this burden. We just need to go a step at a time, like at the beginning."

Beliza had been cuddling Ilka, gently rubbing her throat how she liked, but the drake moved willingly enough when the sorceress leaned forward and reached out to him. Jaush came forward at the invitation and leaned into her embrace.

They hadn't met lips that often while knowing each other, but they did now. They shared a deep and lengthy kiss, leading to them stripping off their cum-stained clothing. Beliza willingly opened herself for him, relaxed despite her hunger, accepting his offer of pleasure and comfort for the first time since she'd told him she was pregnant.

They coupled on top of the coins and gems within the safest cave of the Deepearth. His skin still tingled where the Dragon's seed had touched it. With one hand stroking her belly, his tongue tasting her neck and breast, his own cock servicing her with care and attention, he listened to her moan.

In the middle of it all, Jaush thought he sensed something … *different*

… within her womb.

Nah. Can't trust my senses as usual in a Dragon's Lair.

Chapter 10

Jaush stood facing one rock wall. The Dragon was behind him, his breath hot on his neck. One muscular arm hooked around from the right and crossed his naked chest, the rough and unnaturally hot hand gripping the opposite shoulder. The bua's arms and hands were unrestrained, and he used them to hold firmly on to stone.

To hold on to something as the black beast took him again.

"Fuck!" the Elf blurted, shocked to feel bumps and ridges added to the sensation of his netherhole stretching. "Y-you changed shape again!"

"It's no larger than before, young one. As agreed."

The Dragon hissed in pleasure as he sank in deeper, leaning to lick the bua's pointed ear. The same, extremely slick saliva which vastly eased the passage of his prick now warmed that ear to burning; Jaush didn't think it was because he was too aware of Beliza watching.

"Is it pleasurable?" Sargt asked with another thrust in.

The young Davrin didn't need to answer aloud as his host lightly reached around, finding his cock heavy and hard as well. Jaush shivered as the rough thumb smeared his own pre-cum around the head.

"A pity Beliza shouldn't wrap her lips around this," the Dragon cooed, fucking him much more gently than he had to. "Imagine the glorious agony as we flanked you, front and back … ?"

Jaush guessed that Sargt had probably given the sorceress a teasing wink right then, but he still stared at his own dark hand gripping the wall, one foot stepped up on a small rock to give their frank and overtly sexual provider access to fuck his asshole as he wished.

Jaush also knew why the Dragon teased his sorceress, and it wasn't because she had to share him. Sargt had confirmed what Ilka had told her mistress: any real sex with the Dragon would kill her baby.

Very simple.

That at least offered as a solution to their worry and primary problem living in the wilderness. In exchange for Jaush swallowing Sargt's cum the next time, Beliza was told she would probably recover from such a miscarriage in about the same as if she ingested the right extraction from the right plant or mushroom, though they still didn't know which those were.

They hadn't traded for that knowledge yet.

"What does 'real sex' with you mean?" she'd asked after watching the first few interactions between the males. Though confused about it, she wasn't as hostile as she might have been.

At worst, she was likely feeling left out, or a bit jealous, and worried. Probably protective, too. Jaush has witnessed a combination of all of this when she saw the aftermath. It took him quite a while for his head to stop spinning whenever the Dragon left his gooey semen inside of him, regardless of which hole he used.

Sargt had indulged the sorceress in an answer without payment that time. "For you? That would be our auras merging, mage. On a direct level."

Beliza had frowned. "So if you are ... um ... inside Jaush, and ... ?"

"And you start touching him, especially if you make him cum," the Dragon completed with a suggestive grin, "that counts. Our bua would act as the conduit."

Beliza had only watched them thus far, still undecided whether to take that final step. So often she appeared as aroused as she was wary of being so.

Jaush was relieved and grateful that Sargt was doing as he promised, granting her time and respect — and lots of food — to have her choice to decide. She hadn't leaped at the first chance to abort the pregnancy, which sort of confused the younger Davrin. The hesitation might be from the bad dreams having stopped. For once, she was sleeping well and never hungry.

The long-term decisions are best not made tired and hungry, his Mother had once said.

It's more than a lack of bad dreams and good food, Sargt murmured privately in the younger male's mind as Jaush felt his back hole stretch a little more than usual around the Dragon's tool.

Huh?

Oh, yes. She considers the truth that you are the sire of her newest catch, Jaush. Not those other wizards who forced themselves on her. She is in awe that you are willing to do this for her. She did choose you, after all.

It was lust, Jaush thought back, his balance shaky and his cock aching. He'd enjoy so much having her touch it as he was getting fucked. *Sh-she said I was just a bua. It makes sense; I wasn't magical enough or old enough to make her to do anything. Then I went and got her pregnant somehow, just after weaning … *

Ohhh, don't start doubting yourself now, Jaush. Sargt fucked him harder as he drew closer to climax. *I was ready to disregard and eat you at that first meeting. I did not expect to see one such as you arrive from either city after all that has happened. You are all products of your environment, after all.*

Either city? he asked, his vision blurred, and his head starting to get groggy as his flesh tingled with pleasure. *What happened?*

Oops! Sargt chuckled, huffing as he pushed his rigid, irregular cock again and again through the Dark Elf's tight ring. *That's not for free. But see how you lower the guard of mages? What's more, I recall no recent creature who isn't a mage who can look me in the eyes as you do. Quite a talent of willpower you have, despite your lack of significant magic. I wonder if that is peculiar to the Baenar alone?*

Sargt paused as if he might be contemplating that curiosity even as he rutted his bua, perhaps to distract his pleasure and draw this out. Their thought-link hadn't quite faded, however, and the Dragon instead focused intensely on the younger male's clutching hole, on his scent, and the back of his neck which he wanted to bite … .

★ … *oh, yes … Yesss.*★

"AH!" Jaush cried aloud as Sargt took him abruptly, all the way to the hilt, holding tight to his hips and pressed flush to his backside.

The Dragon snapped jaws onto the Davrin's nape, his tail coiling around one thigh to cling tighter still. Again Jaush's guts filled with hot, magic-soaked cream, and he trembled with the need to cum himself.

★*Delicious.*★

Sargt hummed in satisfaction, coming down slowly and moving his cock in and out a few extra times before pulling out completely.

"Shit … ohhh, shit …" Jaush groaned, stumbling in Beliza's general direction before flopping down onto the coins and rolling onto his back.

He gripped his erection, intending to jerk himself off quickly, but his sorceress swatted his hand away and took hold of it herself, staring down at him with a flushed face and intense lust.

"B-Beliza — ?"

She leaned down to kiss his mouth first, squeezing his cock gently. He moaned, and she pushed her tongue into his mouth, kissing him deeper before breaking it off to lift the skirts of the dress she had borrowed from Sargt's hoard. Jaush sniffed deeply and caught her familiar scent, groaning again as she straddled him and aimed his prick.

"Bel!" he gasped, growling as she plunged her hips down, impaling herself. Her body was hot and tight, every stroke as slick as his own netherhole was right now.

"Jaush, oh! Yes!"

She fucked him hard, shrieking in pleasured joy as he gripped her clothed waist. How he held out for even three strokes of her wild riding mystified him.

"Oh, Goddess!" she cried, nails digging into his shoulders, and the rush overtook them both.

Jaush's own cry locked in his throat as his prick shot off inside her, her sex milking him to her own satisfaction as she coasted, her heart pounding. She leaned down and kissed him again, and they panted together, his cock softening as they caught their breath. She put her arms around him and held tight.

"The two of you are indeed very interesting," the Dragon murmured thoughtfully from a safe distance away.

With such an invitation, Beliza didn't wait to engage their host again. That was alright. Jaush could barely tell which way was the ceiling, so he merely listened drowsily.

"What price for one conversation as to what is so interesting about us?" she asked. "I know Ilka surprised you."

"Yes, and she enjoys watching and feeling what is between you as much as I do. Don't you, purr-box?"

Beliza's familiar fluttered her throat in simultaneous annoyance and agreement upon her guest ledge generally just above Sargt's head — though only when he allowed it.

"You tease when you should be bartering, Sargt."

"Feisty as ever, lovely sorceress. I envy Jaush knowing that juicy cunt so worry-free, you know. Wise of him that he does not take it for granted."

"Ask'im 'bout th'other city," Jaush murmured drunkenly.

Beliza turned to him. "What other city? And how does that relate to us being inter ... .? Oh."

Sargt chortled, saying nothing aloud, but Jaush could imagine him waving his hand for Beliza to speak her mind while his tail swept back and forth along his coins.

"If there are two cities, then you know both. If we are curiosities, then ... we fit in neither?"

"Not bad," Sargt agreed. "Far from the Truth, of course."

He did this a lot, Jaush noted, as his sorceress growled in irritation.

"What price?" she asked again.

"Your lineage," Sargt said immediately. "And Jaush's. Explain them to me, as you know them."

"That's complicated," she said. "And I don't know it all."

"Then I'll trade as is appropriate for what you *do* know, my lovely, untouchable scholar. Let us speak a while as poor Jaush recovers from

74

being wrung out and hung to dry."

Six quad-spans. Another half a turn.

They'd been held like possessions and entertainment, practically as part of the Dragon's Hoard, for six quad-spans now. The exchanges went on and on. Jaush justifiably could have chafed much more at this than he was; he could have grown impatient at Beliza seemingly not deciding, not saying or signing to him that she would stop the pregnancy or not.

Instead, he reflected that he might be a barely literate Noble, and that in name only, but he still understood plenty about his mature sorceress. She must see enough benefit in the dance to keep the Dragon interested and patient

Most important was that they did not want for food. Sargt brought them more than meat, giving permission to use a few of the items in his hoard for cooking. They had the time to prepare the greater variety in more complicated forms than raw or mashed or quickly seared travel rations.

A lot of the Dragon's choices for their sustenance were hard to reach or find; high-risk delicacies, all beneficial to a gestating mother, and Jaush got his full share as well. A nice change of pace for as long as it lasted.

Adding to this were the sleep and the sex, which were peaceful and mind-sweeping, respectively. Jaush had worried that Beliza's renewed and intense interest in coupling with him every time Sargt satisfied himself would come with far worse humiliation if her respect for him plummeted.

They'd all noticed him getting an erection every time Sargt even hinted that he wanted sex, which was with stunning regularity as he didn't seem to be getting bored with the young Davrin. The ancient male teased him and Beliza plenty about the hovering possibility of a threesome unlike either of them had known, if only the sorceress would make her decision.

Usually in the heat of things, Jaush wished she'd go for it and jump in with them.

Yet that wish went away, every time, as soon as the Dragon lust faded, and the young sire regretted even thinking it. Jaush lay in awe of the sorceress's willpower and self-control as Sargt tested her conviction, and especially as his sorceress continued to treat him well, thanking him for doing the "slut work," even asking how he was holding up.

I think you were right at the start, Beliza. This agreement is changing me somehow ...

He bit the inside of his cheek and answered his usual, "I'm holding up well, Beliza."

Finally, there was the knowledge.

Jaush was aware that Beliza used their situation to its fullest for knowledge. Conversational exchanges with Sargt grew more frequent than before, and it was interesting what puzzles Sargt and Beliza were able to put together. Jaush only listened, often with a sore mouth and tingling netherhole, a strange heat in his gut, and his hands feeling like they could shatter stone if he were but to grip it.

He learned the most wondrous things about the Deepearth and the Baenar. Compared to what Beliza had suffered in the Sanctuary before running away with him, Jaush didn't think he had anything to complain about being little more than the play toy in all this.

"Out of curiosity," Sargt said one eve, paying an answer forward after Beliza had provided him with the answer he'd requested, "I asked Y'shir what his old House's name was. He answered D'Shauranti. Does that ring a bell?"

Beliza shook her head. She had long ago stopped trying to direct the conversation or practice any of the intrigues of bargaining she'd learned at the Palace. It just didn't work with Sargt. "No. I have not heard it or seen it written down, but ..."

"But," the Dragon completed for her, "D'Shea. Aurenthin. Similar sounds each in that one older name."

Beliza and Jaush both nodded.

"Could I meet Y'shir Matalai'ko?" Beliza asked yet again.

"I think that is as dangerous an idea as it is interesting," Sargt said again, happy to repeat himself to the persistent sorceress. "Vuthra'tern has become even more isolated than Sivaraus, despite their intentions in breaking away from their Queen-Mother. The influence of the Abyss dogged them, followed them. When they settled, it became permanent."

"You do not like the Abyss in your Deepearth," Beliza said.

Sargt shrugged, wingless for the moment and only a little larger than the Dark Elves while retaining many of his Draconic features. "The Abyss refines what the Deepearth is, challenges it to remake itself, for better or worse."

"But you do not welcome it trying to influence you," Jaush guessed. "Just as the mind flayers and their Elders may not lay claim to you, either."

Their host grinned. "Correct, young one."

"And if I'd been tainted by the Abyss, you wouldn't have even accepted sex for barter. That was how we were 'different' than you expected."

"Insightful. Although, Beliza was tainted when I captured her, willing her to die. Her bond with Ill'irkya'e has helped cleanse her to become more what a Dark Elf used to be." Sargt looked at the sorceress directly. "You owe this small Dragon-kin a great debt, accepting such a risky bond with you when you called, mage."

Hearing her name, the shadow drake lifted her head from her mistress's lap, her tail flicked happily at the praise from the Great Drake. Ilka peered up at Beliza, who stroked her in all the places she enjoyed, making her purr with contentment.

The sorceress studied her "familiar" with affection and a degree of wonder. "Dragon-kin? What are the shadow drakes to you that they are 'kin'?"

Sargt smirked. "Will you describe to me two rituals, in detail, which you witnessed among the Priestesses? Your choice."

Beliza exhaled on a nod. "Done."

"Very good. The drakes were some of the earliest to make their home in the Deepearth with me, and the shadow drakes discovered the cracks in the vault, and not only warned me but keep them mended as they pass between shadows."

Beliza seemed to grasp as little as Jaush. "Cracks? Vault?"

The Dragon grinned. "I'm not sure you have enough knowledge to trade for an explanation of how that works."

"Well … at least clarify, you don't mean blood-kin?"

Both he and Ilka shook their heads. "Kinship in form and function. Not dissimilar to many races of the Surface, especially the highly sentient ones like the Elves and the Tundar."

"Tundar?"

"You call them Dwarves."

"The Tragar?" Beliza asked with a bit of a curl to her lip.

"Them. There are others more common."

"Do you call us kin?"

"I do." Sargt enjoyed her expression a moment before going a step further. "I've rutted both Elves and Dwarves before."

Beliza made a belching sound, and Jaush couldn't keep his laugh down before she slapped his thigh. The Dragon continued willingly.

"You are among the most passionate and fertile of races. My play doesn't harm the balance of things. But …" Golden eyes landed on Jaush. "You are the first I cared to take within my own home. Before, I found you all on the Surface."

"The break with the Valsharess." Beliza seized on this, finally connecting many small hints she'd received over the quad-spans. "The Davrin of Vuthra'tern were trying to return to the Surface?"

He winked, pleased she had figured that out. "Correct, dear sorceress. There were no Baenar at all down here. Your very presence has changed many things in a very short time. The other cave-dwelling races are still reeling."

"And from what you've each said," Jaush spoke up softly, and the other two focused intently on the youngest here since he almost never interrupted them. "House D'Shauranti might've made the break possible but couldn't join Y'shir Matalai'ko with the others. The Valsharess split us up and made us forget."

"Far-seeing and ruthless," Sargt replied, "as she has always been."

"You knew about our Queen when she first brought the Baenar down here from the Surface?"

"How could I not? She is as powerful and insane as the Baenar come.

I could claim a certain kinship with her as well."

Sobering in its way to think the Davrin Queen and a tiny shadow drake familiar might have something in common with a Dragon in Sargt's eyes. But the Great Drake seemed open to indulging Jaush, so the bua kept asking questions on the assumption he had earned the courtesy to ask without censure. Whether or not the powerful male answered was a different matter.

"Why did She come down here? Why did She bring us to the Deep-earth?"

Sargt considered for a few moments as if he wanted to answer but still weighed the heft of it, and Beliza did not interrupt.

"There was a large enough threat at the time that it was possible the Baenar might have been either exterminated or too-quickly altered to continue serving in their role. They would leave a large void, and the Naulor and the Yungar would be the next to fall if outsiders should fill it. Your Valsharess sought to have her people survive, even in exile and in darkness, and serve their purpose."

"Which is?" Jaush asked.

"Something like what you are doing now, Jaush, but on a much grander scale."

"I don't understand."

"You aren't meant to."

When they paused, Beliza spoke. "You make the Valsharess sound far-seeing and wise."

Sargt shook his head. "She *is* far-seeing, but I would say more desperate than wise. This one choice may balance all she has done before and after, or it may not. Certainly some, like yourself, may always hate her for what she has done to you."

"But … you won't destroy us as a race for invading your territory," Jaush said.

"The Baenar have added to the Deepearth, young one, and you have taken nothing away you did not already lose yourselves." Sargt smiled almost with appreciation. "The loss to the Surface is my gain, I am begin-ning to see. Especially with you two warming my den and my hoard with mutual lust and life magic."

The younger male felt his face grow hot as too many explicit memories returned all at once, while Beliza covered her abdomen at the mention of "life." Jaush noticed, rubbing his palms together as he thought about something which had come to him when he'd last touched her bare belly with his hands.

"So," Sargt said with striking bass in his voice, "since we are sharing thoughts more fluidly at the moment, are you going to tell her, Jaush?"

"Huh?" The bua snapped his attention back. "Tell her what?"

His stomach tightened as the Dragon winked but said nothing more. Beliza and Ilka pinned him with expectant gazes.

Ah, damn it all ...

Jaush breathed out and gave it a try. "I think I'm getting stronger. Some of my senses are sharper, too. I haven't so much as scraped my skin or bruised myself in spans, though I still ... feel everything."

He glanced up at his sorceress, testing her mood. She watched him with curiosity and concern then looked at the Dragon.

"Each being responds differently to various pressures," Sargt added, looking smug. "Our Jaush tempers like a fine blade. In fact, that part about sharper senses, tell us what you have noticed."

Jaush glared at Sargt. *You already know.*

I have for some time. She still does not.

It's not fair to her.

She has had plenty of time to consider and will not break under a bit more pressure, young one. She desires to bear your offspring but is still too proud and knowledge-hungry around me to confirm it. Give her a nudge. You have more than earned it.

Jaush rubbed his hands again, and Beliza asked, "What? What is it?"

The young male swallowed. "I ... can feel the magical aura in your belly when I touch you and pay attention. That's ... never happened to me before. And the last time I put my ear against your middle ... ?"

She nodded. They'd been lounging in afterglow after he'd only had the energy to crawl half-way up after helping her cum one more time with his mouth. His arm around her waist, head resting on her belly, her fingers combing his hair …

He was nervous when he said it.

"I heard two heartbeats, Beliza. There are two babies in your womb."

Beliza uttered a cry of shock, lifting her hands to cover her mouth as the sound faded into the cave. She stared at him with widened eyes, and Jaush couldn't tell if either that sound or that face was one of denial or …

Or something better. Something hopeful.

Sargt chuckled in deep amusement. "So, if House D'Shea and House Aurenthin has come back together to breed anew, does that mean House D'Shauranti is risen from the ashes?"

"Not yet, and not like before," the sorceress murmured, holding her belly with both hands, her eyes bright and full of thought as Ilka shifted with her mistress's excitement. "But … if I bore them …" She looked at Jaush. "How would we … ?"

That was the next step Jaush hadn't spent a lot of energy thinking about until the sorceress uttered it out loud. How would they care for not just one infant but two of them entirely alone except to become tolerable servant-guests of a Dragon?

"You aren't interested in raising a Baenar family, right?" Jaush asked Sargt directly.

The Dragon shook his head in amusement. "Not in the least, my delectable little slut."

Jaush nodded. "Just checking."

Chapter 11

2152 S.E., Vuthra'tern

THE OLDEST MALE DAVRIN IN VUTHRA'TERN WAITED FOR THE DRAGON TO COME again. Y'shir was wary of acknowledging hope but grateful for the scent of change.

As far as he knew, in the last five centuries since his people had settled here, he was the only one to lay eyes upon the Great One while he was awake. That first meeting had stirred some of the elder male's deepest memories outside of his magic.

The first in a long time.

Some of his current Priestess-Matrons claimed to meet with the Dragon in occasional Reverie or rituals. All the stories claimed that his den was close by, while odd, unexplainable events of magic drifted through at times. The Blade Song Grandmaster would never openly doubt the Priestess-Matrons but wondered privately. They only used this idea for petty and short-term control.

Even the Queen-Seer Ishuna hadn't claimed alliance with the Black Serpent, in part because no one at House Ja'Prohn or House D'Shauranti would allow that claim to stand without proof. It held while the new city had Xala Ja'Prohn, the General whose strategies had taken the Great Cavern *from* the Dragon, and while his own Mother, Lizabet D'Shauranti, was alive.

Her disciplined training had ultimately won the Davrin their new home in the first place.

Y'shir had grown into one of Sivaraus's elders, having always looked up to the General and the Sorceress Supreme. He'd aimed to be as wise and strong as them. Male though he was, no one had mastered Blade Song as well as he had.

Xala had passed away with surprisingly little violence, unlike his easily impassioned Mother and Matron. The General had been the last Davrin who could talk grounded sense to balance their visionary Mystic-Queen. Once she was gone, the decline began. Looking back, the changes had only seemed slow because he'd not been able to recognize what had been brewing just beneath the altars within the Priesthood.

When it all came to a head, the demands of the Spider Queen were not to be denied.

As frightening and terrible as Ishuna's deceased sister had become in the Red Desert, Ishuna herself had eclipsed that when She released the Driders and the Sathoet both upon Her own people. Up until then, these gifts from their Goddess had been the defenders against the rest of the Deepearth after chasing the Black Serpent out.

With Braqth's creatures, the Davrin held their new borders until the Houses were well established, stable, and could not be easily expunged. They were safe from being eradicated, as their Queen had promised.

But the promises didn't last.

Perhaps he had been too old even then, too tired to fight anymore when the Matrons in favor of the Break had come together as Priestesses of Braqth to carve out new borders for Vuthra'tern. He understood their weariness, at least.

Their smaller population had been constantly attacked since their escape from Sivaraus. None in the Deepearth had been willing to leave them in peace or let them find a way out back to the Surface. They'd been preceded by their Valsharess's reputation at every turn

After more than a century of nomadic existence, the Matrons were using the same tactics once used on them, and someone had listened to the promises of Braqth. They began bearing and using demon-bred sons to enhance their magic and status over those they ruled, receiving unique gifts never seen before, and causing more than enough fear and misery both within and without to finally set those borders into eternal iron.

Y'shir knew now he was trapped, expecting to die here while the younger ones forgot who they'd been. The purpose of the rebellion against the Valsharess, which no one seemed to recall anymore, had failed at last and could never be rekindled.

Even the great House Ja'Prohn which Y'shir had joined at the expense of his own family was irrevocably changed, among the cruelest of those tainted by the Abyss. Seeing this caused him more sorrow and regret than he felt he could bear some cycles.

The only relative blessing he could hold was that while the Matron-Priestesses gave birth to half-demon sons like in Sivaraus, there were no Driders here. Vuthra'tern did not need a Drider Keeper, for none of their children were condemned to become twisted, half-living monstrosities no longer functioning as Elves.

Y'shir had been waiting for over a turn for the Dragon to return, after asking him about his old House. After stirring so many memories.

Perhaps the Great Drake could trade for some answers, some understanding, though it would be yet more knowledge which may only die with him, as it had General Xala and later, Tala, his Daughter whom he'd had left behind in that last battle.

"GRANDMASTER! GRANDMASTER, COME AND SEE! YOU'RE BEING SUMMONED!"

Y'shir acknowledged the summons formally to the excitable, young cait, as was her due. "Yes, First Daughter Mikiri. I am coming."

The whispers were saying House Dar'Prohn had captured something very interesting in the Deepearth. Something that could work in their favor to remain the First House, as was their right.

"No one with our lineage and history is more qualified or entitled," their Matron often muttered. "Why any would challenge it is beyond me."

The eldest male had lived enough centuries for his hair to have changed to solid gold, which he kept in a very long braid. Unhurriedly, he walked where the child led him, expecting to be brought to the dungeons.

They turned to the left wing, the one where they kept political prisoners away from the criminal or bestial, and Y'shir heard the raging and terrified screaming of a female. He altered his expectations, wondering who House Dar'Prohn had taken this time, instead of what had been found out in the wilderness.

At the prison door, he soon discovered both his questions were equally valid.

Who ... ?

"Let me go!" she shrieked as three guards and two mages struggled to place her in restraints to both further suppress her magic and so she couldn't harm herself. "I'll kill you! I'll kill you all for what you've done!"

He had never seen this Davrin in Vuthra'tern before; he was certain she came from outside of it. She spoke differently, her aura flared powerfully, and she was too old for him not to have either met or heard gossip of her. She was heavily pregnant as well, probably carrying twins. This would never be kept secret until this close to birth.

She must be a Noble sorceress from the Valsharess's City.

What was she doing all the way out here?

"You see it already," his Matron smirked in satisfaction behind him. "Not getting dull in your old age, Grandmaster?"

He bowed his head to her. "She is of those serving the Unnamed Queen, is she not?"

"Yes."

"Where did you capture her?"

The Matron Dar'Prohn nodded to her Head Guard, allowing her to fill in the blanks while she observed their captive losing her struggle inside the cell. She chuckled as a second guard cried out in pain.

"Sentries caught their trail toward the waterfall," Head Guard Berus told him, "and scouts tracked for spans before I finally had to go out. We caught up with them, rounded them back closer to here before trapping them."

Them?

"There were more?" Y'shir asked.

"One more, a servant-fighter," the Matron said dismissively before Berus could speak, though she nodded and picked up the thread again.

"Her bodyguard, as far as we could tell. Wouldn't stay down and wouldn't surrender. We finally had to shove him off a cliff."

"A pity," the Matron said. "I would have liked to interrogate him before placing him on my altar."

The pregnant mother heard that. She screamed in such mournful agony, a despairing pitch and tone he had not heard since the nomadic days of their population. Lancing pain shot through his chest to listen. The guards quickly and viciously gagged her, and Y'shir swallowed.

He was not just a bodyguard.

"And what do you need from me, Matron-Priestess?" he asked respectfully, bowing. "Head Guard?"

"There's a drake that wouldn't leave us alone and followed us here," Berus said. "We injured it, but we can't trap it. Keeps slipping free no matter what we do yet doesn't go away, it's like her own damn shadow." She shook her head. "Doesn't make sense to me. What about you? Heard of it before?"

Y'shir stared at them before looking in at the prisoner while they set and strengthened the magical restraints to hold her on soft bedding laid over the stone. Padding had been attached to the corner walls.

At least they didn't lash her down onto her back.

The sorceress-mother could sit up or lie down on her side as needed. He felt a tinge of bitterness thinking that was the most kindness he could expect any more from the House he'd once fought beside.

For whom he had given up everything.

Careful. These thoughts have been too long buried to bring them up now ...

He cleared his throat. "The sorceress cast an animal-guard spell on the drake. It is compelled to stay with her. I imagine she wanted a pet, and a useful hunter and forager of the wilderness. Given enough time and separation, the spell will fade, and it will fly away if the compulsion doesn't cause its death first."

The Matron nodded. "What I thought. Very well. Put it out of its misery if it continues to harry us, Berus."

"Yes, Matron."

Cold and calculating crimson eyes returned to the writhing, powerless prisoner. "How close would you estimate is she to birthing, Y'shir?"

Somehow, despite being the eldest weapons master, he had gradually taken on side-role of healer as well, appraising their female warriors who became pregnant. Ironically, he had more experience in this matter than many of the young mothers here. Every generation, his current Matron-Priestess seemed more and more youth-like to him.

"I would have to examine her more closely, Matron," Y'shir said. "It isn't as easy to tell when there are two, and she is already under great stress. This could trigger early contractions if we don't calm her down."

Matron Dar'Prohn tapped her fingertips eagerly together before catching herself — a childhood habit she was still trying to break — and nodded. "Twins. Excellent. Good, I'm glad you see it, too. Do what you must, Grandmaster."

Those were exactly the words he'd hoped to hear.

Y'SHIR HAD NEEDED TO USE A VERY SMALL AMOUNT OF SEDATION POTION TO prevent the foreign sorceress from going into labor that very cycle. He broke his visits into many small ones with minor updates that first eve, hoping to glean as much insight as quickly as he could.

He heard many unusual things on his visits, in addition to the pestering drake, that made him reconsider whether they had heard the last from the sorceress's protector.

"I'm telling you, he didn't bleed, Grandmaster," one injured soldier told him while confined to a cell block meant for interrogations. "This fucker ... I got him! Dead by right! Sword tip square in the gut! Fucker took it full and grunted, didn't spill a drop that wasn't sweat when his intestines should have been at his feet!"

"Wild story," another in a different cell commented.

"You weren't there!" she shot back, her heart pounding with insult.

"Probably just a stone-skin spell that would wear off with enough hits," the other retorted. "You just didn't get lucky enough. I'd think the Matron and Head Guard would be on high alert if you really met an invulnerable Davrin sent from the Valsh —"

"Don't say it!" the first fighter hissed. "Her agents will find us! It's bad enough they dragged that swollen sorceress here, ready to pop out Abyss knows what! Could be a sick trap for all we know!"

Y'shir at least knew why this soldier was in prison if she didn't know enough to shut her mouth. Fear like this would spread to the other Houses like fire, and the other Matron-Priestesses would demand the strange sorceress's execution and sacrifice along with her babies as soon as possible. Maybe they would do it before the children were even born.

Although, that hasn't happened in a while.

Y'shir guessed that the Matron intended to quietly incorporate these mage twins into her House. Something about this had triggered greed over security, and the other Matrons would make her pay handsomely for it if they knew about it.

The Matron would keep one example — this soldier, who would be dead very soon in a private ceremony — to convince the others to take the "gag potion." They would never talk about what they'd seen out in the wilderness or whisper where these children had come from.

The fourth time the weapons master visited the pregnant prisoner, he removed the gag gently once she agreed to be quiet. She managed a firm grip on his wrist as he examined her belly, and he let it stay there. Her eyes blazed and glistened with tears as she stared up at him, afraid and desperate for herself and her unborn.

She finally spoke past the sedative. "Wh-who are y-you?"

The accent was similar to how he remembered his Mother.

Y'shir bowed his head respectfully. "I am Y'shir Matalai'ko. I will not harm you or your children, honored mother. I am here to tend you."

Her eyes widened as far as they would go, and he read that she knew his name.

"Oh ... ! Y-you're a grandsire of my lineage. H-House D'Shauranti?"

Something cold and hot at once pierced him, and he stared at the unfamiliar sorceress before checking that the guard was still outside. He put a finger to his lips, signaling silence before he moved his hand deliberate and slow.

★What is your name, daughter?★

Even the Matron hadn't learned that yet. He knew he was taking advantage, but ...

I must know.

She could read the sign, thankfully, but only after some mental translation. ★Beliza D'Shea.★

He shook his head, face showing confusion. ★D'Shea?★

★D'Shea,★ she repeated deliberately with trembling hand and quivering bottom lip. Her eyes teared up before true tears dripped down her cheeks.

He hadn't seen a female Davrin cry in sorrow for decades.

★We are half-House,★ she told him. ★Magic side. House D'Shauranti not exists, but D'Shea is, with House Aurenthin, warriors.★ Signing this caused a whimper to escape her throat. ★Killed my consort-sire! My warrior!★

Goddess, what have I done ... ?

"Please ..." she whispered.

He shushed her, encouraged her to sign.

★If see Ilka, tell her, run away or they kill her also!★

★Ilka?★

★My familiar. Shadow drake.★

It can't be ...

★Please, grandsire!★

She could tell. She *saw* him more clearly than any of his betters. She knew he was different, because so was she.

"Alright," he spoke aloud, glancing to assure no one new had arrived. "You seem healthy, honored mother, just relax. I will get you what you need."

He paused. Should he tell her what the soldier had said about her bodyguard? *Perhaps not.* Perhaps it would only lift her hopes when there were none.

How do you know who I am? he asked. *Did the Valsharess tell you?*

Beliza shook her head desperately. *No one remembers. No one! I discover it. You confirmed.*

How?

*Dragon. Black Dragon ... *

Ah.

So that was why the Great Drake had brought such an odd questions for him more than a turn ago. Y'shir had been waiting for the Dragon to return and, in some way, he had. This prisoner might be his thrice-great granddaughter, and she would have been newly pregnant and in contact with the Black Dragon back then.

Had she come to find him? She came bearing children from his old House, which were sadly destined to be used and kept a slave as he was. Beliza herself wouldn't survive here; she already showed too much emotion. After so long, the twists had turned, but now he was so old, he may never see how this ended.

The impulse to imagine the Black Dragon even crueler than his Matron was tempting.

It might also be that he is more merciful.

CHAPTER 12

2152 S.E., THE DEEPEARTH WILDERNESS

THE GIFT OF THE TO'VAH WASN'T WITHOUT ITS DOWNSIDE.

Beliza and Ilka made a strong showing against their attackers, keeping the casters and most of the fighters off him when their small family had been ambushed.

There were too many of them to win.

All Jaush and Beliza could do was try to seal off an escape once they reached the right tunnel, although that lead commander and her trackers had been following them for spans and weren't giving up anytime soon. Too late, he realized they'd been herded into the wrong tunnel, back to that fucking waterfall as they'd made a circle.

Far above and all around them, the cliffs were sheer.

Cornered at the edge of the chasm, Jaush had taken multiple sword strikes, bolts, and spells which damaged and singed his clothing, tools, and weapons. The last slam of a blade's point right in his abdomen had felt like someone punching him with a fist, knocking the wind out of him before he knocked it aside.

Finally, the lead female simply rammed him with her shoulder, pushing him over the cliff and far down as Beliza screamed for him.

He landed among slick rocks sprayed with roaring water.

For a while, everything was black.

When he came aware, Jaush was soaked, chilled, and partially naked. His clothes were in tatters, his hair singed, and most of his tools and weapons gone. He wasn't bleeding, however, and not a single bone was broken. He had something of a headache and a clear recollection of his landing alongside every strike leading to it.

Since being allowed to leave Sargt's lair, he and Beliza had learned the sire of her children was unimaginably resilient. Jaush resisted injury, burns from excessive temperatures, diseases, poisons, and toxins as well.

Their attackers had discovered of this quickly.

Jaush was never ill anymore, but where it came to sex and violence, he could still feel ... *everything*. The pleasure in orgasm was more intense while the force from a blow could be as stunning or crippling as it should be. Yet, he always got back up. The pain would pass.

Jaush would never have imagined that a turn of being mounted and inseminated by the Dragon of the Deepearth would have had that effect on him. Ever since they'd made the decision to leave Sargt's lair — for Sargt made it clear they must not give birth to their twins among his hoard, or he would "keep" them — Jaush had used this gift to take all the risks for Beliza and his unborn twins. He had even given her his old ring of protection.

The young Aurenthin could be much bolder getting them food, and until now they'd been able to drive off any threats with spells and persistent blade dance and tricks. Jaush had helped them evade the Davrin from the other city for as long as he could, though the urgent need for food drove them to keep moving dens rather than hiding long-term.

Beliza had run until she couldn't anymore; Jaush had fought for them, until he couldn't anymore. There had been too many Davrin this time, and they had learned from past defeats. Too many of his own kind, and like him, they wouldn't give up. They had Beliza cornered and had finally pushed Jaush out of the way.

Now he was awake, and he knew what his first step was.

Find Vuthra'tern. Discover where they've taken my family.

THE BORDER PARTY HAD MADE IT EASY TO TRACK THEM BACK TO THEIR CITY. They could have hidden their tracks much better, but instead of assuming arrogance, Jaush took it as a warning that they might be expecting him to show up again.

He left no sign behind himself, though he expected sentries and magical wards out in front. Jaush already knew he couldn't charge in. He might be very hard to kill but they could still capture him.

They would enjoy having a second opportunity to try.

Ilka signaled him when he drew close to the border. He heard the familiar burr of Beliza's companion, one no other Davrin would recognize as having come from an intelligent creature. When she didn't emerge or climb down from the crevice in which she hid, Jaush climbed up to her. He smelled the blood even before he saw her.

Damn them.

A break in her left wing left her unable to fold it down or fly. A bolt from a hand-held crossbow was still lodged in her hind leg. The shaft was splintered from where Ilka had been gnawing on it trying to remove it. She wouldn't have survived if not for escaping through shadows.

"Let me take you out," he whispered, reaching in and leaving his hands open. "We'll get the bolt out."

She whimpered on a gurgle, her smaller ribcage moving in rapid breaths, and she blinked at him with too-moist eyes.

Shit. Of course it was poisoned.

"Ilka," he whispered, "don't bite me, alright? I need to bring you out or I can't help."

Not that he could help a lot anyway. He didn't have much left from the fall he'd been able to salvage: a dagger he'd fished out in a side pool, his pants and boots, some rope, and the tatters of his shirt tied around his waist.

Everything else including half of his hair was gone. Anything more delicate had been water-logged and useless, and he'd already eaten the soggy rations while he could. He'd stuffed his belt and whatever pouches still clung to it somewhere it might dry or might not. Assuming he could ever return to that spot.

At best, Jaush might be able to bind the bolt hole in Ilka's leg, though he had no idea how to set a broken wing bone on a drake.

Damn it. I need a mage for this. Hells, Ilka needs her mage.

"Is she alive?" he murmured.

Ilka knew what he meant.

"Was when I escaped," she croaked. "Scared. Mourning."

"Mourning?" His heart sped up beyond his control.

"Us. Not babies."

Jaush exhaled in subtle relief, aware he should be concerned what would happen to Beliza if Ilka died. He focused on getting the bolt out of Ilka's leg and using his water to wash out the wound before binding it firm with the pieces of his shirt to stop the bleeding.

Ilka didn't complain beyond the unavoidable squawk at the bolt being yanked out, accepting his pitiful efforts in tending her afterward.

"You know a gap in their borders?" he whispered.

"To fit one big as you?" she asked dryly, shaking her head. "As closed as Sivarausss …"

Jaush sat for a while, squeezed in a crevice of his own to hid his outline and heat signature. He kept Ilka warmer and more comfortable as she shivered from the slow poison, thinking on the enormous stack of problems that had piled up quickly.

He wanted Beliza back. He'd promised her she wouldn't have to give birth yet again in captivity among Priestesses, but he wouldn't be able to reach her by himself.

Ilka had sneaked out of the borders when she was injured, but she'd seen enough while inside. She described it to him in brief murmurings as she had the energy.

Sounds like I'd have to enter the Queen's own dungeons to reach Beliza.

He'd never done that before. He had only reached places above them, within the Palace itself where servants were allowed. That was how he'd met Beliza in the first place, and even then, he'd had help. *Contacts.*

"No contacts here," he murmured aloud, more to himself though the shadow drake responded after breathing in painfully.

"Gold-hair mage," Ilka said with a wheeze, "compelled me to him. When I left Beliza alone."

"Gold hair?"

"Ancient Davrin. Hair turns yellow."

Jaush had never seen that before, though he'd heard that the Valsharess was turning that way. *An old, male mage?*

If he was still alive after all this time, did that make him more or less dangerous than the young females which had attacked them?

"He compelled you, then let you go," Jaush nudged the drake. "What did he say? Anything?"

Ilka whimpered. "Message from mistress. Go away, or be killed if seen again."

"So he knew she had a familiar, and delivered a message for her?"

A tired nod.

"He compelled, but did he harm you? Was it he who broke your wing or poisoned you?"

The shadow drake shook her head despite how weakened she was. At least the old mage wasn't bloodthirsty in capturing and torturing smaller creatures when given the opportunity. That was something.

A lot of good that does when I'm out here and the gold-hair is in there.

Chapter 13

2152 S.E., House Dar'Prohn, Vuthra'tern

"What is wrong with her, Y'shir? Why is she weakening like this?"

The weapons master bowed his head. "I believe I was wrong in my initial assessment, Matron-Priestess. This sorceress has an older and stronger magical bond with the drake. It's not an instinct-suppression spell. The drake has been injured and is dying somewhere out in the wilderness, and she weakens with it."

"Will it kill the twins?"

"I do not know, my Matron. It could."

"Should we cut them out now before it gets worse for her?"

Only through immense effort did Y'shir not wince to hear that.

"Mm. My recommendation is she needs a few more quad-spans yet for them to be full term." He hesitated. "If you will it, I can find the drake again and mend it. It should restore her health, and we will have time to study this bond."

"Perhaps learn what she did, exactly," the Matron Dar'Prohn pondered, nodding. "Very well. I will it, Y'shir. Take whoever you need and find that drake and bring it back here if it needs so badly to be with her."

Y'shir bowed his head and left.

He took a large risk in asking absolutely no one to go with him, but he was the Weapons Master of House Dar'Prohn. He was still the elder advisor they asked about unusual situations like this, and almost any in which the Matron needed discretion.

He'd earned it simply by not talking about House business to those who had no need to know. He even agreed with his young Matron now; the fewer who knew about this pregnant sorceress, the better.

"I need a few wild mushrooms," Y'shir told the sentries on his ride out on a House lizard.

The sentries nodded; they'd heard this before. "As you will, Grandmaster."

The ancient mage was not randomly searching the Deepearth for the drake. When he had called the loitering creature near enough to speak outside the prison, she became afraid of his magic. The poor creature would not let him touch her, even to neutralize the poison.

He'd forgotten how loyal to their chosen mage some familiars could be. Y'shir using a strong spell on her and telling her Beliza's message too soon had been a mistake. When he saw she was about to escape, he had compounded it by putting a magical mark on her so he could sense her again if she got close.

She had not drawn close ever since. That was four cycles ago.

From how Beliza seemed now — unable to rest, feeling phantom pains and poisons which could not easily be explained — the creature was suffering and would be dead before long. If not for the demands of the mother's belly, the sorceress herself might not have eaten.

You can be as overbearing as your Matrons, old Elf, he thought tiredly as he searched for that mark, hoping he could mend what he had frayed out of shocked ignorance and urgency.

Later that cycle, he found it, and therefore found the drake. Having magically deadened all sound and scent from his mounted approach, Y'shir had the luxury of confirming Ilka still breathed. She was at rest in a young bua's arms, who sat in a crevice somewhat above Y'shir's head.

Ah-ha. You live.

The weapons master felt genuine gladness for this, that Beliza's protector was there, trying to comfort her familiar and give her water.

Then the young fighter tensed, ready to spring up out of his crevice.

97

"I mean no harm, Jaush," Y'shir said, maintaining both hands on his saddle ridge. Lifting empty hands into view wasn't considered a show of surrender for mages as it was for soldiers. Quite the opposite. "I'm sure Ilka would appreciate not being jostled."

The youth stilled hearing his name, appraising the older male quickly. His eyes, nose, and ears all noted something about him; the bua wasn't studying the mage's aura, that was obvious.

"You're the gold-hair," Jaush said bluntly.

He had nearly the same accent as Beliza.

Y'shir smiled a little. "That I am, I suppose. I am here to heal the shadow drake before it is too late, both for hers and Beliza's sake."

Ilka barely paid attention; she hadn't the strength to make her choices known. All decisions rested on the young fighter's shoulders.

"She told you my name, gold-hair?"

"Unintended, but yes," Y'shir replied. "She spoke it in Reverie, remembering the last time she saw you by the waterfall. She willingly told me you are from the warrior House Aurenthin and are sire of her twins. Is this correct?"

Jaush looked extremely wary. "How is she?"

"Alive but suffering alongside her familiar. Come down. Once Ilka is tended to, we can talk."

The youth strained his senses, trying to determine if anyone else was nearby. Y'shir waited patiently but hoped the bua only held out so long.

"You're alone?"

"I am."

Jaush frowned. "If you can sneak up with a riding lizard, you could be masking others."

Y'shir nodded. "I could. You can't really know, can you? But I have as much time as you're willing to waste, Jaush. I am not the one with a dying familiar in my arms."

The bua wouldn't be pushed that way. Stubbornness marched visibly right up his spine into his bare shoulders. He sniffed in an odd, feral way, as if he had been raised in the wild with beasts.

"Toss me the ring on your left, middle finger, Gold-hair. I'll come down and hand you Ilka, and you will heal her without wasting more time."

Y'shir tilted his head. He saw no magical aura in this youth; Jaush was not a mage. The white gold ring he'd asked for was plain and indistinct, but it was the one most advantageous to ask for in negotiations like this.

How had he known?

"Hm," the mage considered then shrugged easily, preparing to tug off his ring. This was the second interaction with his own race in the last span that didn't stink of the Abyss.

I want to know more.

Y'shir tossed it with intention off to the side and witnessed Jaush's stunningly fast reflexes for himself. Beliza's protector reached out and unerringly caught the ring before the mage could do more than blink, and The elder mage glimpsed no aura strong enough to suggest he was using spells or objects.

The soldier's story about one fighter-bua holding off multiple House Guard at once seemed plausible.

Jaush slipped the pale ring on his own finger before he brought Ilka down gently. Y'shir dismounted and reached for the drake, able to smell the bad blood and decay within the crippled creature.

"Please guard us," Y'shir asked Jaush as he sat down cross-legged upon the rock, cradling Beliza's familiar, "and be patient. This will not be easy, or quick."

"Just don't kill her to hurt Beliza," Jaush agreed, "and I won't tear your throat out, old one."

Y'shir smiled to hear that and nodded in agreement, promptly setting to his work.

"You have known the Black Serpent," Y'shir stated to confirm.

"Yeah. I have." Jaush smiled oddly, gently stroking Ilka's throat pouch as she hummed in between small bites of dried meat the young male partially chewed and then feed to her. "He mentioned you, grandsire. Oldest living D'Shauranti, aren't you?"

The Grandmaster exhaled. "And the last, as I have heard from Beliza. Though the spirit of the House may live on in both of you, and your twins should they be born."

"The Black Dragon said that, too."

Y'shir nodded soberly. "Jaush. If you were to free her, where do you mean to take her?"

The youth's smirk faded, and he shook his head. "Far from here, that's for sure."

"Back to Sivaraus?"

"No. We left for a reason, grandsire. Did she tell you?"

"Tell me what?"

"That the Priestesses have been breeding her and her grandmothers like bloodstock. They only want House D'Shea to have more mages. Everything else they're given to do is a distraction."

Y'shir frowned. "Odd. Are you sure?"

"It wasn't me being fucked under compulsion and kept in a soft room, grandsire. I only know what she told me."

The elder male couldn't blame Jaush for his abrasiveness, and his blunt manner was rather refreshing, even if Y'shir mentally winced when he mentioned the soft room. Clearly, Matron Dar'Prohn intended the same as the Valsharess for his granddaughter.

"Where do you plan to raise two infants out there?" he asked again, his tone serious.

"None of your damned business, mage."

"You have no plan. You are aimless."

The bua smirked. "But not clueless."

"Jaush. Consider —"

"Consider what?" he barked. "That I'll give my children to either fucking, Abyss-mad city?"

"A family like yours won't survive long out here," Y'shir said firmly, "especially if at least one Matron here knows you exist. She has laid eyes upon Beliza's aura, grandson, and she will hunt you if only to make sure you don't bother her. If she captures you, she'll rip apart your essence and feed it to the Abyss."

The bua was furious with the unnamed female's threat.

"I can also tell you she wants these children for her House — "

"Why?!"

"Shh!"

They paused, listening around them. Y'shir's sound ward seemed to be holding. He continued.

"I do not know yet. It is clear to me, however, that you are the one with the greatest endurance and resilience for living in the Deepearth itself. You survived a fall from the top of a cliff without breaking a bone. You were struck with multiple poisoned edges and arrows, and you haven't so much as a light fever. You are far beyond a normal adult soldier, never mind an infant or a nursing matron. No one can keep up with you, however you came to be this way, and you know *despite* this that you cannot always protect them."

Jaush wouldn't even grant a hint about his nature.

The old mage sighed. "I am asking if you would rather watch have any of them — Beliza or the twins — taken or eaten later? Weakened by disease or poison or injury, where you can do nothing but hold them as you've held Ilka, to watch them slowly die?"

The youth narrowed eyes at him. "As opposed to what?"

"As opposed to seeing them into the care of elders of your choice —"

"Who? You?"

"Yes, grandson, I would" Y'shir said in solemn promise. "If Beliza stays, I will look after her and those infants with all my remaining days."

Jaush gave him an odd look. "Days?"

The weapons master flipped his hand. "A ... word from our Surface time. The time of light, versus the time of darkness. Like counting a cycle of earth pulses down here."

The young male stared at him, a glint of hope coming into his eyes. "The Surface? Do you know how to get there?"

Y'shir felt most of his energy drain away with the necessity of dashing that solution upon the stone and grind it underfoot.

"Jaush ... if I knew, this city would be living beneath the Sun right now, not wallowing in despair and blood sacrifice. This is where I have failed the worst.

"And after so long since the Valsharess led us down here, I could not tell you if claiming a home up there would be any easier or less bloody than it is down here. For a small and vulnerable family, it may be just as dangerous. There would be different diseases for young bodies to withstand and a long adjustment to see normally in daylight. Especially for those who have never seen the Sun in their life."

Jaush lowered his head, reassuring himself that he held a healed, hungry, and easily resting drake in his lap. After a long moment, finally, he nodded his head. "You're doing a good job convincing me it's hopeless, grandsire."

"The odds are long and against you," Y'shir said. "Beliza may have fought as long as she could beside you, much to expect of any carrying female, but now she cannot. Will you let me *help* you decide what's best for them?"

The youth looked up and frowned at him in the same way he had just before asking for his most powerful ring of teleportation.

"Get me inside to see Beliza, grandsire, and I'll discuss it with her."

"Wow, look what Y'shir caught!" one sentry exclaimed.

"The Matron will be very pleased. That's the little fuck that bit off Yuta's ear, isn't it?"

"Is that what you have to do? Shine a light on it from both sides and it can't vanish? Neat! Can't wait to see the thing roasted on a spit."

"As you were," Y'shir suggested. "I shouldn't be delayed from delivering to the Matron-Priestess."

"Of course, of course, ancient one."

Y'shir rode farther down the slope and easily into Dar'Prohn land. He chuckled softly. "That worked even better than I'd hoped. You're quite the distraction, Ilka."

She growled testily with the string still wrapped around her muzzle, her wings tucked close, and her tail lashing irritably. She was indeed the most obvious thing to look at, with two small balls of light flanking the collapsible cage strapped to the haunches of his riding lizard.

Jaush was cloaked with an illusion spell suggesting a rough texture if the sentries checked beneath the riding lizard's belly, as they were supposed to do. The spell proved unnecessary when they had forgotten to look much beneath the level of the illuminated drake.

"They're complacent around me," Y'shir murmured when it was safe.

"Tells me you're in a rut," Jaush muttered back from where he clung underneath.

"A good thing for you, here and now. You remember the command word if you must use my ring?"

"Yeah."

"There are only two charges left. If you must jump in, you can only jump out once. If you jump out first, you cannot jump back in without being stranded."

"Got it. Will the Matron notice it missing from your finger?"

"I have a similar one to replace it, and she has little reason to check the purposes of my rings anymore."

"Maybe she does now. She's got a valuable prisoner or three."

"Fair point. Let's neither of us get complacent."

"YOU HAVE IT. LET ME LOOK."

Matron Dar'Prohn tromped impatiently around the small cage, shielding her eyes from the light which kept the shadow drake from leaping out.

"Clever, Y'shir. What took you so long?"

"The drake was nearly dead from poison and infection, Matron-Priestess. See her hind leg, there? It took time to mend her. I could not bring her here until I did. Has the sorceress grown stronger while I've been gone?"

The Matron scowled down at the persistent pest to her hunting party. "She has. She is in Reverie now. It was interesting."

"Shall we reunite them, Matron?"

"To what purpose, Grandmaster?"

"If she is a familiar of the old style, which I have not seen since I was a child, Matron, then it will be obvious in the sorceress's aura."

"And how does that help me?"

Y'shir shrugged. "You will have a direct method to interrogate her, Matron. She will answer any questions you ask. Harm the drake and she will feel it without it harming her unborn. Though bear in mind if you kill the drake, the sorceress's magic will be crippled, at least for a time. It would be as if someone killed your own Sathoet son, Matron-Priestess."

The younger female hissed at him the same as the drake did.

"Be silent, Y'shir! Do not ever speak that again."

"I apologize, Matron. Shall we?"

"PESHNEL. STOP POKING AT IT."

The Sathoet grunted and sat on his haunches in disappointment just beside the brightly lit cage. His claws were lightly blooded, and he licked the drake's blood, grinning malevolently at Ilka. She coughed a bubble of rank air back at him, making him snort and jerk away, shuffling back a bit more.

"So," the Matron-Priestess began, ignoring the animals' bickering. "Beliza D'Shea, is it? And you are from the cursed city, Sivaraus?"

Beliza's cheeks were already wet with silent tears as she kept a desperate gaze on the well-being of her familiar, much to the derision of the other female. "Yes."

"Say, 'Yes, Matron-Priestess,' Beliza."

The sorceress bit her lip as a shudder passed through her. "Yes, Matron-

Priestess."

Matron Dar'Prohn pleased with the swift compliance after having had to wait more than a span to get this much from the prisoner. "Tell me what you know of your unborn children, Beliza."

The other blinked and looked at her. "Huh?"

"At this point, any mother knows something about her baby," the Matron cooed, strutting closer. She bent over, letting soft breasts beneath her Priestess robe hang against the fabric. "I want to know what you've dreamed, little mother. Or Peshnel begins shredding the drake's left wing. Speak truth to me now, and her wings stay intact. You may even touch her."

Beliza glanced at Y'shir, her hatred easy to see, much to the Matron's added pleasure. "I dreamed ... th-they will both be watched by the Dragon of the Deepearth."

Matron Dar'Prohn's eyes widened in surprise and eagerness. "Truly? Why so?"

"He'll be curious, nothing more," she admitted, clearly reluctant though aware the Matron had several lie detectors set in place.

The only defense Beliza had before now was her illness and high resistance to compulsive-speech spells. She could be silent, though she could not lie under such pressure.

"Nothing more? Oh, darling Beliza, do tell me what would have garnered his interest in the first place."

The sorceress huffed a laugh and tried to breathe deeply. "They gestated in his den, among his hoard. For a turn."

"Gesta ... ? You don't mean to suggest that large cock somehow mounted a Davrin?"

"What?" Her face became very hot as she imagined that. " ... N-no! I-I had already caught!"

"You had. Was it by that bua we killed?"

Beliza's expression turned murderous. "Yes, by that bua, you phlegm-sucking pucker-cleaner for the Abyss."

The Matron went for the pregnant Davrin's throat.

Y'shir cleared his throat in a hurry. "Matron. Matron, please! This is beneath you."

Goddess, when did his own leaders grow so crude and petty with no self-control? Not only this, but his own well-practiced control grew tenuous the more he watched the genuine distress and response from the descendent of his Daughter.

This reminded him how little was genuine where he lived now, except for the fear and gluttony, the exploitation of pain on others.

The Matron stood up slowly, taking a smooth breath and straightening her robe. She turned around and stepped up to Y'shir. He looked at her chin, as he must, and waited.

There was a beat before she struck him so hard, he stumbled to one side. He listened to her exhaling as if some massive pressure had been released as the Matron walked over to comb through her son's mane.

She extended her hand for the softly hissing snake whip he kept for her. "Next time, Y'shir, I don't care how frail you've become over the centuries. You'll feel the venom of Braqth for speaking to me so."

"Yes, my Matron-Priestess."

"Good. Now. Let us begin again."

EVENTUALLY, THE MATRON HAD TO LEAVE HER INTERROGATION. SHE COULD not continue to neglect happenings back at the manor when a third messenger had come for her. Fortunately, she had gotten enough from a weeping Beliza to be satisfied for one eve.

"Tend the drake's wounds, and make sure the babies remain healthy before you leave, Y'shir."

"Yes, Matron-Priestess."

Fortunately, the Priestess had taken her eagerly sniffing son with her, and the Weapons Master saw the change of the guard himself. This allowed one magical charge on his ring to be saved for when it was truly needed.

★Thank you for your control,★ Y'shir signed as Jaush stepped up in uniform.

The youth shook his head. ★Don't thank me. I wanted to stab her as she walked past.★

★Satisfying for two moments, for which you trade everything.★

Jaush signed back with a dark grin. ★Do you know from experience, old sire?★

★Not in exactly such a scenario, but yes.★

★Ah. Sorry, then.★

Y'shir shook his head, dismissing it. ★Come in and talk with her. I will help Ilka and set the protection wards. You will have some time and quiet at last.★

Jaush nodded and stepped into Beliza's cell to kneel beside her. He waited as quietly as possible and took his time convincing her that he was really there.

"Jaush!" the sorceress whispered. Shock, awe, delight — it was all there in her living breath.

They lunged into a kiss of a kind Y'shir had not witnessed in decades, and he protected their privacy with dampening spells and proximity wards. Then, with a soft snap of his dry fingers, one light went out beside Ilka's cage and shadows appeared on one side. The drake immediately slipped outside of the bars, tired and sore as she looked pathetically up at Y'shir.

"I am sorry, small one," he murmured, leaning down to collect her and cast something to soothe and heal her as she thrummed in her throat. "You are as brave and devoted as her chosen sire. Your bond is genuine, and despite how it can be used ... am grateful the Davrin can still experience familiars such as you."

"I think she's the only reason the Dragon let us stay at first," Jaush murmured as Ilka next slithered eagerly into a welcoming sorceress's lap.

"He was curious," Y'shir guessed, "testing your ... well, your Surface magic. Not the Abyssal."

The couple glanced at each other but then nodded warily.

"I never thought of it that way," Beliza whispered, cradling Ilka on one side since her belly had taken most of her lap by this point. "But ... maybe because it worked on a Deepearth creature."

"And Dragon-kin," Jaush added.

"I recall a bit of that at the beginning as well," the ancient Davrin murmured, "but it tapered off very quickly with the change of environment. I thought we'd lost it."

As we nearly have Blade Song.

"And your dream is true?" Y'shir asked Beliza. "The Great Drake will remain curious about your children if they are born?"

Jaush shrugged. "He doesn't have a lot else to do, it seems."

The elder male nodded, wondering about this invulnerable bua living with the Dragon and his sorceress, but gestured to the both of them instead. "You are here. Talk with her as you wanted. You may not have long to make your decision together. I will keep watch."

"WHAT ARE THESE?" HE WHISPERED ON HER MANACLES AND NECK COLLAR WHICH had no locks or mechanisms.

"They are resistant to spells and suppress my aura. I can't take them off."

"Can Y'shir?"

"Probably, but his Matron will know instantly. She taunted me about it."

"You believe her?"

"Yes! She doesn't need to bluff, Jaush!" She seized his hand, pointing at the ring. "What's this?"

"Ring of teleportation. How I was going to get you out of here."

She shook her own restraints. "Only if you want to take my head and hands off in doing so."

"I'm not leaving you here like this! The cunt can't just take all of you away from me as if it's her privilege!"

"Try convincing her it isn't," Beliza muttered bitterly, shaking her head. "It's just like Sivaraus here, Jaush. That city had you, and this place has Y'shir."

"So you want to leave. Run away again out into the wilderness."

She shook her head, surprising him as crimson eyes glimmered in the single glow over by Ilka's cage. She spread both hands over her belly. "I have to stay. I can't run anywhere, not anymore, and expect them to live much beyond their first breath."

His face barely withheld total collapse. "Bel ... no."

"Something else I dreamed but haven't spoken of yet," she said, testing her restraints to touch his face. "The Abyss will follow me again. Having caught me a second time, it knows me too well. If I'm with them, it'll latch on to them, too.

"But you ... *you* can still outrun it, especially with what Sargt gave you. You can choose a place for our children, Jaush. Don't let the Abyss see you now, for then they'll never see you leaving with them. Just as they never saw when you left with me."

"Beliza ... I ... !"

She took both sides of his face, wetting her palms as she did so. Neither blinked. "What I want, Jaush, is to use Matron Dar'Prohn to give me a safe delivery of our children. With Y'shir here, this can happen. Then I want you to take them back."

She kissed him, all lust and love, regret, and sorrow from the last two turns in that one taste. "And don't tell me where you decide to go next, my Dragon Warrior. Just go."

CHAPTER 14

2152 S.E., VUTHRA'TERN

JAUSH WANTED TO CHANGE THINGS, BUT HE DIDN'T HAVE THE TIME. ILKA WOULD stay with Beliza, but he needed to go.

Or the Abyss would see him.

He didn't go back outside the borders, however. Now that he was inside, he was staying inside. His Dragon-keen senses proved more than enough to keep to the fringe here, as he had back at Sivaraus.

Even though there wasn't a central populace and a large market where he could disappear, every House had their own small market by which trade happened with other Houses by invitation and armed guard. Each new cycle led him easily enough to another small nook or back gully or overlooked garden which wasn't worth the guards' efforts to peer into every time.

Jaush didn't mind having to move every cycle, either, as he waited for his children to arrive. Much as he had adapted to having Beliza with him when they'd left the City, as much as he had fallen into the need to always think of *her* first and himself next, his spans spent shifting around Vuthra'tern reminded him of how he'd spent his time before leaving Sivaraus.

It was certainly easier to get things accomplished when he was alone. He still didn't know what he would do about things when he had two infants in his arms, he certainly couldn't continue doing this. But he needed to decide.

As I promised Beliza.

Y'shir was right. He couldn't just run out into the darkness and expect delicate, baby Elves to keep up. They needed a Mother even to have a chance.

Bel ... why would you just give up and die like this ... ?

Her voice answered in his memory, as he remembered she'd told him before they'd ever left the Palace of Sivaraus.

I only want to walk free for a while, Jaush. Do you agree not to get too attached? You're still so young. You promise you will move on when I am finished walking?

He had promised. Or "agreed," anyway. But then she had lived such blood-rushing, heart-pounding adventures with him. Then she announced she was pregnant. They had met Sargt. Most of all, she had decided to keep the twins, and he though ...

Well, I thought things had changed.

With the Abyss dragging them down, perhaps things never really had changed for her. Not as they had for him.

Dragon Warrior, she called me. He smiled. *Better than Dragon's Sheath, I suppose.*

Jaush.

Y'shir. How close is she?

Close. The first has dropped low. Thank you for meeting me. I should not be long.

What do you want?

Bluntly? I want one child to keep, while you take the other.

What?!

Let me explain.

Fuck off!

*Jaush — *

Read me carefully, old one, if you even dare think to hold one back the moment I come for them, I'll fucking kill your Matron, then you!

Y'shir gave him an odd look, then smirked.

Jaush paused. *What?*

*I *want* you to kill Matron Dar'Prohn, grandson.*

He stared at the old Davrin.

Y'Shir continued. *In exchange for providing a good home, food, and hopefully a weapons apprenticeship for your infant daughter, please kill the Matron Dar'Prohn and her Sathoet for me.*

Jaush narrowed his eyes. *Why?*

Y'shir bowed his head respectfully. *Head Guard Berus and her force is more than enough to keep the other Houses back if our Matron should perish suddenly. She has been through this before.*

Oh? She has?

Indeed. When our current Matron poisoned her Mother. Berus is a level-headed leader, and the Matron's First Daughter, Mikiri, is young and malleable, though she learned to evade most torture from her Matron-Mother.

And if you have Beliza's daughter but not her son?

The mage twins will both disappear. I have a plan to explain the arrival of another infant at our House, not Beliza's. While Mikiri grows up, Berus and I can cultivate change I would like to see in House Dar'Prohn. A better home than it would be now.

Jaush could read either utter sincerity or a lack of duplicity, though both counted to him.

His ancient grandsire continued.

I would like to provide for my great-granddaughter as some small payment to the House I left behind, Y'shir signed. *I would help you and Beliza, if you let me. I can free my granddaughter as she wishes to be freed, before the Abyss corrupts her familiar. I can help provide you with a healthy son and care directly for your daughter. You may take the killing stroke of our current Matron if you want it. She will be readily replaced, as they have been each century since we settled here.*

Y'shir paused then shrugged lightly to add, *You will also be saving the young son of a servant, a friend of mine, who is set to be sacrificed in praise of the birth of mage-twins at our House.★

Jaush ground his teeth, gripping and kneading the hilt of his blade as he tried to think. He couldn't. This was too much.

★I will give you an answer the next cycle.★

★And if Beliza gives birth by then?★

★Then if your Matron does something stupid and ends up dead, you know we have a bargain, grandsire.★

LATER THAT CYCLE, BELIZA LAY STILL CHAINED TO THE SOFT, PADDED WALL. SHE tried not to clutch her unnervingly quiet daughter to her chest too hard as she worked to breathe out the second.

"G-Grandmaster?" she whispered. "It's kind of numb, I can't …"

"You're doing well, Bel. I can see the head. Have you the strength to go again?"

"D-Don't have a choice. Not as though I can leave him in there without his sister …"

Y'shir smiled at her and chanted a pain-soothing spell as Ilka nervously shifted about the shadows of the cell, unable to stay still with what her mistress was feeling. Not only that, but the old mage knew Ilka didn't trust herself to be right next to the sorceress right now. She might chomp one of the babies.

Because that's what the Abyss would want her to do.

All four of you will be free of this cell soon, in one way or another.

Y'shir stroked and coaxed Beliza's belly, bending to his comparatively lighter work as the guards watched and listened to the new mother from the outside. They were ready to update the Matron in a moment.

Come on out, little bua, your father is waiting to take you away from here.

After the second twin was born, Y'shir was wiping down the wet bundle as one of the guards called for the messenger.

The Grandmaster made eye contact with his great-granddaughter and mouthed, "Names?"

The sorceress was still gasping, her forehead damp and strands of white hair sticking to it. She asked, "What was your Mother's name?"

He blinked but answered, "Lizabet."

Beliza nodded, looking down at her curled, nursing Daughter. "Izabet Dar'Prohn, if all goes well …"

With an unexpected quiver in his arms, Y'shir bowed his head in thanks and acknowledgment. He glanced down at the son, wiping out his mouth so he could breathe fully, even if he wouldn't cry. "And … ?"

The sorceress beckoned with her free arm, determined to give each child one good feeding. The great-grandsire placed the tiny Davrin onto the platform of her still-squishy belly, and Beliza coaxed him into a position where he could not help but smell the milk.

Only when he attached to suckle did she murmur, "Jaek Aurenthin."

"Izabet and Jaek." Y'shir bowed his head, then Beliza caught his gaze. She added intensely, "Neither of them can be named D'Shea. Tell him that."

"I will, honored mother."

Jaush was probably the only Davrin in Vuthra'tern who recognized the sound of a shadow drake keening in grief.

Ilka's long, loud, unceasing cries pulled him out of an unsettled Reverie as it reverberated on their side of the cavern, drawing confused servants and guards cautiously out into the otherwise still eve.

Too late, he thought, yet he immediately collected all he owned by habit, already dressed in the stolen colors of House Dar'Prohn.

He was ready to move yet again. If Ilka was free, even if she might wish she weren't, hopefully that meant Beliza was, too.

The twins must be next.

Beliza's mourning familiar provided the perfect distraction as many of House Dar'Prohn's "best" tried to target or capture the damned animal as it made such an unwelcome ruckus. The bodies rushed around, and Jaush simply rushed in among them.

At one point, he recognized Head Guard Berus and made the mistake of meeting her eyes. She focused directly on him, her sharp, intense eyes narrowed for an instant ...

Then she looked away and bellowed out an order to her nearest. "Get the fucking drake! Go!"

He moved on, and she didn't follow him.

Y'shir must have told her. Fuck. Fuck ...

He made it closer to the prison where he was just in time to spy the weapons master escorting his Matron, his robes stained with blood. Each of them did well to cloak the presence of a baby in their arms, as if they were a mere sack of underroot buds.

To Jaush they held something more valuable than Sargt's entire hoard.

"Blast the beast if you must!" the Matron shouted at them on her way by. "Capture it if you can!"

Not too soon, wait, wait, the young male recited to himself, joining the back of the group escorting them to the manor.

He wasn't sure if Y'shir knew yet he was there, but he'd go in as deep as possible. He could still hear Ilka frequently moving around the cavern, leading them on a chase as she sought to relieve her pain. Perversely, he hoped the drake would keen so loud and long it would make the coming child sacrifice harder for the Matron to administer.

Once they reached a large, spotless lobby, the beautiful and cruel Priestess spun around to face her weapons master.

"Give him to me," she ordered.

Y'shir did not hesitate to hand her the second twin as Jaush struggled to keep his heart from giving in silent rage. Matron Dar'Prohn nodded in satisfaction, looking between the two squirming infants against her chest before lifting her chin to the old male again.

"Retrieve Qiren's third son and meet me at the altar. After that, assist Berus in recapturing the mage-less familiar."

He bowed gracefully. "Yes, Matron-Priestess."

"And Y'shir," she added just before he turned away, her arms full with his babies. She moved her hips in such a way that the snake whip made a sound, one fanged end moving on its own. "It's been a while since a Matron needed to add to that mass of scars on your back, hasn't it?"

"Your Grandmother, Matron-Priestess," Y'shir answered calmly.

"You've grown lax. Twenty lashes for letting Ilka escape. Thirty for giving Beliza too much sedative that she died!"

Y'shir's face changed a lot, showing dread as he shook his head.

"I misjudged her blood loss, Matron, please," he began, beseeching and begging in a way that nearly convinced Jaush the old mage meant it. "Ilka said she could help if I —"

"Silence! Get the servant's bua. Now." She turned around and spoke confidently over her shoulder. "I hope you have plenty of healing paste stashed, because your incompetence in this matter will see it all used up. We're lucky neither child came out crippled."

Y'shir watched the Matron leave with most of her guard, though he signaled two of them to stay: Jaush, and another he didn't know was in on this or not. Exhaling, the weapons master nodded to each of them and signed for them to follow him to the servant's quarters.

Qiren had already tried to hide her bua even though it was pointless; Y'shir found the bua in a matter of moments, pushing the toddler at Jaush to hold. The servant threw herself at the eldest male, no actual tears on her face but her expression intense and bold with protest.

"Weapons Master, please, no! Not my son! Talk to her!"

"I have, Qiren, and the Matron has decided," he said stoically. "I cannot change her mind. May you have a daughter next time, as the Matron is likely to let her be."

The young female servant shoved herself away from Y'shir as if he was a diseased pile of rags, baring her teeth and rushing from the room to slam the door with enormous force.

Anger to cover fear and grief. Jaush understood that, at least.

"Carry him," Y'shir ordered.

Ever since they had entered this room, there was a stark difference in Y'shir's expression and body language. The old Davrin came across like the guiding military trainer the "weapons master" was supposed to be, despite Jaush only having seen the wizard and the healer sides of him until now.

When one survives as long as him, one must have multiple identities.

Nonetheless, Jaush glared back at his great-grandsire. Each understood they had not yet agreed on his offer to adopt Beliza's Daughter. Jaush wagered now he'd be ordered to strap Qiren's son down on the altar himself.

Refusing to cooperate or accept Y'shir's offer wouldn't prevent Jaush from taking back his twins at some point. It would only determine whether it was before or after the ceremony, and whether this blameless child would be dead and fed to the Abyss.

The servant's bua began to struggle as they walked out, beginning to understand that his separation from his mother was not good. He whined and growled, withholding loud bellows as if he expected to be struck, though he kicked and pushed at Jaush's hold as he was carried into an ornate worship hall. The main room and side halls and offices took up most of the Right Wing of the manor.

The Abyss won't see you leaving with them, as they never saw you leaving with me … .

Beliza, he sighed, still numb in thinking her gone. *The Abyss probably will if I interrupt a blood sacrifice.*

Yet if he killed the Matron himself, he gave up his Daughter to Y'shir. That's what he'd said on impulse to the ancient male.

Goddess damn all conniving, old cocks.

Why would Y'shir just allow all this to happen for so long, anyway?

Jaush could wonder the same about Beliza and her past. He could wonder about his birth House Aurenthin and what the Valsharess and the Priesthood and the Sisterhood had all wrought. At least now he had some idea what his House had done to be where they were.

He'd been out on his own too long, and too much had changed. Beliza had given him two tender, nameless infants, and he had no idea what he could do for each of them over the next sixty-plus turns.

Beliza's urgent, frustrated voice returned. *As much as the Davrin hate and fight among each other, we need each other when it comes to breeding.*

Jaush watched Matron Dar'Prohn smile at his children and hand them carefully to her ritual assistants with a warning that they should not be so much as bruised. The Grandmaster waited patiently despite all the trouble he was in if this assassination attempt failed.

The other soldier beside him glanced quickly at him, giving away that he knew. He expected a coup, and he was eager.

Jaush had to make the decision.

Y'shir wanted a cait. He was able to make things well for her, he promised, if only this Matron died right now. The Grandmaster could do much better for a cait in Vuthra'tern than Jaush could offer as an Aurenthin back home.

Yet a son ... ?

Matron Aurenthin liked her sons. She never had a need to sacrifice any son, hers or the servants. She had even given them freedom to leave.

The Matron turned his way and pointed. "You!"

Jaush jumped, startled, and almost dropped the servant's bua as the toddler whimpered loudly.

"Bring him here."

"Yes, Matron-Priestess," he muttered, moving forward over the spotless, polished floor with the hot, fearful burden in his arms. He accidentally kicked some of the sand-salt mixtures on the floor, spreading the grains in a loose fan. The Matron cried out in immediate irritation.

"Step *over* the circle, fool!"

She was eager to put that snake whip to use and didn't give him the chance to appease her in any way. Her Sathoet son chuckled, and Jaush didn't think before turning to shield the child, letting the strike land on his back. He felt something weird prick his skin but not break it, though his shirt tore and something Abyssal hissed with disappointment.

"To'vah ..." the snake-whip whispered.

The Matron froze, her eyes widened. "What ... ?"

Fuck.

Jaush shoved the poor child as low and far away from him as he could and turned to tackle the Priestess straight on. He landed on top of her, ripping the snake whip out of her hand to toss it away.

"Stop — !"

Several crossbow bolts glanced off him as Jaush threw a punch hard enough to break her jaw. She yowled.

Oh, fuck me, that feels good ...

The ritual helpers hadn't acted yet; they'd been trying to find a place to hand off the infants in their care. They settled for a chest sitting behind them on the floor. When the two mages began to cast at him, Jaush heard an abruptly escalating chime, as if a blade spun around impossibly fast. Two daggers landed in their throats.

"Ilya-nah GESH!" the Matron screamed, her pronunciation off from her swelling jaw. Still, her aura exploded in an icy blast, knocking him off with force, even if he didn't feel the frigid ice-burn.

The young Sathoet was on him immediately, face-to-face, gripping, biting, ripping, and clawing. Any other Davrin would have been mangled, and the fight would be over.

Jaush pulled a boot dagger, kneed the Sathoet in the crotch, and stabbed him in the eye, twisting and grinding it in. The demonblood could not even scream; instead, the creature gnawed his attacker's other arm in sheer desperation but didn't pierce his dark skin.

"Peshnel!" the Matron groaned through gritted teeth, her voice halved for not opening her mouth all the way. "Y'sh'r! Kill'im!"

She glanced around, saw the Grandmaster and the one soldier with him gathering the twins and the toddler and fleeing straight out of the altar room. The guards who had shot crossbow bolts at the would-be assassin weren't anywhere to be seen.

Jaush threw Peshnel off, crippled but alive, and got to his feet. His Dar'Prohn uniform was torn to shreds but the only blood on him was that of the Sathoet.

"You ..." she hissed, pushing desperately to her feet. "The bua Beliza was bleating for! Berus saw you fall. Wazit tha' ring?"

His own jaw shut tight as she mumbled her questions; he glared at her, wishing to discuss nothing with her. Jaush charged instead, and the gout of flame erupting from her hands set his clothes on fire but did not slow him.

Jaush fell on top of her again, letting her own spell wash over her as she grunted and roared as she could with a broken jaw, trying to roll them to smother the flames. He resisted the roll and let himself burn, able to detect the heat but feeling his skin adjust and toughen the magically hard levels.

He couldn't even feel her fingernails, but he could smell her robes catching fire. Her eyes stared straight at him, showing fear.

He grinned. She panicked.

Once again, he was thrown off from magical force as the Matron used one of the rings on her right hand. She swiftly rolled and muttered a spell to cause her to be soaking wet in an instant. She smoldered, partly naked as blackened clothes hung off her and most of her hair gone. Peshnel whined, writhing half-blind toward her, twitching uncontrollably as the dagger remained lodged in his eye.

"Wh-what are y-you?" she gasped. "No Davrin bua's this pow'rful …"

"You shouldn't have taken her," Jaush said, his voice quivering with rage. "You shouldn't have imprisoned her again. It made her want to *die*."

The Matron-Priestess shook her head, glaring at him with only one eye as the other swelled shut, white eyelashes burned off and the lid covered in blisters.

"What d-did the Cursed Queen do to you … ?"

"Not nearly as much as you just did."

Jaush yanked his boot blade out of Peshnel's eye and stomped the demonblood's hand before it could grip his ankle, breaking a bone. The Dragon Warrior was still shaking, hot with fury.

"You can't have them. They aren't yours."

Jaush slammed the dagger into the Sathoet's temple, making the demonblood go still. Finally, the Priestess screamed in agony similar to poor Ilka outside.

"No one's coming to help you."

She peered around the empty altar room, seeing only herself left to stop the foreign Davrin on her lands and in her manor.

Ilka keened and continuous voices shouted too loudly to hear what was going on in the altar room, and Jaush witnessed her disbelief and contemptuous rage that both the Grandmaster and the Head Guard had betrayed her to this. Her one eye raked over him again, searching desperately for the source of magic which had bested her as she clutched herself like there was a hole in her chest.

"The Dragon sent you," she said hoarsely, her mouth bleeding.

Jaush shrugged. "Not really."

"Which House are you, assassin?!"

He refused to answer, approaching her for a third and final time.

"I think assassins make less noise, Matron."

"JAUSH."

Y'shir intercepted him into a narrow, secret passage as he had run back outside of the altar room covered in blood. He held both twins and jerked his chin to lead him into a room the Grandmaster had clearly prepared ahead of time.

"Clean up. Get dressed."

Water, soap, a basin, a towel, and a change into fresh, dark travel clothing. A pack of provisions and a belt with familiar tools, a short blade and a sword. Jaush looked at him.

"You want me to leave now."

"You must," the old male said. "Berus and I can handle the fallout, but you will complicate matters significantly. If your Daughter is to be safe, no other House must know there is any connection to the Valshraress's City in this."

Jaush gritted his teeth but stripped out of the ruined uniform to scrub himself down and redress. "So we have a bargain?"

"We do. I will look after her, Jaush, I swear this. She will do well here."

"What about Ilka?"

"You don't have time to coax her to come with you, and she will likely stay in this area while she grieves. If she follows you, so be it." Y'shir paused, watching him hurry. "What do you plan for the brother?"

"He's coming with me, as we agreed. Right?"

"Correct."

The old warrior-mage waited but exhaled when Jaush wouldn't tell him anything else. "She named them."

Jaush had grabbed the towel, paused, but then started rubbing himself dry. "Okay?"

"Izabet and Jaek."

Jaush nodded. One Noble name and one common name. Even she had known.

"She does not want either of them known as 'D'Shea.' She wanted me to tell you that."

He felt his stomach turn and needed to take a deeper breath as he nodded and continued to outfit himself. "Understood."

When all that remained was to lift the supply bag, Jaush instead reached out for the female twin. "Can I hold her just once?"

Even now the old Davrin was worried as he kept hold of Jaek almost as collateral, wary of handing his granddaughter to her too-young sire with the teleportation ring on his finger.

"Relax," Jaush huffed with a laugh, cradling his daughter, and taking a deep sniff of her infant scent. "We made a bargain."

Y'shir nodded. "That has meant less these days with the young."

"I'll keep it, grandsire. You just raise her better."

"I will do everything I can, surrounded by the Abyss and the Deepearth as we are."

Jaush nodded. So had his Mother done, he only now came to realize, and that even without the conscious knowledge of what they'd lost. He rubbed his lips across the unbelievably soft forehead before handing her back to don the provisioning pack and then trade for his son.

"Use both charges to get as far from here as you can," Y'shir said, holding Izabet as tenderly as any sire could expect. "And please listen. Return to your City if you want Jaek to survive."

Jaush said nothing as he focused on where he wanted to go.

A moment after he spoke the command word using his grandsire's ring, he and his baby vanished in a silent burst of magic.

CHAPTER 15

2152 S.E., THE DEEPEARTH WILDERNESS

THE YOUNG WARRIOR SAT ON ONE SIDE OF THE TUNNEL, HIS BACK BRACED ON the stone. Jaek grew anxious on his lap. There had been a little milk inside a skin to start with, possibly from Beliza if she and their grandsire been planning that far in advance.

Jaush didn't really want to think about that.

Regardless, the milk was gone already, and he had to admit he had little idea what he was doing.

Both charges on the ring were spent, and he was as far away as he could go and be sure where he'd end up. Unfortunately, a fair bit of the time he'd saved leaping over that distance in an instant had been spent moving no closer to Sivaraus.

He was waiting outside Sargt's den, or as close to it as he could determine, hoping foolishly that the Dragon would come by this area again soon.

Jaush might have to start hurting himself on the Wards if this took too much longer, but he dreaded doing that. If the Dragon's wards made him pass out or run away in fear, Jaek would be defenseless, even if it might — *might* — get Sargt's attention more quickly.

Attempting to break into a Dragon's Hoard proved unnecessary.

Abruptly, Jaush began to weep over what had happened, feeling Beliza's absence keenly, as he hadn't dared allow himself to feel it while she'd still been alive. It figured that the moment he'd believed he had the privacy to cry, when he could no longer hold it back regardless, that Sargt strode in out of nowhere to make this as awkward as possible.

Sargt eased a large, bipedal, wingless body down beside him without words at first, observing Jaush as he held a tiny baby close to his chest, able to do nothing but ignore the infant's persistent signals of hunger. It grew harder every moment.

"Help me, Sargt," he muttered.

The Dragon exhaled, his body language relaxed and calm. Jaush hadn't looked at his face yet but sensed no irritation that he'd come back to his door.

Still he said, "You knew it was just sex, right, Elf?"

"Yeah," the young male replied readily, his own irritation arriving as a hard, hot core in his chest. "If you think I couldn't tell the difference between you and Beliza when we were fucking, you've been asleep too long."

"Quite possibly. Just checking." Sargt chuckled, craning his neck a bit to study the infant in his lap. "Cute. Looks like you."

Jaush huffed in skeptical comment. "Thanks. Aren't you going to ask what happened?"

"I already know. You went too close to Vuthra'tern. Impressive that you made it back out."

"Beliza didn't."

"It seems you had the advantage for survival."

The young male withdrew his boot blade and pressed it point-first firmly into his wrist. "Only because you did this to me!"

His hand started to tremble from the effort. When he removed the blade, his skin was unmarked. Jaush didn't return the weapon to its sheath but dropped it beside him instead.

Sargt nodded, unsurprised as these signs had been showing long before Jaush finally left the Dragon's den. "Indeed."

Jaush glared up at him, his pulse showing in his throat as he thought of something he wasn't sure he could face. "Will I ever be able to die?"

"This quality will fade with time." The Drake grinned suggestively. "As long as I don't continue cumming inside you."

Jaush's gut warmed and his body responded well to the teasing, yet his mind shouted, *No!*

No. He had to think about Jaek.

"How long before this 'quality' fades?"

Now Sargt deigned to look a little embarrassed, though he mused aloud as if he enjoyed doing so. "Mm. Truthfully, I am not sure. It has been a very long time since I enjoyed one Elf so frequently for so long. The world was different then."

Meeting Jaush's glaring stare, the Dragon chuckled. "Remember what I told Beliza, Baenar. Every being responds differently to various pressures. This is how you responded, Jaush. Not every sentient I fuck is altered the same way, if they are much altered at all. Even with me, it takes two to determine that."

Sargt noted his stubborn denial. "Despite what you may tell yourself, you were no powerless puppet but a conscious participant in your own development. Something I tend to enjoy, believe it or not."

Not powerless, even with curtailed options. And no one would understand how he'd changed, not even his Mother.

Unique, then.

Jaush was unique, even in all Davrin history. He'd have to wait for the To'vah gift to fade.

Meanwhile, Jaek whimpered aloud, begging to nurse from his own Mother, and his sire's heart ached to hear it.

"I still need your help one more time, Sargt," Jaush said. "You can name your price as long as Jaek makes it back to my Mother well before he starves."

Sargt hummed. "That gives me the idea of a bargain, but it's not a full one. You can do better."

"Fine." He lifted his head to look up at the brilliant, gold eyes. "Is it within your ability to take Jaek and me safely to House Aurenthin within the borders of Sivaraus?"

The Dragon scratched the short, coarse bristles on his chin — more for show — as he thought for a moment. Then nodded. "It is, yes."

"Can you do it in less than a cycle?"

"I can do it in less than a mark, if you like. You might lose your meal, but the baby Baenar would be alright."

"Good. That's what I want. What is this worth to you, Great Drake?"

The large beast rumbled quietly in thought, something his infant son seemed to be listening to, though he hadn't yet opened his eyes.

"We can begin with the ring on your finger."

"Its charges are all burnt out."

"I know. That's why it is only half my payment."

Jaush pulled the ring from his finger, holding it in his fist for now but showing he was willing to part with it. "What else?"

"I would like to meet your Mother."

Jaush started. "What ? You —"

Sargt grinned at him. "Will you introduce me when we arrive? I will stay no more than a mark in her house."

"But you'll endanger my *entire* House!" Jaush blurted. "If the Valsha-ress found out, the Sisterhood would — !"

"Very well," Sargt waved a clawed hand. "I will stay no more than a mark *and* none but you and her will recognize me for what I am. I will be in Davrin form, and quite non-descript."

Jaush still considered. "Just meet her? You don't want anything else from her."

"I'll ask nothing else from her, Jaush." The Dragon extended his hand, palm up. "Do we have a bargain?"

Jaush turned it over in his mind. His son would only grow hungrier, and he wasn't even sure there would be a Davrin mata available to feed a newborn.

His Mother would think of something, if only he could reach her.

"We have a bargain, Sargt," he said, placing Y'shir's ring in the large, scaly palm.

"Done," Sargt replied, closing his clawed hand around it.

CHAPTER 16

2152 S.E., HOUSE AURENTHIN, SIVARAUS

MATRON KURIA AURENTHIN WAS IN HER OFFICE, GOING OVER WORN, RATTY ledgers just to get a brief idea if she had a rat problem. Some rats were very large and had pointed ears, and what they found valuable enough to take varied in the shade of hunger. Envious ones weren't in abundance around here, but there were plenty of spiteful and desperate. Tempted as she was simply to execute all pilferers she caught — she hated thieves taking from her family's mouths — if she did that, she wouldn't have any meager guard or servants left.

Usually it was better to "repurpose" them and discover just what they'd found so tempting at House Aurenthin in the first place. Braqth knew there wasn't much.

She didn't hear the door open, no servant made an announcement, so to hear a voice behind her startled her badly.

"Mother?"

The chair overturned in how fast she shot up to her feet, spinning around with blade drawn. She saw two Davrin buas, both smelling as if they'd been out in the wilderness for a very long time.

She blinked to recognize one of them was her youngest son, who took a protective step backward, shifting as if to hide something from her. Kuria saw it anyway.

Jaush was holding a baby.

The Matron did not lower her blade just yet as she evaluated the stranger with him. He looked perfectly common, just like a contact Jaush could bring back from the black market or the fringe of Sivaraus. Could, but never had. Her bua wasn't that foolish, at least until now.

The stranger smiled and signed an oddly formal greeting that clashed with his grubby appearance. ★Salutations, Honored Mother. You are younger than I expected.★

"Who is this?" she asked Jaush aloud, ignoring the greeting. "How did you get in just now?"

"We got in by magic," he answered. "And this is … ah … the Dragon of the Deepearth. I asked him to bring me back here."

That kind of announcement could only go over so well. Kuria's mind crowded with too many questions at once, and she flatly didn't believe him.

"Hold on a moment," she said, pausing the arising debate as she stepped around her office, activating her strongest ward items to prevent their raised voices being overheard by the servants. After some more pointless questioning, she insisted on proof before they could move forward.

"Sheath your sword, Matron," the stranger said, still smiling, "and I will provide that proof."

She did so with an odd lack of reluctance, she thought, and the Dragon — for it was indeed him — proved it by touching her hand and shifting his face and body right in front of her. He became a golden-eyed, black-scaled, white-horned draconic reptile in one smooth transition, then just as easily returned to the unremarkable male Davrin form in moments. During that time, contact with his skin let her "taste" his age, and she could barely breathe for a moment, let alone speak. They held eyes for the entire time.

"Mm," the beast hummed. "Perhaps now I know where he gets it."

What in the fucking pit had her son been doing in his exploration?

"Jaush," she said at last, taking a step to be closer to him and farther from the magical creature, who watched her far too curiously without speaking, as if he patiently waited for his turn to sort a few things out. "You have returned. It's been ..." She paused to think. "Not three turns, but still sooner than I expected given what you told me. Back so soon?" She pointed to the bundle in his arms; she recognized the small noises it was making. "Because of this?"

Her youngest nodded, very much distracted by the infant. Neither of them had ever much bothered to be anything but direct with each other — something she'd always liked about her youngest. He sounded worried when he asked, "Are you glad to see me, Matron?"

Kuria exhaled with a small, astonished shake of her head. "With both a newborn and the Dragon in tow, I'm not sure, honestly. Maybe House Aurenthin is about to be wiped out at last ..."

"I have agreed not to cause this event, Matron," the Dragon said, his deep voice not really matching the lithe form he'd taken. "You need not worry, as long as we are discreet."

She looked her fantastic "guest" in the eyes again. "And you will tell me why you are here?"

The Dragon-Davrin smiled at her, obviously amused and enjoying this. "When we get to it. I am patient. I understand we have trespassed quite unexpectedly into your den, and you are most gracious about it, young Matron."

Surreal.

Kuria moved next to Jaush, indicating she would look at the baby. He lifted him and pulled back the blanket but didn't offer to hand him over. Interesting. The moment she looked at the tiny face, she smiled without thinking. This infant was true Aurenthin.

"You brought me a grandchild?" She peeled back the blanket a bit more. "Ah-ha, a grandson."

Jaush stared at her, frozen in some nameless fear for a moment.

"He is yours, isn't he?" she teased when he didn't answer. "He looks like you did."

"Told you," the Dragon commented on a snicker, and Jaush snapped out of his stupor to glare at him before looking back at his Matron.

"He ... is mine. His name is Jaek."

Kuria nodded, thinking as the little face grimaced again with hunger that something must be done about it. There were three matas nursing at the moment, one of them her personal healer. Bryl was probably the best choice for discretion, at least until they could work this out.

"One moment. Let me summon Brylthara."

As they waited for the healer to come to the office, the Matron insisted on gently lifting the bua out of her son's over-protective arms. Based on how Jaush was lost on what to do with his hands now that they were empty, it told her he had been traveling with this child for a while now. Her grandson certainly needed a bath as well as her son, but one thing at a time. Kuria found a comfortable hold easily and nodded in satisfaction even as the infant squirmed with the change in location.

"Now, before Bryl arrives. Who is the Mother? Give me the short version."

"Was the Mother," Jaush said, and he clearly thought she would care about that detail most. "She will never come to claim him."

Certainly useful to know. She nodded. "And the deceased Mother? Who is she, and how did she die?"

Her son swallowed. "Uh. Beliza D'Shea. Died shortly after giving birth in the wilderness."

D'Shea ... ?

Kuria nearly lost her composure as her mouth dropped open. "D'Shea! What ... ? How could you say no one will try to claim him?!"

"No one knows he exists!" he cried, pleading with her. "Beliza made me promise not to name him by his Mother's House but my own!"

"He'll most likely grow to be a mage, Jaush, and he has our eyes! Someone will notice he exists, and probably the Sisterhood! They'll come to take him and then you'll be interrogated about what you've done!"

His face shifted to one of grief. "You mean you know ... ?"

"Know what?" She exhaled on her jangling nerves. "That every Matron before and including me has seen 'accidents' explain the missing Nobles too regularly? That we are the only Noble House who does not train mages or offer acolytes to the Priestesses, even as we give recruits for the Sisterhood and never see them again? Whether or not anyone talks about it, there has been something of a pattern with us. The Valsharess Herself has always had it out for us. We're her kicking bag."

The Matron looked down regretfully at baby Jaek, biting her lip. "We won't get to keep him once he shows mage potential like his Mother, and the Valsharess will want to know where he came from."

Jaush was trembling, a bit in shock as he could not think of what to say. Before this topic could continue, Brylthara knocked, and Kuria signed at both son and Dragon to hold off on it until later. It would give her time to think.

After due diligence, the Matron allowed her healer in to bear witness to the arrival of her first grandson. For good or for ill …

"I need you to feed a Motherless newborn for me, Bryl, until we come up with a better solution."

"Umm …"

The House healer looked down into the blanket. Bryl was indeed as observant as her Matron, as she glanced immediately at Jaush, pinning him with a stern eye and an arched eyebrow. Jaush fidgeted as he used to under her care. Yet … she did not seem to notice the other "Davrin" at all. Instead, Jaek's squirming and muffled protests returned her attention and she shrugged nonchalantly and reached for the baby.

"Ahright. Tits out, then, I s'ppose."

Kuria chuckled to hear her brusque and often crude healer acquiesce, giving her a place to sit where she could open her shift and settle Jaek into position. Bryl gasped to feel him latch on.

"Oh, fuck … ! Little one is desperate, Matron."

"You have enough milk for both him and Chaya?"

A nod as she studied the tiny face. "Should. For a bit, anyway." Then she looked up. "Has the Aurenthin eyes. You wanna tell me what's going on or can I guess?"

"Guess," Kuria offered, waving her hand.

"Ahright. Jaush quickened someone's womb out on the fringe, and she lumped the burden on him?"

Kuria looked at Jaush, crossing her arms. His face was easy to read; it wasn't true.

"No," he said. "I mean … yes, I did get her pregnant, but she wanted it. We were too far from help when she gave birth. She died soon after."

"Ahright," the healer said with a shrug, just as content with that explanation. "Too bad for her, then. An' you want your Matron-Mother to take the burden instead and adopt him?"

Jaush's mouth moved without sound and looked at his Mother. Kuria sighed.

"I will consider, Bryl. We could use more hands around here, but there are a few things we need to discuss first in private."

The healer nodded. After some not-so-quiet nursing as Jaek sucked and swallowed, breathing with such urgency that, as she switched breasts, Bryl commented that she was surprised the babe didn't choke.

Jaush and Kuria exchanged glances with each other during, each checking that the Dragon Davriu was still here. He stood unobtrusively along one wall of worn books, seeming to study the faded script as he remained silent. The two of them could still see the shapeshifter, but Kuria doubted that Bryl sensed him at all.

Unnerving. Where else could he stroll in, unseen?

"Ahright, that should do it for now," Brylthara said again as Jaek detached from her nipple by default when he abruptly fell asleep and could no longer suckle. She pulled up her worn shift onto her shoulders and looked at the Matron. "Want me to get him cleaned up? He's pretty smelly."

Kuria was about to nod and accept when Jaush spoke up. "I-I'll do it. Could you bring a basin and bucket of hot water here?" He looked at his Matron. "No one should see him until we've figured out our story, right?"

Bryl snorted inelegantly. "Like I don't know the secret passages inside and out around this place, bua? And sorry, I'm not lugging buckets of hot water all the way here. Someone would notice that, too. 'Sides, he's going to be digesting that milk fast and when he does, we'll need more supplies than a bucket of water. I've already got it all in my quarters with Chaya already, just let me take him for a bit." The healer bowed her head at the Matron. "You let me know what you plan to do."

"Accepted, Bryl. Thank you. Make sure no one sees him until then."

"Can do."

Jaush didn't like this but with the two females overriding him, he chose not to fight. When Bryl left through the masked passage, he looked just like a too-young mother losing sight of her baby for the first time.

Kuria privately shook her head, astonished. She hadn't expected to meet her son again after his travels, and all this would have been more amusing if Kuria didn't also see a great deal of recent suffering on his face.

She knew that was inevitable when he told her he was leaving for "a few turns," she'd had no reason or method to stop him. Jaush would experience some pain, learn some things, and if he survived, she'd meet a more mature child than the one she'd raised. Whatever happened with this baby seemed to have cut deeper than she had expected, however.

"So how in all the Abyss did you get a D'Shea sorceress to bear you a child, Jaush?" she asked. She huffed an incredulous laugh. "How did you even meet one?"

The Dragon was paying attention now, content to watch the show as Jaush finally felt the fatigue Kuria knew from experience would surge up as soon as the baby was taken care of.

Her youngest of three, not even a century old, sat down — nearly fell down — into a chair without asking her if it was alright. He rubbed his grimy face, running his hands through his short hair. She noticed that it seemed unevenly shorn, and maybe not even from something as crude as a dagger.

Fire? No, no. There are no scars …

"I can't easily explain, Mother," he admitted, not looking up. "It started when one of your 'friends' wanted someone to steal something out of the Sanctuary, and I took the job."

Kuria's mouth twitched. "Did you succeed?"

"Yeah."

That's my bua.

He saw her expression of satisfied approval. Anything to pick at and annoy the Priestesses without getting caught, it had long been this way. He relaxed, so she prodded a little more.

"But you unexpectedly met the sorceress as well."

He nodded, his face warming with the memory. "She was one of the scholars. I know we're never supposed to trust mages, but ... she was different. She was ... older than you."

"The mages do tend to live longer, more value to the Valsharess," she acknowledged, reflecting that in his circles, Jaush had probably never gotten to know a Davrin older than three hundred. She as a Matron hadn't even reached that marking stone yet, and she had no older advisors for her House. They had long been killed by something, leaving her the oldest female with power, bearing three children before she reached her second century.

"I ... helped her escape the Palace," Jaush admitted, flat and honest and direct.

Uh-oh.

"Escape," she repeated. "The Sorceress House is influential. They are hardly kept in the dungeons, Jaush."

He showed real emotion, passion entering his voice as he communicated more personal hatred for the Sanctuary than he ever had before. "They might as well be, Mother. Beliza wanted out. Your 'friends' gave me a way to make it happen without fully revealing what we were doing, so it wouldn't get back to you or endanger them."

Fucking Goddess. Kuria glanced at the still-silent Dragon, who was grinning. Almost too eagerly. He was enjoying the story.

"I might've heard some gossip about that," she admitted. "A sorceress going missing, no dead body discovered. I didn't pay attention. They just blamed the Sisterhood again."

Jaush nodded. "As we expected."

"But you're confirming that both the Valsharess and the Sisterhood know they didn't take this sorceress anywhere, and they didn't kill her."

"Correct, Mother."

"Fuck the whirlstone," she muttered with a sigh.

The Dragon chuckled. There was a definite suggestive undertone to it. She looked at him again, and they locked eyes. The false Davrin-shape shifted just enough to show her the golden sheen again before changing back. He was teasing her.

Shaking her head and breaking loose from his gaze, she looked back to get the rest of the story. "And this sorceress caught from you."

"It was an accident," Jaush muttered, strength going out of his shoulders, "and we didn't have any potions out in the wilderness."

"You said to Bryl she wanted it."

"At first she didn't."

"Well. I'd think there wouldn't be enough food, either, unless you shacked up with somebo —" Something hit Kuria just then, and she looked again at the Dragon in her office. "What was your part in this?"

Jaush groaned, very low, but she still heard it.

"As you figure," the Dragon said smoothly. "They stumbled into my territory, we bargained, I fed them — a lot of food, truth be told — allowing your grandson to grow."

Kuria frowned. "D'Shea did want him, then?"

The Dragon shrugged. "Eventually. Jaush and I made a deal that gave her time to consider."

"Why would you do that?"

"I liked his bargains."

"Why did she die giving birth in the wilderness, then? Couldn't you have made another bargain to save her?"

Both males paused long enough — even the ancient non-Elf — for Kuria to know there was something they weren't telling her.

"I didn't want to bargain again," Jaush told her, lifting his head to look at her. "I thought … we had a plan that didn't depend on the Dragon anymore."

The creature chuckled, winking at her son but looking back at her. "Jaush did right by Beliza that way, Matron. A Baenar Mother should not give birth in a Dragon's den. Take that as simple wisdom if nothing else."

Kuria grunted, nodding to accept before looking at Jaush again. "And she knew you were House Aurenthin?"

Her son nodded, seeming wary, waiting for her to bring up something. She figured what it probably was: that she'd asked about the details of the bargains. He didn't want to tell her.

I doubt I need to know.

Not only moot, but it was not her business except as it brought the Dragon here and now into her home. She'd kept her fringe contacts — her "friends," as Jaush put it — this long by being one of the few Matrons to not snoop into personal deals to use as threats. The result was all that mattered this low on the status bar. She, her Mother, and her Grandmother were remembered for this.

This was a Dragon her son brought home with her newborn grandson, alive and well. He was only asking her for help on exactly how to take them back.

"You must have made quite an impression on a sorceress, of all matrons, Jaush," she said, folding her arms and starting to smile. "But then, I knew you were going to be trouble the moment you came out of me. Nothing has really kept you in or out when you want to wander someplace else. Like seeping water or air, no one notices until you're already in."

He relaxed, dared to smile. Just a little.

Matron Aurenthin looked to the Dragon-Davrin then. "As far as you know, Great Dragon, does anyone else of note in Sivaraus know about this?"

A shake of his head. "No. Only you and Bryl have seen Jaush within the city borders in almost three turns."

"And is there a way you could suggest we might hide a mage-son in plain sight? Is it possible?"

The Dragon perked up. "Maybe. That would take magic on its own, of course."

Jaush stood up then, confronting the Dragon. "You said you wouldn't ask anything of her!"

"I am not," their guest replied coolly. "Your Matron is doing the asking and is more than capable of negotiating on her own terms."

"You enjoy bargains of all kinds," Kuria said bluntly.

He nodded with a touch of glee. "I can even grant most wishes, if you want it enough."

"Mother, don't," Jaush warned.

Now she could tell where part of the hard-earned experience had come from. Her youngest had matured a lot in a short time, despite his excitability now.

"This may be worth discussing," she said to Jaush. "As you must have learned with D'Shea's pregnancy, we could choose to do nothing, but that won't stop your baby from growing up. I would like to keep him, but it is not that simple. Sooner or later this will return upon us."

"Don't do bargains with him!" he replied intensely, enough to have not been moved by her reason.

"To keep Jaek will mean dealing with either the Valsharess or this Dragon," she said, her words hard as a hammer drop in the forge. "Or we find another place for your son. I can't keep him here at the expense of my whole House."

Her son was starting to hear her, and she pressed on. "We have no magic, Jaush. We've always had to barter for what magic items we do use. You brought us a magical son. We must deal with that somehow."

Her youngest looked pained, even as he didn't argue the position they were in. Jaush exhaled, blinking his eyes as they began to glisten. She tried not to stare.

"Well ... then you should at least make an informed choice," he said quietly.

"I'd certainly want to," she said, glad he was opening up. "Do you have more to tell me?"

She could see his pulse in his neck for a beat or two. "What I've learned ... it could get us killed, Mother."

She chuckled, a little dark and much more defiant. "So what else is new? And what happened to my laid-back, wandering son to be so filled with doom? Come, then, I'm listening. What do I need to know?"

At first, he was very quiet, and she had to come closer and lean in to listen. Kuria absorbed the first details her son gave her of what he'd learned from the scholar Beliza D'Shea, believably confirmed by the Dragon. It made sense in hindsight, but Kuria's stomach began to get hot as she straightened up.

"We were once House D'Shea?" she asked softly.

"House D'Shauranti, the fighter-mages," her son told her. "But that name will make us vanish if spoken outside this room. Then our entire House will disappear. House Aurenthin has only fighters."

She nodded; she knew that was true. "Beliza knew her Mother and Grandmother were probably abducted Aurenthin. And they've been breeding our mages like livestock under a different name in the Palace? Why?"

"House D'Shauranti rebelled against the Valsharess and lost," he said, his heart pounding. "That was what the records said. It was over half a millennia ago but we've been forced to forget even while being punished. That was why Beliza needed to leave. She discovered too much, remembered too much … I-I helped her."

"Why you went out into the wilderness with her," Kuria muttered, thinking. "Aurenthin and D'Shea together … ? That's likely why she kept your child."

"One reason," the Dragon said, agreeing and disagreeing at the same time.

She harrumphed in acceptance of that and reopened negotiations. "Can my grandson be hidden in plain sight, Dragon? And if so, how?"

"Yes, he can be, and by suppressing the mage within the mind before it becomes aware." His arms crossed and his jaw tilted with a certain arrogance. "I make sure the Elf simply never taps that part of his essence."

"So he … wouldn't grow into a mage, he'd be like us?"

"Correct, practically speaking. He lives as one of you, and the Valsharess none the wiser."

"And the risk?" Jaush interjected, glaring at the Dragon.

"None, really." He paused. "Oh! Unless there is a trigger."

"I knew it," Jaush muttered.

Kuria frowned. "A trigger like what?"

The Dragon scratched his chin. "Myself, of course, but also deep enough of a mindlink with a psion would do it. You would want to keep him away from Ornilleth and Tragar regardless, I'd think, but especially because they might 'awaken' his magic."

What's an Ornilleth?

Jaush's tone was accusing. "What possible good could this do to take

139

away Jaek's birthright?"

"Your Matron would be allowed to keep him for his entire life, obviously," the Dragon pointed out. "And a suppressed mage doesn't sire mundane or suppressed children. House Aurenthin would start producing mages again."

Jaush's eyes went wide as Kuria touched her lips in thought.

Fuck.

"That could become troublesome very quickly," she commented.

"Troublesome for who, exactly?" the Dragon asked her with a certain coyness.

Good question.

The Matron paced a bit, imagining such a thing. Her eldest Daughter was already learning the ropes; if something happened to Kuria — which often did for Matron Aurenthin while young — then Julen would take over. But she wouldn't know. She'd be unprepared, as would her own young Daughter. If she didn't survive but one of Jaek's children took over . . .

Even the Matrons could be unprepared for what might arise within them.

She shook her head. "It wouldn't work, suppressing only one generation. The Sisterhood would just start over culling our mages again, one at a time."

"How many generations would you desire, then, Matron?" the Dragon asked.

"What does it take?" she asked curiously. "Would it be difficult? Is the risk of missing one high?"

"Not at all, Matron. It is something I can do in my Sleep. A Bargain once made is seen complete."

She believed him.

Kuria looked at Jaush, who was clearly torn and afraid for the future of House Aurenthin. He shouldn't be. He had given her the best possible chance to make any lasting effect on the rest of Sivaraus from her position.

Our House had been powerful enough once for them to want this from us, powerful enough to be able to rebel openly, once. And now we are powerless and kept alive simply because we deserve to suffer for that insult. Because we lost.

Now the Dragon offered a way to change their bloodline …

No. To return it back closer to what it once was. With new potential and new experience …

"Why do this, Mother?" Jaush asked quietly.

She pursed her lips. "Because they deserve to be challenged in all ways, without pause or leniency. Nothing ever changes if we stop testing the limits. You've seen that with your own eyes in the market, Jaush."

The Dragon purred, shifting with clear interest. "How many generations would you desire, Matron? I can suggest what it is worth to me, and within your ability to pay."

Kuria wasn't sure what to ask. Well beyond her lifetime was necessary, but the longer it went, the higher the price he'd ask, and the greater chances House Aurenthin may simply disappear before the mages came forth again.

She wished she could see it all happen, could guide its direction, but it wasn't likely. She knew better than to cling to the idea of aging long and well. She had this chance to do something for her House and come what may. She may never even be known for it, but that wouldn't matter.

Mage children would return eventually.

The Matron Aurenthin stepped to her desk, opening a small box on top and lifting out her game of chance. Jaush recognized it and perked up, as if this meant more than it had.

She smiled at him a bit. "What?"

"Um." He settled back down. "I taught Beliza that."

Kuria grinned at her son, who was more like her and how she could have been had she not been born First Daughter. She chose a few pieces and gave them a toss. Both males came closer to witness the results.

"Six generations," she said aloud, looking at the Dragon in Davrin form. "All House Aurenthin offspring, including commoners and servants, which come from Jaek Aurenthin must not tap their inherent mage essence if they are to live and have children right beneath the Valsharess's nose."

The Dragon's eyes sparkled with gold, and he purred more loudly, nodding. He winked again at Jaush. "You didn't tell me your Mother was a gambler."

"You didn't need to know," he said frankly.

The uncanny lack of fear or awe Jaush showed for the Dragon, and that the beast of legend let him get away with it, spoke volumes of their implied past to help Beliza through her time to give birth.

"I'll remember you said that," the Dragon said. "Although if you do not wish to be bound by the Bargain, Jaush, it is best not to bear witness to it."

Jaush understood this on a level Kuria knew she did not — not yet — and he said, "You will not take her away for any length of time. We need her here."

Yes. They always have.

"I can work with that," the Dragon said.

"What is your name, then?" she asked. "If we are to make a bargain, Great One."

"Jaush calls me Sargt," was his reply. "It is enough."

"Very well, Sargt." Kuria nodded toward Jaush. "You need not worry; you have seen me negotiate with the fringe since you were little."

Her son swallowed, both wanting and not wanting what was offered; probably how it had been from the moment Beliza told him she carried. Kuria stepped forward to take hold of his grimy face, making him look at her.

"You've made some extraordinary choices, and I am glad to see you, Jaush. You and little Jaek. I will take the burden from here and assure all you've done can move forward and not simply die with you. The other Matrons underestimate their sons. In the future, House Aurenthin will show them why they shouldn't. I want this, you understand?"

Jaush listened to every word and nodded, and again his eyes teared up. That was new. She chose to overlook it again, as she had many small quirks about him, and pressed her lips to his forehead. She tasted dried sweat and dirt, and something much deeper, from very far away.

Her young son reached around her waist to embrace her, shocking boldness for a third-born child, and she realized only then how strong he'd become.

There is still more to the story, even now.

She looked forward to hearing about it, living vicariously, and to glean the value to be had when Davrin returned from the deep wilderness.

Kuria reached back to peel his arms away when she had given him a few breaths to compose himself, and Jaush released her willingly.

"Follow Bryl and go see your son," she suggested. "She can teach you useful things to care for him."

Jaush nodded, deciding that he didn't want to stay, even if he did give Sargt one more warning glare before stepping out through the secret passage. Kuria waited until all sound was once again protected, and she turned to face the Dragon head on, folding her arms.

He smiled at her with engaging charm.

Now all that remained was the price.

CHAPTER 17

2153 S.E., HOUSE DAR'PROHN, VUTHRA'TERN

Y'SHIR ROCKED IZABET AS SHE SLEPT, EACH OF THEM IN THE "PRESENT" TOGETHER for the first time. *At last.*

He didn't have to think forward, need not anticipate the next danger from their enemies or plan his alliances. His resources were secured while few others guarded the little foundling niece to the late Matron, who was no threat to the surviving Daughter. And everyone believed him.

Izabet was an "accident" from among the House Guard by the recently deceased First Son. This meant something to Y'Shir at least, that young Venic's own suffering — her death and her stillborn child — had not been forgotten.

Even if we must build a lie to remember.

He enjoyed the short time he had alone with Beliza's daughter.

"Turning blackness into purpose yet again, D'Shauranti?" the Dragon asked from behind him from over the left shoulder.

Y'shir didn't move or look away from Izabet, though he bowed his chin in the direction of the Great Drake. "With such blood spilled at all times, what else can I do to hold our heritage against such odds?"

The strong, bulky guest settled himself into a chair without asking. Finally, Y'shir turned his head to look.

The old Elf recognized the shadow drake, Ilka, resting in the Dragon's lap. She was quiet and asleep, exhausted to a degree few animals ever had to suffer in such consciousness clarity. Y'shir was glad to see her recovering from the torture and death of her mistress.

The Great Drake spoke while gently stroking the shadow drake behind the wing with the pad of his thumb, in an odd mirror to Y'shir with his granddaughter.

"I grant that the Houses under the Valsharess are more stable than any of yours, but with far less inheritance, ironically. Still. Fewer coups in Sivaraus, with older Matrons — at least among the top tiers. They can afford to leave the true brutality to Fadele and the Sisterhood."

Y'shir frowned hearing that name. "Fadele is still alive?"

The Dragon nodded with a playful smirk on his reptilian lips. "She finally found a way to give herself a real cock. She's changing the culture, as you have long desired to do, but with less forethought and more appetite."

The Grandmaster shook his head, losing *any* appetite he may have had. He remembered the young, angry warrior he'd tried to train in Hand and Heart despite not being a mage. He'd only succeeded in the Hand, and later realized his mistake in giving her even that.

"We belong in the Deepearth," he said.

"That you do," the Black Dragon agreed, "and I do enjoy the company I'm curious, though. How long does the Council of Eight exist without replacing a member as they will need to do now, hmm?"

Y'shir grimaced. A "Council" was what the Matron-Priestesses of each House called themselves when they could stand to be in the same place with each other, to attempt formal negotiations. "Never more than a decade."

"So the 'elders' among them are still children bickering. Why do you constantly teach children who won't listen, Y'shir? Why stay?"

The blond Elf looked down at Beliza's daughter. "Because not all is lost. Had I not stayed, I would have missed this."

The Dragon grunted, gently stroking Ilka's back as her throat pouch fluttered in her sleep. "Loyal to a fault, old Elf. You ever question your methods, Blade Singer?"

"All the time, Great Drake."

"Do we still have a Bargain?"

"Of course. A Bargain once made is seen complete."

"Good. You will see me again, then."

The Dragon stood up with Ilka curled horizontally in his muscular arms. He spoke aloud now what they hadn't discussed since before Y'shir had convinced Jaush to give up one of his twins.

"You have your baby granddaughter now, Y'shir, as you wanted, and I'll not claim this one. In exchange, at the time of my choosing, I will want to choose a grown one."

The Grandmaster nodded. "So be it, Lethrix."

2153 S.E., THE PALACE OF SIVARAUS

ISHUNA WALKED AROUND IN A SQUARE, LIGHTLY TOUCHING EACH TAPESTRY TRAP-ping her within the stone. She thought she had found the threads which needed to be tugged out and clipped, the end burned off with a flame so it wouldn't cause the rest to unravel. Three or four of them this time around, and she had handed them off to the High Priestess without looking too carefully at them.

Now everything seemed peaceful again. As peaceful as it could be with ash storms constantly sweeping her chambers within her Reverie, staining the underside of her slippers black, and she would have to walk for a long time before she stopped seeing new footprints adding to the circle.

This time, when the dark outlines finally started to fade, Ishuna stopped by a small crack of light where tapestry met the floor. She looked around her, confirmed she was alone, at least for the moment. The storms had gone and Ishuna didn't hear the Voices. Her reward for each Vision diverted to help her Spider Queen. For a time, she could be alone.

She deserved to be and die alone, after all

Now curious, the aging Davrin kneeled and poked at the crack of light. The tapestry moved, as did the picture, waving slowly, implying a giant breath of air on the other side ...

And the lack of a stone wall.

Dare You? A Voice whispered. *Dare You Now ... ?*

Ishuna reached under. Her fingers touched sand. She knew it would be red in color, and it made her want to weep.

Except she was dry inside. She could weep no longer.

Crawling on her knees, Ishuna ducked beneath the border of the tapestry and crawled out, squirming, and struggling to take firm hold of the ever-shifting grains. She had to dig herself a pit before she could slip fully under and once again be blinded by the Sun.

"Oh. Hello, Mother Weasel. It has been a while."

"Lethrix."

With heart pounding she pushed herself up, her purple and gold robes heavy and trying to drag her down to sink into the sand. She had to look up at the Black Dragon. He wasn't as large as he had been in physical form when her forces had chased him out of the Great Cavern, but he still looked exactly like himself.

She wondered if her eyes would turn more golden every time they met like this.

"You are awake?" she asked.

"For now." He looked around them as the wind churned the sand around them, diluting their voices. "You are alone."

She nodded, trembling, and feeling small, like the second-born, strange mystic she had once been. "Only you seem ever to find me so."

"You crammed your way into my domain, Dark Queen. Your Goddess enjoys it here but even She still explores."

A pause as she noticed how blue the Sky was today.

"Mm. Why are you here, Lethrix?"

"There's no fun in that for one such as you, Ishuna. Your people have proven themselves interesting to me. I believe I've changed my mind about the Ornilleths having the advantage."

Ishuna stared. "Why?"

He tilted his great head, the crown of horns brilliant white in the daylight. "For a while, you each only made cracks. Now some of your people have discovered how to mend them. You will become once again, but this time within my realm, and I thank you for it. I cannot wait to see it. Something Mazdek has only been able to describe to me until now."

Ishuna trembled, sensing this could not be good for her Goddess. This could only be a wonder. A true mystic wonders for her race, and something she only dreamed about. The two Truths were never the same thing, and this made her afraid now as it would likely tear her in half.

"What is it you want?" she asked.

"I already have it, Dark Queen. You need only Do as you must."

He opened his wings, sweeping down to cause a cloud of red dust to obscure them, give her cover and the urgent need to dart back beneath her tapestries for shelter.

"Sweet Dreams, Ishuna."

CHAPTER 18
2153-2385 S.E., SIVARAUS

JAUSH LIVED TO BE OLDER THAN ANY BUA OF HOUSE AURENTHIN HAD ANY RIGHT to. He survived to be older than the age his Mother had been when she died, and he lived to see Jaek grow and learn who he was. He saw much of Beliza their son, even without a conscious awareness of magic.

Though, his sire could never say so.

As adults, and each raised by the Matron Kuria, Jaush and Jaek were more like brothers over enough decades, supporting their sisters and younger cait cousins. Then Jaek sired his own children, and Jaush alone watched with silent trepidation for what they would become.

When his first great-grandchild arrived and all before him remained House Aurenthin, Jaush exhaled with relief.

For as many reasons as they may suffer from as many events which might make him want for something else, one promise held true. Jaush did not see the betrayal of what his Mother had paid on their behalf. None of them expressed mage potential.

Jaush couldn't even know how many Aurenthins might have been mages if the past had been different.

The elder warrior found himself on the fringe more and more often once he passed two-fifty. He even returned to the deep wilderness, learning the shadows and the holes in the system which worked without any magic whatsoever.

The To'vah gift was still with him this whole time, if in lessening strength; he still didn't bleed even if his speed and strength were slowing down. The risks became riskier and the fights fairer, even as he kept his actions balanced so as not to spawn too many stories of a Davrin bua who couldn't be stabbed, poisoned, or set aflame. There were a few such stories, but never of rising concern for those in power.

Eventually he found himself in a place he swore he'd been before.

"I'm pregnant, Jaush."

Reine. She was a caravan security mistress who'd taken a liking to him while on her payroll. He'd genuinely, tentatively felt something for Reine, as he had no one since Beliza.

"Why tell me, Reine? It's your choice."

She'd smiled wryly, her belly already showing by the time she'd decided to mention it. "I'm keeping her. I just wanted you to know before we go deep on circuit again, since I'll be gone for a while." She paused. "Thanks."

Jaush had blinked. "Uh. You're welcome?"

The "Dragon Warrior" was well over three hundred when a street urchin tried to stab him with her free hand after he'd seized her wrist, catching her with her hand in his pocket. He stared down at the grubby face, thinking how much she looked like a young Reine.

"That's not how you do it," he'd whispered down to her, twisting the blade from her grip with enough pain to convince her to listen. "You'll get your fingers sliced off that way."

Her glare was just like her Mother's.

"She died," the youth answered too casually when Jaush had finally won enough trust to be able to ask about Reine. This had taken several small hunts locating the little urchin. She wouldn't say more, only confirm her Mother's name.

"Gotcha. Well, little cait, do you want to learn more? I know a lot. I've been around a while."

She appraised him with a squint. "Yeah, you look old."

Jaush grinned.

Reine's daughter was smart and bold as she'd been; she proved better at tactics than Jaush once she understood the patterns that he'd set in front of her. His tips and tricks and her own raw talent and grit made her difficult for the City Guard to catch.

His bold and brave cait even started making a name for herself in the black market while Jaush, as always, kept off to the side of things. He had often been thankful they looked nothing alike, or she wouldn't have the chance to become the youngest Guild Mistress in the making.

Later, someone had made a mistake somewhere, or someone had said something, or they simply came for reasons Jaush could do nothing to prevent. Either way, the Sisterhood found them at last, deep in the slums.

The worst of it was that he believed that they would beat his young daughter to death before his very eyes.

"No ..."

Mercifully, they stopped when Red Sister Prime stepped in. She looked around, evaluated all their prisoners, and she stepped straight toward him.

Her sword point rammed into his gut and punched out the other end. The pain was worse than it had ever been, and he could feel the edge of the blade sawing back out as she withdrew.

Jaush held the front wound, his own hot, red blood spilling out. Though stunned at first, he lifted his head to look at the Red Sister Prime with an odd, cocked smirk on his face.

She sneered down at him. "Don't know enough to die, ass-whore?"

The Prime stabbed him again, drawing much more blood, and he finally collapsed. His daughter didn't cry out once; just as he'd taught her.

The Deepearth grew darker still.

Good cait. Cooperate with the Sisters. Don't try to save me. My time has come at last ... .

oldest female after having some fun with her.

Spitting out the taste of blood as she got her leathers back into place, Fadele sighed satisfaction, feeling the pressure drain away at last.

She stalked around the broken down den, evaluating the black market prisoners, and made eye contact with the young cait that reports had told her was the "real" leader.

Fadele didn't believe it.

Striding up to her, the Prime loomed over the bruised, bound cait held by the Red Sisters, her lip curled as the youth stared over at the deceased male. This chaos-raiser of the black market was almost grown, almost …

A bit young for the tests, but …

The strength of will Fadele saw when she seized the stubborn cait by the jaw and forced her to look up. She could meet the Prime's eyes and not twitch.

Fadele wanted her.

Sisterhood can remake this one. Time's just right.

"What's your name, sweetmeat?"

That one stubborn refusal would be her final rebellion.

The Prime punched her. "What. Is. Your. Name? Or you can end up like him right now."

The cait glared up at her with a bloody lip, glancing one more time at the gutted male on the floor. She nodded acceptance of her fate.

"Rausery," she answered.

AURANKA THE KEEPER

A TALE OF MIURAG
BY A.S. ETASKI

2350 S.E., SIVARAUS

SHE SMELLED THE DUNGEON. HUMID WITH BODIES, STENCH ALL AROUND HER; moans of misery with short, piercing shrieks of nightmare not far away.

"Push, Auranka."

She had never heard this tone before or heard Her so near. Not aloof as a ruler speaking to a priestess, but familiar. Not dispassionate and bored, but vested.

Auranka blinked rapidly in the dark, her eyes slow to collect anything from the shapes around her. There was plenty to see but she felt out of practice. Her eyes were dry.

"M-my Queen ... ?"

Her mouth could have been stuffed with dwarf moss for how well it worked, though her tongue touched the tips of her teeth easily enough. Blinking her eyes helped, and finally, she could see Her face without candles.

The Valsharess looked down at her sternly. "Push. Now."

Push? Push what?

She couldn't feel anything below her lips as they began to tingle.

"H-how did I get here?"

"Silence."

Purple robes rustled as She turned toward Auranka's feet and spoke to another.

"How soon?"

"Anytime, Valsharess."

The Priestess's stomach clenched down on itself from the inside, and she gasped to realize how big and round it was. Auranka couldn't see her feet or her crotch in how it blocked her view, but she could see her legs parted wide.

She was naked, and someone was between her legs.

Finally she could *feel* something. Her chest filled with hot rage.

"Phaelous!!" she cried. Her hoarse voice broke.

"Push, Priestess!" the Queen barked. "Deliver your daughter to us!"

Her distended belly contracted, and Auranka gasped, trying to come up on her elbows as the Headmaster disappeared behind her bulge. Her breasts were larger than she remembered, the nipples long and purple, leaking … something.

I hope that's milk.

She had almost no strength in her arms. They were scrawny, her hands thinner and weaker than they used to be. All her jewelry was gone, even her anklet. Her legs barely moved. She could not push herself up, could not sit, much less reach for the young wizard's throat as she wanted to.

Her body ached as if realizing how long it had been resting comatose to the world. Part of it was already hard at work, doing what it was made to do without her leave or even conscious thought.

"Oh, Braqth," the Priestess wept, attempting to bear down again.

"Crowning," Phaelous murmured.

"Push, Auranka."

She did.

Again.

And again.

Until something rose up and tore free. She screamed. Some of the other prisoners screamed back.

"Cut it."

"Soon, my Queen."

"Now!"

Auranka's Dark Sight swam; her nether regions burned and throbbed. Something whisper-light swirled around her, then something *crawled* on her hypersensitive skin.

Several somethings.

"N-no ..." She swatted ineffectually, drunk, and sluggish, weak from her efforts.

"Stop immediately! You shall accept Braqth's gift, as you agreed!"

Auranka's hands trembled as she tried to still them, as the four large, black spiders clambered over her. They chimed excitedly; they were happy to see her awake at last. They had been guarding her so long ...

They belonged to her, and they knew it.

She had no idea who they were, or why she could understand them. One crawled forward onto her hot, slightly deflated stomach, up her ribs and onto her milk-heavy, left breast.

She sank her fangs into her.

"*Aaaa!* Stop!"

The Priestess's voice wheezed after the scream, pathetic in her state. "Braqth's Will, child."

The other three spiders took the cue to crawl onto her breasts as well, injecting their own venom, spoiling the nourishment she might have given to her newborn. At once, her four guardians shriveled out before her eyes to become dry husks.

Simultaneously, her flesh swelled as a new, sick heat invaded her. Not just her blood began to boil but her aura surged out, any magic she had flowing beyond her reach. She did not know how to stop the hemorrhage.

"She will reshape your purpose, Auranka," the Valsharess said, holding a fluid-covered infant wrapped in silk, "as I shall reshape your body. We will not have you as a Priestess any longer. Not with what We have seen of your future."

Any longer? What future?

She had not even trained in the Sanctuary for two turns. She was the newest, not yet initiated. Why even accept her, by the Queen's own blessing, if she was only to be executed before finishing the training? What had she done to deserve this?

158

Phaelous came to my bed ... I did not trespass, I did not poach ...

Her joints ached and a horrid, new strength flooded her atrophied muscles, rebuilding them by force. She convulsed, and that was when the wizard reached forward.

Auranka gritted her teeth, glaring at him as he collected two husks of the spiders who had bitten her, leaving the other two in her cleavage. Crushing them in his fist, the Headmaster glanced toward the Valsharess for permission before bracing himself.

Slowly, Phaelous pushed his fist into her elastic birth canal. It felt as though she were giving birth to a smaller twin.

"*Rrraugh!*" she shrieked in protest. "G-get ... .out ... !"

The young wizard lingered with his hand inside well past the wrist and he murmured to set off a spark from his fingertips. Magic traveled from her womb to erupt behind her eyes. She convulsed again, and when he slowly withdrew his hand.

He left the spider husks inside.

Auranka could barely utter another denial as the Valsharess flicked Her long fingers and made her open her mouth without touching her. Auranka held it open while the Queen plucked up the remaining two spider husks and fed them to her like dried mushrooms.

"Chew," the Queen said, patting beneath her chin.

She did, staring up at Her, making a feeble attempt to peek at her tiny daughter. She swallowed the dead arachnids, still boiling inside but now something else compressed that heat. Now something was trying to get out, to break out of her very skin!

"You will never betray Braqth, Auranka. No one will. You shall remind them why they must fear Us. You shall forever guard the tunnels and caverns of the Deepearth around Sivaraus."

The sickness inside her arose, clutching to her back, digging in with claws made of black shadow.

"Now ... Change."

It took her, overwhelmed her body, claiming every vulnerable place at once.

It would Become her.

Auranka screamed.

Uncounted decades later, in the Drider Pit

" … No! Please, no! I've done nothing! It wasn't me!"

"That didn't work for the Matron, and it's not going to work now."

"Shut up, Kini, before I stuff a ball in your mouth."

The caits had little need for pomp or circumstance, for their Matron had already forgotten about him. Apparently, Kini had not betrayed her to the point where she wanted to make the trip out here herself. She would be satisfied to hear the description later from two of her personal guards.

The strong caits shoved Kini over the edge into the pit, uncaring if he broke a limb on the way down. He rolled, helpless to stop himself until he reached the bottom. The fall wasn't vertical; in theory, the slant of the ground was enough to crawl back up, but that was part of the hopelessness.

He was too dizzy to stand up, and the top was too far to outrun what would soon come out of the cavern. Even if he did reach it, he had nowhere to go beyond where she could not follow.

What do I do now?

Servants whispered that even the Sathoet shrink back from her on the rare occasions she returned to the Palace or Sanctuary. He had never known anyone who saw her provoke that response. One would think that many eyes would recall a giant spider — one with the entire torso of a Davrin in place of the head — strutting around the inner sanctum of Sivaraus, but that was not the case.

Yet Matrons assured them every turn that they had seen the Drider Keeper beside the Valsharess before.

The guardsvrin above taunted him as Kini shakily got to his knees. Stone and dirt lay beneath him, but his eyes also detected the gossamer threads of old webbing caught over a few pebbles and covered in dust. There was more of it, and it looked newer as his eyes followed it toward the open maw of the abyss into which he had been condemned.

"Mealtime, Keeper!" yelled one of the guards, who was elbowed by the other as she hissed about drawing other things in the Deepearth.

"Like what?" she challenged the other. "What else would dare come near the Pit?"

"Well … There's no guarantee that she won't try to pinch us as well, is there?"

"Oh." The loudmouth fell quiet.

To his right, deeper in the cave decorated in threads of spider silk, he heard footsteps. Not skittering, giant claws as he expected.

Feet. On two legs.

"Maybe we should go," the second the guard whispered, unnerved by Kini's body language and the way he stared, as unmoving prey upon the ground.

"And not witness this for the Matron?"

"We'll make something up. He's not coming back either way."

They came to an agreement.

Kini was, at once, glad when they left him and desperate to call them back. Was it better to be eaten alone? With no one to wince at his suffering or shout to acknowledge it, even in insults?

Before he decided on an answer, the figure came out of the cave.

She looked like a regular Davrin. His Dark Sight spotted Radiant patterns suggesting bright copper eyes, white hair, and normal skin. She wore a simple, sleeveless gown, her muscular arms on display and long legs revealed by slits up both sides. Her breasts strangely large, and her white hair hung loose down her back, possessing no decoration whatsoever. She wore no jewelry, no sandals on her bare feet.

"Who are you?" she whispered.

He cringed. The sound felt like a pincerworm trying to nibble its way inside his ear.

"I-I am Kini, mistress."

"Have you any chhildrren, Kini?"

He blinked. "Yes, I do, mistress."

She stepped closer, and he gained his feet without her protest. Once the details were clear to them both, she smiled almost playfully. His heart kickstarted into a sprint inside his chest.

This heavy-breasted Davrin had fangs like a spider. The dark spots around her Davrin eyes easily mimicked the multiple sets of a spider's. Kini had thought her bare arms smooth, but there were short, stiff, black bristles — not unlike the sensitive hairs on a spider's legs — protruding through the skin and lying back along her forearms, and longer ones crowning her elbows.

Auranka the Keeper.

His executioner!

Kini dropped to his knees once again and trembled.

"Rissse, Kini," she commanded. "Follow me."

He glanced up to see her regal back and gait, the rolling set of hips and hypnotizing backside beckoning further to obey her.

He gained his feet to follow.

Why did she not have the form of a Drider, as the tales said? She looked almost normal! She could speak, and she had called him by his name.

How often did she creep through Sivaraus, then, when a mere cloak would prevent them from looking twice at her? Could the stories be exaggerated, invented by skittish "witnesses" like his own escorts, who never stuck around long outside the pit?

Could there be something he would witness that even the Matrons did not know? Perhaps he was not going to die, or if he was, then not in the manner he thought.

What will happen to me?

In a way, he was glad that the guards had left him. He had nowhere to go but here.

The inside of the cave was beautiful, like the spider garden he had once glimpsed inside the Palace. Webs of artistic design decorated the cave walls, creating murals and tapestries which would change on a whim. The strands were softly luminescent, a light blue color, allowing him to see greater detail, like in the candle spectrum, but so gentle that the light soothed him rather than make his head ache.

The Keeper had a nest as well, woven of the same glowing stuff, and not as sticky as he might've guessed when he watched her kneel down to crawl upon it. She rolled over as smoothly as if she lay on simple moss. Her dark, curvaceous body provided a stark outline upon the light blue bed. Her eyes were indeed like copper, and her dark gown was actually purple.

"How many?" she asked him as he stood about two body lengths away.

Kini was a good servant; he remembered her previous question to which this would be her follow-up.

"Two, mistress," he said. "That I am sure of."

She smirked, resting on her elbows, her biceps well-defined. "Are you a wizzard?"

"No, mistress."

"Then you cannot be sssure."

Uncertain of a reply, he bowed his head and folded his hands.

"Why are you given to me?"

"I am innocent."

"Thisss does not anssswer the quessstion."

Kini shuddered at her plain annoyance. "Charged for switching a box in a ceremony."

In the following pause, he waited with half a flinch ready that he forgot any honorifics.

She watched him steadily, unblinking, and tilted her head. "Which cccceremony?"

Did she not really care, or was she noting it only to punish him later? Trying to moisten his mouth, he swallowed with a dry throat.

"The Taming of the Stable."

She showed fangs again. "Mere embarrasssment, or actual damage?"

"Embarrassment."

"Thisss would be why the Matron isss not here."

Kini chose to lower his eyes rather than answer, his gaze landing upon her strong, lengthy legs. Tiny, black claws curved off the tip of each toe, and a few more of those thick bristles grew down her calf and off of her heel.

"The Valsharesss approved thisss?"

"How am I to know, mistress? Perhaps not."

"Frivolousss."

His heart thumped harder once again but for a different reason. Perhaps Auranka was her own type of independent judge, as well as the queen's executioner. Perhaps she would pardon him, offer him a stay.

Her two normal eyes slid down and then up his form. He wore his simple, long-sleeved shirt and matching pants.

"Lie with me."

Kini didn't know if she meant what he thought she meant. For certain, she told him to join her upon the nest. Now instead of thoughts of pardon, he had thoughts of a bargain.

It always comes down to sex with the matrons. Always.

Perhaps if he pleased her—

Tremors passing through him, Kini stepped closer to kneel on to the glowing blue webbing. He prepared himself to be trapped. Maybe he would be spun into a cocoon like a proper insect.

When his hands and knees came onto the nest, he noticed the nest had no noticeable temperature, neither cool nor warm, but it was soft and smooth, not sticky.

He wasn't trapped yet.

Next to him, Auranka lifted her arms languidly to rest them just above her head, watching him. His eyes were drawn first to her breasts but then her hips shifted sensually, as did her legs as he ended up studying her the whole way down. She parted her legs wide, the silk of her dress falling to cover her crotch but revealing to him everything else from hip to toe.

"Touch me," she said.

Kini dropped any pretense that he wasn't truly fucked. He swallowed again and did what he was told.

Shifting over in between her ankles and gently moving her silk to where he would not be kneeling upon it, the bua servant slid his fingertips along the edge of her dress until he reached her thigh. Gently, he pulled the fabric aside like a set of drapes, glancing up once to see whether she showed any fang before focusing on her sex.

Auranka possessed no white fur upon her mound; by his practiced eye, it had not been plucked but simply did not grow. Likewise, her labia were not soft or puffy; he could not tell whether she was aroused or not and had to touch to be sure it wasn't a trick of the shadow.

No, it isn't.

Framing the opening to her slit were hardened ridges, as if her nether-lips had petrified into a protective outer shell. The legend of the Drider Keeper was not an elaborate hoax on the people, even if she wasn't really a Drider.

"Tassste me," she hummed.

"Uhhh …"

Fool. Do not be squeamish now.

Kini settled onto his stomach and elbows, shuffling closer before cupping her thighs right up against her ass. He focused on how normal those felt as he squeezed. He kept massaging her as he lowered his face and ran his tongue along the chitinous ridges surrounding her hole first before searching whether she had that all-important, sensitive nub hidden somewhere

His tongue touched … something, but then Auranka chuckled and shifted away from him slightly, so he couldn't touch that particular spot.

"You want to live, I presssume."

He nodded.

Her hips relaxed; she settled back down. She had not given him different instructions, so he resumed licking her. She was strange; her sex was dry and tasted like a musky perfume further reduced, concentrated until it was almost crystalline. It caused his saliva glands to tingle and produce more spit. The sensitive skin around his lips puckered and tightened.

"Rissse up," she told him with that penetrating whisper. "Presssent, so I may feel you."

Shit …

Kini pushed himself up off the nest and moved closer so that his knees were against Auranka's soft thighs, making sure that his crotch was within her reach. Braced on her elbow, she reached forward to fondle him, finding him completely flaccid. He awaited her displeasure.

"Did you ever watch your chhilddren nurssse from their mother?" she asked, keeping her touch on his penis and scrotum gentle and exploratory.

"Yes, mistress."

"Tell me what you sssaw."

The bua shifted, uncomfortable as she kept playing with him; he was becoming turgid from the persistent rubbing, but his memories of silently observing an adult servant nourishing a future servant clashed in his head.

The memory caused many thoughts to pass through his mind but none of them were arousing.

"I saw … her and her baby. Her head was always up as she held him, watching around her. She always saw me, so I did not try to hide."

"Shhe wasss guarding."

"Yes, mistress."

"Go on. The baby?"

He considered as she rubbed him through his pants. "Eyes open, more often than not, except at the very beginning. Always single-minded."

"To feed and live."

"Yes, mistress."

"Shhhow me."

Auranka loosened the rope belt around her waist with one hand, releasing his genitals to undo the knots which held her gown to her shoulders. She lowered the purple silk to reveal her breasts, generous and full, the dark purple nipples poking out like a mother who had recently given birth.

Kini stared as she shimmied and shuffled off her gown to kick off of her feet; he moved quickly to get out of the way. Once naked, Auranka cupped her large breasts in her hands and arched her back. Her piercing, predator's gaze never blinked, never left him.

"Shhhow me. Nurssse like your chhild."

Well, it would probably taste better than her cunt.

Kini crawled closer and Auranka's hands left her breasts as she reached for him. She drew him close, one of her palms cradling the back of his head as if he was indeed that infant he described. He latched his mouth onto one plump tit and immediately began flicking the nipple with his tongue, swirling it around the pebbled areola as he massaged her other breast.

"No," she hissed. "Not like a sssire. Sssuckle like an infant. Draw in mothersss nourissshment."

Momentarily confused, Kini shifted the hold of his mouth to a much more basic one, closing off any air and sucking by sheer instinct.

He wasn't expecting anything except her strange, dry skin, so when the milky fluid suddenly coated his tongue on the first draw, half-filling his mouth on the second, Kini either needed to swallow the sickly-sweet stuff down or allow it to drip out all over her.

He swallowed.

It burned. All the way down inside him.

Auranka kept her hand on the back of his head, disallowing him to lift it from her breast. "More. Drinnk more."

He shivered in her arms and nursed, sucking and swallowing more of her hot and wet milk. Sticky and sweet, it made him dizzy and nauseated as it seemed to infuse his very blood. His cock finally responded, stiffening to an almost painful level as the drugging told him by long habit to expect to be mated.

He rubbed it against her hip.

"Yesss," she whispered.

Her legs remained apart, though she did not touch herself or demand that he do so; she kept hold of him while he nursed.

Kini had not realized how empty his stomach had been, how *hungry* he was until she fed him. He pressed his hips desperately against her, knowing only these two things: the sucking and the humping.

His Matron was forgotten, the fellow servant he'd been chosen to seed forgotten as well. Blue and purple and white played in threads and patterns within view of his open eyes. The black bristles on the Keeper's elbows seemed to grow.

Unsure how to speak, Kini simply stopped sucking when he was full, chewing and gnawing on the tough, long nipples in play. Auranka purred and rubbed his hair, reaching to tickle his rampant cock pushing against her hip.

"Rrroll over, baby," she whispered.

Reluctantly, he took his mouth from the wet teat and his crotch from her soft skin. He rolled onto his back, and she followed him, stripped him utterly naked, tearing the clothes, then encouraged him to keep rolling. She pushed at him until he was on his stomach.

His eyes fluttered as he grew sleepy, his heart beating in time with the pulse of his naked cock pressed in between his stomach and the gossamer spider silk. The Drider Keeper straddled his thighs, massaged his buttocks and lower back before she leaned over him and nudged her smooth, hardened crotch up against his crack.

Above him, she made a disturbing clicking noise with her throat as she shoved harder at him, hooking a hand beneath his hips to force him to arch his back just a little. She pressed flush against him, and something popped. The sound was like cartilage slipping across itself but muffled by their flesh as it absorbed the impact.

Kini felt her penetration; it was like the times his Matron had filled him with water using a tube, wanting to "clean him out." She'd made him wait, standing before her while holding it in, until he could barely stand it.

This was much faster: the claiming, the cool squirting, and the finishing thrust before the Keeper pulled out of him again. So fast, he could only contemplate what she had left inside him after the fact.

It didn't hurt. Soon, it was warm like the milk in his belly and made him want to climax as he shifted his hips and pressed his penis against the silk webbing. The stuff wouldn't seep out of him; it was already being absorbed. As it did, he pondered whether it might dissolve him from the inside, like a metaphysical corrosive.

Something he'd never even realized he owned was breaking down.

His Keeper left him there, and he fussed from one basic need not yet taken care of, poking stiffly into the web bedding. The only memories he seemed able to focus on were the nursing and the helpless submission.

When he grew hungry, he called for her.

After a time, she answered.

She fed him again from her breasts, and he sucked hungrily, single-mindedly, working to fill his stomach again with her nourishment. He got too rambunctious this time, tiny fangs he just discovered pricking her nipples and her breasts as he tried to chew on them again.

She became irritated and spun the sticky stuff around his knees and around his torso, trapping his arms as he was forced onto his stomach again.

This time he knew to arch his back and receive her care for that other part of him. The stretching, the coupling, the warm injection flowing into him once again gave him something to contemplate for the next few cycles before she would return to feed him again.

He needed to eat, or he wouldn't grow. He wouldn't gain the same bristles and fangs and number of long, deadly legs that she had. If he didn't eat, he wouldn't grow big and strong enough to learn how to hunt from her, to do as she did, roaming the caverns.

He wanted to look like her. He wanted to learn.

Mother knows best.

Rohenvi

A Tale of Miurag
By A.S. Etaski

CHAPTER 1

2818 S.E., HOUSE THALLUEN, SIVARAUS

HER MATRON GRIPPED HER WRIST. IT HURT, BUT SHE BORE IT BRAVELY.

Rohenvi did not blink, even as she felt her Mother's gaze in the pitch dark like a hot blade pressed to the hollow of her throat. She was pulled closer, stubbornly down, until Matron Siranet could whisper without anyone else hearing.

"You can never show what you really are," the dying Elf hissed. "Y-you are my sole heir, First Daughter. S-soon you will be Matron! Make it quick. L-leave me to suffer and you sh-shall run afoul my l-last weapon. It will come for you instead of them. Kill me ... Quickly ... !"

"Where did they strike you?" Rohenvi asked, feeling the tremors begin in the scalding, sweating body.

The Matron clutched her Daughter's hand and clumsily slid it to cover her waist, where Rohenvi could just feel the break in the fine fabric. The hole was very small.

"Quickly," the Daughter agreed, embracing her Mother tightly to her and reaching for the hard-cased needle at her own belt.

This was the closest they dared be to each other in six decades, when the inevitable tests arose between them. Sivaraus was watching.

Would the all-too-necessary heir be a puppet to the Court? A cait pliable and useful to her elders but lacking the necessary initiative to maintain power after her Matron's death and thus dooming the House's standing.

Instead, would Rohenvi be a subversive competitor undermining her Matron's and House's image well before her time as she dealt with the plots of any siblings?

Or, finally, would the First Daughter be a cooperative extension of the ruling Matron during her lifetime, loyal but always ready and waiting for her Matron's passing?

This last option was the best-case scenario for any House, assuming there were no latter-turn regrets to fray what should be clear severance at the end. Matron Thalluen had worked hard to assure this cut was clean, and Rohenvi would not disrupt it now.

The Daughter used the same puncture wound made by the poison dart to deliver the glass needle, breaking it and letting the rare toxin leak in. Rohenvi had been holding on to it for three turns now, staying out of the city plots as her Mother willed it, making her seem the pliable puppet to the Court …

Until this one eve.

Siranet's Daughter had waited out in the darkness to see if her strong, determined Matron made it out alive. She had, but it wouldn't last. Finding Rohenvi, her Mother had pulled out the dart in her haste; her Daughter would have to find and recover it before she dared leave.

For now, Rohenvi held her Mother, feeling the heat lessen and the rampaging heart slow. In time, she exhaled, silent and sure.

Matron Thalluen's mind would go black; Siranet would fall into her last Reverie well before her tongue and glands swelled up from the poisoned dart, before closing off her throat to choke her. She would be asleep before her eyes would bulge and begin to bleed. The pain of her entrails and her inner organs would cease as her heart simply stopped and her lungs quit drawing air.

The Matron of House Thalluen would not suffer, and she would not leave behind an ugly corpse for witnesses. Whoever was watching would see this, and they would not come after Rohenvi. They would let her live to rule in her Mother's stead, because she did not hesitate to do what needed to be done.

She had proven herself worthy.

Rohenvi held the body for as long as she was allowed without seeming too weak or mournful. She lifted her head, swiveling her head to move her ears, inhaling the scent of her Mother' cooling sweat.

She could sense nothing and might figure she was not being watched, but she didn't believe it.

Soon her Mother's Head Guard came, having obeyed Siranet's last order. Fintre circled around on her lizard mount to wait a little longer before dismounting to help the First Daughter move the Matron's body back to their House.

You can never show what you really are.

Last words as a lesson reinforced. Rohenvi had heard it said many times. At different points in her life, it had meant different things.

She could not show she was afraid of pincer worms as a child. She could not show she was covetous of her brother's new slave as an adolescent. She could not show she was angry at being jilted by a member of a Higher House at the last worship ball at Court, five turns ago.

"Here."

Rohenvi offered the Head Guard her soup; the warrior tasted it without fear and pushed it back. She smirked slightly and ate.

The First Daughter could still feel those emotions, could nurture them if she willed it, they all did, and she could act on them, possibly. But if she *showed* them, her competitors would know those thoughts well before she had any plan in place to deal with them, be it to deal with the adversary or the emotion itself.

Rohenvi lifted her bowl into her hands to drink what her spoon didn't easily capture, lowering it and making eye contact with the stoic fighter sitting across from her. The First Daughter — now the Matron, she reminded herself — licked the soup from her upper lip.

Stoic. That is how her Mother had gotten along for a few centuries, with stoicism. Siranet had done well enough in her short time, had built their wealth and only just now raised their House from Thirteenth to Twelfth. If all went well, Siranet's "last weapon" meant there wouldn't be any immediate retribution.

"How old are you, Fintre?" Rohenvi asked the silent Head Guard.

Her jaw was like stone. "Three hundred three, Matron."

Almost her Mother's peer. Now over double her own.

Siranet had only lived to be three hundred-fifty; she had birthed only one Daughter and had bet everything on that. Rohenvi believed she knew what it was that her own Matron had never been able to show. Not until the end.

Siranet wasn't really a Matron at heart; she was a mercenary hired by herself. Fintre, the Head Guard, was her Second. Her Right Hand. They didn't want to lead an army, but they *did* want to get things done by their own wit and endurance.

Mercenaries also tended to die in their prime, and her Mother was no exception.

Rohenvi wasn't a mercenary, she knew. She wanted to live longer than that and be sure their bloodline would survive by more than the fortune of a single Daughter. If she didn't, it meant her life would be half over in another few decades and it could all vanish in one assassination, as it had for many of the lower Houses, renamed and reformed over centuries.

One hard and stealthy strike, on which the middling and lower Noble Houses were always on the cusp to suffer. The most recent, Rohenvi suspected, was one her Matron had gone out this very eve to prevent.

In this last desire, Siranet had been successful taking fortune into her own hands. It was her last mission.

Siranet should have been a Red Sister or something, Rohenvi thought, burying her expression in a taste-tested wine glass as the Head Guard stood vigilant between her and her Matron's body. *But she came into the title of Matron very young as well. Just like me.*

There weren't that many truly elder Matrons below the Fourth House, those longest-lasting Houses with Matrons who had somehow borne children, raised them, and avoided death past the age of five hundred.

The Matrons were all young compared to the Valsharess, the Red Sister Prime, a handful of Her Priestesses, and the top five Houses. Beneath the Matrons, the average warrior was younger still, as were the servants and the slaves.

Something got to everyone, sooner or later, and no one saw all their children survive to bear their own.

"Your ... Matron," Fintre began quietly, "was glad you did not take after her, Rohenvi."

The Noble cait lifted her head. "Hm? How so?"

A shrug of strong shoulders. "You can be content inside these walls. You figured out a lot of efficiencies Siranet always hated putting her eyes to, much as they needed to be done. A lot of the recent profits and fortune was because you took that off her plate, you split the work. You deserve your inheritance, Matron."

Rohenvi waited, keeping her face placid as she was taught. This was oddly blunt between the two of them, especially using Siranet's title for her. But perhaps it had been this blunt between her Mother and Fintre, too, and Rohenvi was only taking her rightful place in the eyes of the Head Guard.

It spoke well for a relatively peaceful transition.

Rohenvi nodded, trying to be graceful. The Guard accepted that acknowledgment, but it didn't bring out the same level of manners.

"And I take it you enjoy buas?" Fintre asked.

Heh.

"More than Mother did," Rohenvi said, aware that her Matron had barely kept males around long enough to plant the seeds. Siranet might not have gone through a second pregnancy at all if the first child hadn't been a bua. "I also want more children. Four, at least. I've already decided."

Fintre nodded, her rigid face softening a bit to look somber and re-lieved at once. "Good. That's good. Makes it easier, Matron Rohenvi."

She just started to smile hearing how the older Davrin said it then remembered not to.

Easier to do what your rank dictates you must.

Siranet probably only smiled when she was out with Fintre, when no one else could see her. Rohenvi wasn't sure; she was only guessing.

"We will light the pyre at waking, Head of the Guard. You will stand with the rest."

"Thank you, Matron. Long live our House Thalluen."

AT FIRST, ROHENVI DID NOT HAVE TIME FOR MALE COMPANY AT ALL, OUTSIDE of seeing her brother travel from Court to stand at their mother's pyre, to stand witness, before he would be sent back at some point. The siblings had a short eve to talk following the funeral, to plan over a hot drink.

"What newest whispers have you heard at Court, Azed?"

He smirked and shook his head slightly, blowing on the surface of his taze. "They become ever more ridiculous each quad-span, and quickly forgotten when they don't come to pass."

"I am sure I can judge that. Just speak."

"You're wasting your time, Roh. I do not need to fill your head with Court gossip. You want to hear it, you can come to Court yourself."

"I have to stay here and manage our land." She squinted at him. "You never would have argued with Mother."

"She didn't give two hangs about Court gossip. She never asked."

The young Matron sipped thoughtfully. "Why are you at Court, then?"

Her brother, older by only two decades — nearly making them twins — just shrugged. "She didn't want to sell me to another House, I suppose. She bought her information on the streets, she did not have to put me at risk using me as a plant, so she didn't."

Rohenvi planted her fist on her cheek. "Are you grateful?"

Azed looked toward the ceiling, considering. "Court has its own petty spites and dangers, I don't think it is any 'safer.' If that was her aim. I figure she could never decide what to do with me."

With no one else could Rohenvi talk this way; somehow their Matron had not given either of them much reason to despise her. She merely expected them to take care of themselves, be self-reliant, and punishments the Matron's children suffered were no worse than Fintre's among her own Guard — and for very tangible reasons. Even young Nobles could do stupid things to endanger their security — that was the only time the siblings suffered. Growing up here had been more like living in a fortress than a Noble manor.

Rohenvi scratched her chin. "Do you want to come back home?"

Azed blinked but considered the option. He was quiet until her cup was nearly empty, as he weighed a lot in his mind.

"I do," he answered. "But ... well, there is one mention you should know, the only thing I'm sure isn't just gossip. It's coming from too many places."

The young Matron straightened her back and watched her brother, waiting for him to continue.

"Word is the Priestesses have renovated one of their floors in the Sanctuary to house male children, kind of like the Wizard's Tower, except ... I don't know, something like embodiments of beauty as well as magic."

Rohenvi didn't understand. "You mean ... they're going to claim yet more sons from among the Nobles?"

Azed shook his head. "No, I mean they're making new ones. The Priestesses are giving birth to children with mage potential, and they plan to share the males as ... well, the word I've heard is 'consorts.' They aren't grown yet, but they say the Valsharess is going to introduce them at a worship ball in the future, and the Nobles most worthy will be gifted with the first generation."

Rohenvi frowned, looking somewhat ahead and to the side of where a Priestess might wish. "So fewer Nobles will be chosen to be Priestesses? The daughters of the Priestesses will simply fill the ranks, it will become a hereditary position, and they'll just farm the males out for favors and further wealth. The gap between the populace and the Sanctuary will grow."

She thought that might not be a good thing, but Azed shook his head. "That's the odd thing. Whispers only talk about male children. No daughters that anyone has seen. Supposedly a gift from Braqth to increase our Nobles' beauty and magic."

So maybe the Priestesses had already worked out that danger and decided only on male children as less threatening. Could they select the sex that way, then? Had they grown that strong in their divine worship? That level of power granted by their Goddess was frightening to think about, but were the Priestesses making deliberate choices and showing restraint to keep the power balanced in their city?

Rohenvi kind of liked the idea. Better balance in powers meant greater longevity for them all.

The Valsharess is wise. What if we can gain one of those children? Perhaps my first?

She smiled a bit. "We haven't had a real mage in our line in a while. Almost certainly that's why our House hasn't climbed much. All the powerful Houses have a good ratio of children becoming sorceresses and wizards and Priestesses."

"Which benefits nobody but the Sanctuary and the Palace," her brother commented boldly.

Rohenvi frowned at him. "You know, most Matrons would demand I punish you for saying that in public."

"Which is why I do not say it in public, Matron-Sister," he granted with an appropriately gracious bow in deference to her, even as he tried to suppress his humor.

"Do not play so lightly," she warned. "I will punish you if you place House Thalluen or me in a position that gives any excuse to others to doubt our loyalty to the Valsharess. I would rather not, because I know your wit is better than some females and it should not be necessary."

Azed's lingering humor vanished, and he lowered his eyes and nodded. "I understand, Matron."

And so she had made herself plain. *Good.* She nodded in satisfaction.

"If I may dare," he continued somberly, "I thought instead you would like one Davrin with whom double-speak wasn't necessary." He hesitated. "I know I would. I grow tired of the Courts, and my loyalty is and always will be to my House. To you, Matron."

Rohenvi felt her chest tighten like when her Mother had been dying in her arms and turned her cup around on its saucer. She frowned. "If we speak such in private here, and you should mutter something at Court, under some influence … perhaps it is better we do not speak at all about how we would see Sivaraus run. It is not our place."

Azed didn't argue the point. He had already been drugged and abused once. He had confessed to Matron Siranet eight decades ago, when he'd allowed himself to be trapped by some gleeful females shortly after arriving at Court.

This had caused problems for a time, the things he had said — but at least they had been innocuous enough to vanish quickly from the memories of the Court when the embarrassment was fully harvested, and the scavengers found their next juicy bit. New arrivals like him were always most vulnerable.

"Let me come home, Matron," he said, "and I will watch my tongue."

Rohenvi pursed her lips. "What if I need your eyes and ears to tell me when the consorts are going to be introduced?"

Azed did not look surprised to hear that. "Truthfully? It will not give you an edge over the other Nobles. It is not first-come, first serve, it will be by invitation. I would consider other ways of distinguishing yourself, as Mother did. I could help you more with that than listening to insipid rumors cycle in and cycle out, and you would not need to worry about what I might say."

She exhaled. "Give me a cycle and we will talk again about how House Thalluen might be distinguished, to be noticed for the consorts. If I like our plan, you may stay."

Azed smiled, both wry and relieved. "Yes, Matron."

Before he left her suite, her brother paused, watching her. "No one at Court would have given me that option, Roh. That I told you any preference at all means the 'correct' answer is the opposite of it. To keep me in line."

The young Matron frowned. "So you were testing me, brother?"

His eyes were not particularly distinct, red a bit on the dark side. Still, he had had enough taze to be relaxed. "I meant what I said. You do not have to do 'double-speak' with me. But it is up to you, as ruling Matron, how you run the manor. We'll talk again at your tolerance, sister."

After Rohenvi took down her own ward to let him out, and put it back up again, sweeping her room to assure herself privacy, she continued thinking about mages. All Nobles had some basic ability — the standards in privacy and security that no one survived without learning — and only the street commoners might not use magic at all except in pre-made items bought and traded from more powerful Davrin.

Despite the overall youth of the Matrons and the fast fluctuations among them, the final status was still overall consistent with magical strength: the more Priestesses, sorceresses, and wizards in a House's living lineage, the higher up on the ladder they were.

The work was harder when one had to contend with spells and potions, incense, and gems; unlike what some lower Houses thought, winning a windfall of magical items did not make things easier, only more complicated. But managing that complication sorted out the powerful Matrons from those who merely managed resources and added to the Valsharess's army under the Sisterhood.

The consorts, if what her brother had told her was true, would be a new way for Nobles to change their status more quickly. If they were willing to work hard enough with the new influx of talent in their blood.

Yes. Rohenvi knew even before the next wake cycle that she would keep Azed here to advise her.

I accept. I want the blood-sons of the Priestesses to sire my children. As many as I can manage.

Her crotch tingled a little in delight at the thought.

Chapter 2
2820 S.E., House Thalluen, Sivaraus

Rohenvi rarely left her plantation for well over a turn following her Matron's death, as she spent time not only to reaffirm her share of crop farming and mining, but to get a handle on her information network with the Merchant Guild and the House army left behind by Siranet.

A few of the previous contacts were willing to meet with the Daughter, only once Fintre found them and insisted on a meeting. Though Azed could not be present for any of them, his Court-honed insights and opinions discussed both before and afterward were valuable to her in setting up these new arrangements and stabilizing her inheritance.

Only once their routines were stable would she be ready to climb higher once the consorts were formally announced. If there were any outsiders waiting to take vengeance on a new Matron for something her Mother had done, it was easier to see ripples when all else was calm.

So far, so good.

A few other Matrons called upon her, either curious or seeking some kind of deal, but otherwise Rohenvi had to await the next worship ball to be formally recognized as the Matron Thalluen by the Valsharess Herself. That could be anywhere from five to ten turns but alright with her. She had plenty to do in the meantime to keep her busy and build her House's wealth and martial strength together.

All the better to prepare an adult-heavy House for new children.

That was one of the long-wave patterns among the Davrin ruling Houses as well; roughly a century when there were more children to be raised, followed by two or three with few to no new births. Eventually, all the children were grown — like in her House — and now it was time to make use of the dusty nursery again.

It was not this way with commoners and slaves; those births seemed to be happening all the time and it was just a matter of constant training and drilling and negative reinforcement. Rohenvi knew some Matrons delighted in punishments, they were looking for excuses to dish them out and perhaps it eased some of their sexual tastes, too.

Rohenvi knew she took after her Mother in at least one way: the punishments were not pleasurable, only meant to train and show to all that willful transgressions would not be tolerated. The other clear message was that they were an unwelcome disruption to a calm, stable House, and if one followed the rules, they would not be singled out for undue punishment — unlike many other places.

There was an unspoken understanding of good fortune in serving her House. Her Head of Guard Fintre could carry the negative reinforcement out well in the spirit of their late Matron, and Rohenvi did not often have to step in herself — though she made sure to put the fear of Braqth into the first one who did try her tolerance and patience this far.

This old one wanted to see if the new Matron could stand up like their previous Matron when needed; Rohenvi proved that she could. They were also ready to die, so the young Matron did not hesitate to make it a graphic execution.

Otherwise, with enough food, enough protection, and genuine, un-contrived examples of what happened when one did not cooperate in the best interest of House Thalluen, Rohenvi had fewer issues with rebellious slaves, greedy servants, and bitter soldiers than she heard about from many Houses both above and below her.

She could appreciate all she'd accomplished in her first two turns, and so could Azed and Fintre — who always spoke frankly when asked and never bothered with double-speak to kiss her ass and tell her what she wanted to hear. Rohenvi perhaps could not tell them — *As Mother said, I could never show who I really am.* — but she was grateful to her brother and Head of Guard for supporting her as much as they did.

As much as it was in their self-interest to do so, they still did not do it for fear of her. Rohenvi could never be sure if this was typical or a rarity in other Noble Houses, but it worked well enough for this one.

For the moment, House Thalluen wasn't a focus of gossip or drama, covetousness or aggression, and this was where Rohenvi wanted to begin with a solid foundation.

Once she started competing in earnest for the consorts, then more Noble Houses would be talking about Matron Rohenvi Thalluen.

"YOU SEEM A LITTLE ... WELL, BORED LATELY, MATRON," her brother commented over taze, with just enough caution for her to take him seriously.

She frowned. "I've been busy, Azed."

He nodded in agreement and waited for a beat. She rolled her eyes upward and sighed.

"Speak your mind."

He half-smiled. "Usually when I saw a Court Noble acting like you, I knew to hide for fear my ass would wind up bare beneath her riding crop."

"I've not been like that!" she protested.

"Not exactly, no. You have more than air occupying your head," he said, starting to grin. "But the theory is the same."

She wiped the corner of her mouth with a cloth napkin. "So?"

Azed shrugged. "Some have been curious if you take after Mother more than it would appear. You never choose a servant or soldier from either sex, not even to indulge in healthful massages."

She exhaled in annoyance. "Who is talking about this?"

He shrugged. "The servants and soldiers. Mother usually plucked a female soldier or two, ignored most of the servants. The male soldiers never had anything to fear or to look forward to. For our sires, she managed to borrow a Noble cousin of Matron Tiel — always males who could fight, I'll add — for a few quad-spans at a time."

"You are asking me about my recreational tastes," she repeated, narrowing her copper eyes at him.

"Do you have any?" he asked bluntly. "I wouldn't know, I've been away."

"My discoveries while you were at Court are none of your business."

"Granted, but you have been working very hard for two turns, with none of it spent on pleasure. You want balance, Rohenvi, not sex only when you want to conceive. Even Mother wasn't that celibate."

Her expression would have wilted any male except her bold brother when they were in private.

"Here's a question," he began. "Do you know for certain you are fertile?"

She scoffed. "I have no reason to believe I'm not."

"Ah, but if you get a consort, you want to be sure ahead of time, yes?"

Her brows lifted a bit; now she was listening.

"I did learn about a great many potions and spells available for the right price," Azed explained. "To test for conception, to prevent it, to verify or enhance fertility —"

"I know about those, too!"

"But you haven't sought any reputable sources for them yet," he said with certainty. And he would know; he was often her messenger at the market. "You are the Matron. This should be well under your thumb before the worship ball introduces the consorts, not during or after when all the Matrons and their Daughters will be doing the same. And in the meantime …"

She waited. "What?"

Azed placed both his hands palm-down and atop the table where she could see them; an obvious sign that he meant no insult with what he was about to say.

"I'm not sure whether Mother ever told you this, but it is common for important females at Houses and at Court to test conception with a lower male prior to any binding deal for an heir-status male later. It helps the asking Matron's negotiating power."

He was right in that Rohenvi hadn't known about that precedent, but she could follow the next logical conclusion. Otherwise many Houses would have First Daughters with undesirable sires. "Then they drink an expulsion potion?"

Azed nodded. "As soon as they confirm with witnesses that they conceived. The Valsharess and the Priestesses allow this. I am confident they will be watching Matrons who have this history — confirmed fertility — as they decide who gets the first consorts. If you are one of the few who doesn't have it, it will hurt your chances."

The young Matron shook her head slowly and chuckled. "So you ask me about recreation only to persuade me to make that my next turn of ambition, brother?"

He smiled. "You just need a nudge. You didn't know there's a precedent set that makes it acceptable to sample whatever low males you want until you conceive, but I'm sure you'll find you can enjoy sex well enough on its own."

Rohenvi did not thank him for this conversation, even as important as it proved to be. This was the reason that "less useful" sons and daughters were sent to Court in the first place. There was no standard way of conveying things like this to Matrons and Nobles at large. One learned what one learned, observing and picking out truth from falsehood with varying success.

Perhaps it was time she left her plantation for a trip into the city.

"So," Azed asked curiously, "how did it go?"

"Not very productive to be back only the next cycle," she said as if she was sucking on sour fungus. "I was barely able to introduce myself to four apothecaries and confirm Fintre's connection before they started throwing their sons at me! As if I would ride them atop their very counters!"

Her brother smothered a laugh. "I guarantee you that has happened once or twice, Matron."

She made a face at him but commented no further on that. "In any case, I ran out of time."

"Then stay longer," he recommended. "A few cycles."

"Our City has little use for high-class inns," she objected. "Mostly for non-Davrin traders and secret meetings. Matrons don't stay in them even one cycle, Azed. If they are this close, they are expected to stay at the Palace."

"Fair point," he said. "And you do not want to stay in the Palace?"

"I do not want to ask until the Valsharess formally recognizes me. Remember, we are trying to distinguish House Thalluen, not look like a beggar asking for a room to rut in."

"What about the First or Second Houses? They are close to the center and offer high-class rooms to Nobles."

"I shudder to think of the price," Rohenvi murmured, shaking off her cloak before hanging it on a wall hook.

Azed smiled lop-sided. "There's just no pleasing you, is there, sister?"

She sighed. "I thank you for always thinking of alternatives. But I will simply have to keep it to cycle-trips and continue to spend my Reverie here for now. I am not ready to step into the Palace or top tiers. I will go into the City again next span. I have business to attend to and some messages to write."

The unspoken part, on which Azed didn't comment, was the implication that Rohenvi intended to drag a City male back with her at some point. No wonder the merchants were offering up their sons to the young Matron once they understood she was casually "looking." Just as she rarely saw central Sivaraus, few of the merchants had the time or connections to ever see the outer parts of it.

Both Matron and commoner were always working.

CHAPTER 3

2821 S.E., THE MARKET OF SIVARAUS

"MATRON ROHENVI! WELCOME BACK."

"Hello, Polynia. Is your Mother here?"

"Oh! Yes. Let me get her."

Rohenvi waited with a silent Fintre inside, her other two guards just outside the small shop. The main reason she returned to this apothecary for the fourth time was that they only had a young Daughter now. No sons of mating age.

The Matron got a lot of work done as she learned for herself what potions were available to her and her House. She had taken to sampling a lot of them from Hirai's Shop, those besides the fertility and pregnancy detection draughts so it wasn't so obvious what she was doing. Still, the young Matron had had the opportunity to test those on two of her servants. They had worked, so she knew this was a reputable source.

Rohenvi also hadn't made either of her servants try the expulsion potion, seeing the new mother's face when her lower belly glowed a positive yellow after quaffing the detection position. Each servant wanted her child; they were ready. They were planning in their heads, practically as they stood touching their bellies, how they would add to the House's strength. Their Matron approved.

Instead, Rohenvi would keep the expulsion sample in reserve and wait for a soldier or another who might come to her begging for help to avoid a two-turn pregnancy. Fintre had already been quietly dropping the word here and there among the fighters, that there were options if something unplanned happened.

Sometimes it just wasn't the right time or the right sire. Occasionally one had been too drunk, or quite forced, or shamed. Even if few buas would attack a cait outright, that didn't keep other caits from using cowed cocks to humiliate a rival. Sometimes a soldier was just not ready to be a proper mother, not committed, and there was no adoptive mata who would spend such massive resources on another's offspring.

It happened regularly; there was no preventing the common Davrin from fucking each other. They did not have the same reasons to abstain that she did. Why would they? They were commoners.

For her House, Rohenvi preferred early expulsion over the other practice her Mother had heard about to deal with unwanted pregnancies: volunteering babies for sacrifice in the Sanctuary rituals for Braqth's favor, and thus imprisoning the servant or the warrior for two turns, forcing her to bear it before going back to duty.

"What a great way to plant the seed for resentment and disloyalty later," Siranet had said snidely.

Her Mother had never carried out anything like that among her fighting force, and Rohenvi did not want to, either. This might be why her House had not climbed much in centuries, but also why Rohenvi was excited about the consorts.

We might have a way to change things without sacrificing newborns to the Sanctuary.

Rohenvi was doing her utmost to plan her family as well; she knew she would do what was necessary. She understood that the same option was not best for every cait, and it suited how she would run her House.

The Valsharess allowed them all the freedom to do as a Matron saw fit, so long as certain rules were followed.

Better to have all options open.

While Rohenvi was waiting, a city bua entered the shop. He glanced around, holding a package beneath both his arm and his cloak. He blinked to see her present, and she guessed he was weighting on whether his errand with Hirai could wait.

Rohenvi always met one of two kinds of commoners: those with sly glints as they thought to curry favor with her, and those with fear or wariness to set them on their toes. This one was the latter, and she hadn't yet decided if she consistently preferred one over the other. Either way, they always deferred to her.

At least the wariness in this one was the intelligent kind. She trusted her assessment that he was smart the way Azed was, observant and quick of wit behind intense red eyes.

He was pleasing enough to look at, slightly better than common, for a commoner's face. The bua was easily stronger than Azed from harder labor, standing a bit taller and confident on his feet. He might be a century older than her; how City Guard had missed recruiting him was anybody's guess.

In fact, this one was the first bua Rohenvi had seen in Sivaraus that reminded her of Azed and Fintre in one body. She hadn't realized it until she saw it now, but this was what she had been looking for.

He bowed his head and turned to go without a word.

"Stop!" she blurted, and Fintre stepped forward immediately as Thalluen's guard turned outside to block the exit. At the same time, Polynia and Hirai finally came out from the back, alarmed at hearing the Matron's voice raised.

"What's wrong, is anything wrong, Matron?!" Hirai asked, and Rohenvi only shook her head, watching her Head Guard.

"Show what's under the cloak," Fintre ordered the Davrin, low and calm. "Slowly."

He tensed but at least removed the framed, hide-covered box, almost as long as his forearm and twice as wide. He lifted it with both hands to offer toward the counter. "This is for Shopkeeper Hirai. Just components for her potions. They are delicate and apt to spoil if you open them."

"Convenient," Fintre commented, keeping her warrior's eyes on his every move, evaluating him at the same time as she took the box in one hand and transferred it over to Hirai's waiting arms. "What's your name?"

He frowned a little, rightfully concerned. "I've done nothing."

"Strange name." Fintre chuckled at his expression but urged him with a gesture. "C'mon. Your real one. Matron Rohenvi of House Thalluen would like to know."

The young Matron kept her mouth closed and her stance graceful and dignified, as if everything was going to plan; meanwhile Hirai and her First Daughter stared at the standoff in her shop. The Matron stood with poise even though she had no idea how Fintre would have known that, yes, she wanted to ask this one's name. This wasn't the first time Fintre anticipated her needs.

The delivery male smiled then, like there were some private jests in what she'd said. He turned on his feet to bow his head directly to her. "Well met, Matron. My name is Ruk."

She nodded, her face placid with a Noble's mask. "Ruk of what?"

He shrugged. "Of Sivaraus. I travel the outskirts, sometimes with caravans, bringing supplies to the City." He indicated the box Hirai still held. "Like that one. May I have my payment?"

Hirai nodded, collecting herself as the owner of the shop. "Let me get it. Matron? You will not take him until I've completed my bargain? Just ... my reputation —"

"I will not," Rohenvi agreed, although it was curious the way this was playing out. *She shows interest in one male — at last — and all assume she will just take him straight away?* Maybe the stories of other Matrons weren't as exaggerated as she had thought. It was an option, though an impulsive one. *She could get away with it.*

Ruk himself looked disconcerted, even as she came closer to get a better look at him, Polynia and Fintre still looking on.

"Matron?" he asked.

She ignored the question but not his voice at first as she inhaled his scent. The latter should have been off-putting; she could smell the travel he'd mentioned, the dirt, and the aged sweat.

Instead, it brought to her mind moments of excitement her Mother had described to her as a child, following a stint "outside these damned walls." How Siranet sometimes referred to their home, their plantation.

This bua certainly came from far outside what she knew during an average cycle.

"Do you have stories?" she asked him.

"Your pardon, Matron?" he asked, confused.

"Stories. About your travels."

"Oh. Ah, yes, Matron. But you don't want to hear them."

If he wanted to fan my interest higher …

"Does any matron lay claim on you? Any from whom I need to ask permission?"

He was silent, staring slightly up at her eyes with his mouth open. He closed it and remembered to look at her chin, hesitant to answer at first. "Ah … no. Matron. I hire on by the job. I am … in between jobs."

"How do you get away with that?" she asked, intrigued. "Wouldn't any ranking female try to claim you?"

She loved the look on his face; confident but respectful. "They try. Sometimes they succeed. It's short-term on the fringe, though. Circumstances change quickly."

Indeed, they do.

That was the perfect answer, she realized, still staring at him.

He could be claimed for short intervals; Ruk was independent, took care of himself, just as her Mother had always taught her and Azed. He had stories he could tell her, conversation to be had, but he wouldn't want to stay. She would only give him yet another story to take with him.

So appealing compared to the simpering, clinging merchants peddling their dull, cringing, or silent whores to the highest bidder. Rohenvi wouldn't have to answer to another Matron, either. No attached favors or conditions to test her fertility.

"Is there a room I may rent, Polynia?" she asked the younger female behind the counter. "Just for half a mark. Undisturbed."

The fledgling merchant smirked a little but nodded just as her mother returned with Ruk's payment. Rohenvi stepped up to the counter and offered an additional coin to Hirai.

"Private negotiation is all," the young Matron clarified.

The shopkeeper nodded and relaxed a bit. "No bed or desk?"

"Not necessary. Room for my guards would be nice."

"You will have to come upstairs."

Hirai offered a small room with a child-sized bed in it, many odd trinkets and some tiny books lying about, but nothing interesting or revealing about the shop owner herself. Soon enough, it was just Ruk in a room with four intimidating females.

Rohenvi thought he was holding up very well; he had experience negotiating for himself, this was clear. The Matron was privately excited with her serendipitous find and hoping they could come to an amenable agreement.

She couldn't really show it, of course, but she was very direct.

"I would like to hire you for a job, Ruk-Between-Jobs," she said with a formal smile. "It would require you to stay at my House for a time, but you would be provided a room and food, and my House's protection. When you left, you will be paid an agreed sum and, if you like, my guards will escort you back to the center unharmed. You will be free to seek your next 'fringe' job."

Ruk watched her keenly. She imagined him combing over her offer in his mind even as the most obvious use for his presence at her House was still unspoken.

Rohenvi could imagine the Matron of House Bovritz advising her *against* an intelligent male for this task. Personally, she could not stand the thought of rutting with a male unable to engage her with words, regardless of if she intended to abort the pregnancy once she caught.

She had already tried the awkward, wordless sex. After thinking about what her brother had said, she wanted more fun this time.

"You make a sound opening offer, Matron," he granted. "What would I be doing at your House, and for what length of time?"

Rohenvi and Fintre exchanged an amused glance, then they looked back. "Entertaining us with stories of the fringe, giving back a little work to House Thalluen in exchange for the food, and sharing my private quarters when asked. For however long it takes for me to conceive for the first time. You would be helping me test Shopkeeper Hirai's enhancement potions."

His eyes widened a little. He was not surprised to hear he'd be used for sex; he was surprised about the intended outcome.

Rohenvi continued with a large smile on her face. "You will come to no harm as long as you do not thieve anything, harm anyone, do not make contact with another House while you are in residence, and do not speak of my private tastes to any others once you leave. You will also not rut with any other caits of my House. Your body is exclusive to me while beneath my roof, but only short-term. As you are accustomed."

Ruk was appropriately sober hearing the terms. "I see. What happens to me if you do not conceive, either in short-term or at all? I am concerned with such a bargain being open-ended, Matron. I will gladly agree to never speak of your private tastes to others, but if conception fails, will you still let me go unharmed and short-term?"

Rohenvi's expression sharpened. "Do you know yourself to be infertile, trader?"

"Ah … on the contrary," he answered, showing discomfort, "I am aware of a likely daughter, though the mother did not confirm it before she died."

She nodded smartly. "Will you submit to a fertility indicator potion before we leave here if I pay for it?"

He squinted a bit. "Those are not foolproof, Matron."

Rohenvi was delighted with that response. She looked him over once again in appreciation. "Perhaps not, and they tend to make one a little nauseated, I understand. But agree to that and if it is a positive indicator, then I will agree to a fixed period of three quad-spans using Hirai's potions, and if I do not conceive you still may leave unharmed. But I reserve the option to call upon you again if I so choose. The message would come from Hirai."

"Getting a little forward in time, aren't we, Matron?" he commented, daring to tease her if only because she had made it clear she wanted him.

Not to mention this was far more exciting than any other negotiation she had ever done.

"If you do not conceive and I am released, I ask that you not call on me again immediately," he refined. "I would need a minimum period of three quad-spans to maintain all my contacts and remain known for hire on the fringe. Be missing for even six quad-spans and everyone assumes you are dead or compromised."

"Agreed," she said, lifting her chin but smiling. "Do we have a bargain, Ruk?"

He was just nervous enough when he exhaled for her to believe he took it seriously. "Yes, Matron Thalluen. I will take the potion and come to your House for three quad-spans for an agreed sum."

A good sign that he was so confident of the outcome when he took his swig later. Shopkeeper Hirai would know what was going on, of course, but Rohenvi saw no harm in that. Other Matrons did this, and Rohenvi had to test the expulsion potion sooner or later.

Her main concern was having good conversation for the next quarter-turn, in addition to at least decent, functional sex. She did not require him to be a stunning beauty, or sexually talented, or uniquely endowed.

As long as he could become erect and climax inside her, as long as she became pregnant, she'd be content with the stories.

CHAPTER 4

2821 S.E., HOUSE THALLUEN, SIVARAUS

RUK'S TALES DID NOT BEGIN ON THE WAY BACK TO HOUSE THALLUEN. THE traveler sat beside her in the carriage, nauseated from his first test as expected, while Fintre and her guards rode outside on their lizards.

The Matron also thought Ruk was contemplative, possibly reflecting on the fact that he had stepped into a shop to make a delivery and was now being escorted out of the densest Davrin population to a private plantation. Her chosen bua did not seem dazed or bewildered despite the unsettled stomach.

Like Azed. Just thinking.

Although unlike her well-groomed brother, Ruk most certainly needed a bath.

Rohenvi wondered how Azed would react when she got home. She hoped it wasn't with petty jealousy; this had been as much his idea as hers!

Her Head Guard had only shrugged, quite neutral toward the bua trader, when Rohenvi asked her opinion. "As long as he's functional and doesn't cause trouble."

The first was highly likely following Hirai's potion; it even had the side effect of causing an erection in males. The second remained to be seen, but her own instincts weren't sounding off and neither were Fintre's. It was a good sign.

House Thalluen was still standing as they approached on the Valsharess's road. Rohenvi noted this with dark amusement, even as Azed had proven capable watching over things for a cycle at a time when she granted him the authority in her absence and backed it up with Fintre's trusted second, Honaki.

The young Matron could not do this too frequently or there would be talking, and opportunity for conspiracy if another got the right leverage over her brother. She was aware of how many letters he received from Court asking for an invitation to his House, the damned slits.

At least now Rohenvi did not expect to have to leave her plantation again for some time. She would be entertaining her "guest."

"Azed," she greeted, climbing out of her single Uroan-drawn carriage.

"Matron, welcome back," he said with a very Courtly bow. There wasn't a hint of irony in his performance, and the servants always noted that.

She smiled and climbed down, turning to offer her hand to help Ruk out, but saw the trader was already well past the midpoint of stepping down on his own. He realized too late he should have waited for a sign from her. It was surprisingly amusing to watch him try to stop mid-step, half-falling out of the carriage in the process.

Rohenvi allowed herself an elegant, confident laugh as she stepped to make space for the unwittingly jesting male, while most watching servants hid smiles behind their hands as they collected the Uroan and carriage for later settlement. Ruk regained his feet without tripping or falling against her then immediately bowed to show he realized his mistake.

"My deepest apology, Matron," he murmured, his face heating notably in the dark. "My hands are not very clean, I thought I would spare you …"

"I shall let it slide this once," she said. "From now on, wait to be summoned to meet someone new. This is the First Son of House Thalluen, Azed. My brother by blood. Azed, this is Ruk, trader of Sivaraus."

Ruk clearly only guessed when to bow; he began to then hesitated, then confirmed Azed wasn't bowing first, and completed it with passable grace. Her brother's face was placid, but Rohenvi detected some recognizable humor as he mildly lowered his chin to acknowledge the other male.

With his status, Azed did not have to bow to a mere trader, but his Matron-sister did not think he was insulted or contemptuous. He'd never act so openly so without clear cause; he was too smart.

"I am famished," she announced, and Chio from the kitchens stepped forward attentively so she turned to him. "Bring enough for three to the second guest suite as soon as may be. Include taze and something sweet."

"Yes, Matron."

She gestured for Azed and Ruk to come along and led the way herself while the rest dispersed to their duties, and Fintre to her own downtime.

The Head Guard had already thoroughly checked Ruk's person and took possession of his dagger and short sword, the small collection of pouches, a roughly hewn gem, the ring on his finger and earring in his ear, even his payment from Hirai — everything he'd had on him would be kept for when he was leaving, and he would not see them until them. Ruk hadn't had a choice about that.

As he entered her House, the trader possessed only the clothes on his back, his boots, and his cloak. Rohenvi smiled privately to herself. Soon, he wouldn't even be wearing those.

Azed waited while Rohenvi introduced Ruk to his room — not the largest guest suite, that had to remain open for a surprise guest of honor — but it was luxurious compared to anything Ruk had ever seen, she would wager.

The commoner stared at the comfortable bed large enough for two, the private bath, the balcony, and the wide floor space. A desk stood not far from a visiting area with a tray table and three plush chairs. He didn't smile with any greed or glee, but he was aware of the wealth in which he stood.

"This is how you run it warm," she showed Ruk as Azed took one of the visiting chairs, and the tub began to fill with splashing water. "Here is your soap. Now remove your clothing, set them here, and bathe yourself. Put on the robe there when you've finished. The servants will clean your clothes and bring new ones."

"Will I not see this particular set again until I leave as well, Matron?" he asked.

She smiled. "Correct. New habits are best learned in new clothing."

Ruk sighed softly and removed his cloak first to set aside, untucking his shirt from his pants before pulling that over his head. Rohenvi and Azed were both looking him over from their chairs when her brother spoke.

"You have a fair number of scars for a merchant, Ruk," he commented.

"I am a caravan trader, First Son Thalluen," he replied, pausing in removing his boots. "That type of merchant goes into the wilderness. We learn to use a blade out of necessity."

"You can fight?" Azed asked curiously. "How well?"

Ruk shrugged. "Not well enough to evade the marks, First Son."

"I see. What sort of creature caused those on the lower left of your back? They look ragged, like claw marks."

"Rare Deepearth beast," the commoner muttered with a nod, removing his boots. "I ... didn't get a good look at it before they chased it away."

Rohenvi was grinning as she met Azed's eyes. "He has stories."

"Ah." Her brother nodded like this made all the sense in the Deepearth to him.

Ruk dawdled before removing his bottoms, when he would be completely naked. He checked the water level and temperature first.

"I'd like to see the rest of you," Rohenvi said bluntly.

Ruk loosened his belt, but he was tense as Rohenvi glimpsed the first white puff of pubic hair. Finally he simply gripped the trousers and pulled them down, bending over to pull them off his feet. He was mostly in profile but twisted to show more of his backside, probably by accident.

Rohenvi leaned a bit to glimpse his scrotum hanging between his legs as he balanced on one foot before Ruk tossed the pants aside and climbed into the tub. She stared at his flaccid penis until it went out of view as he lowered himself in with some amusing sounds of surprise at the heat of the water. His face was funny, too.

She only realized her smile was too broad and eager, not dignified at all, when a glance at Azed. He raised one playful eyebrow in comment.

What? she signed, her hand hidden from Ruk's view in her lap.

You're acting as if you've never seen a naked bua before, he signed back, blocking it behind his crossed legs.

She lifted her chin proudly. *Not one that was bold enough to bargain with me on his own, and he has traveled. I like his roughness.*

Indeed, Azed signed with a nod of understanding. *No other bartered him?*

No. He is independent.

Interesting.

The sounds from the tub drew their attention back to Ruk, who apparently thought he had only a few ticks to scrub clean, and that was all. No lounging or relishing the luxury, no performance or posing. She always had thought a male Davrin with wet hair and droplets on his skin was alluring, if only he wouldn't speed through each body part like a checklist.

Rohenvi thought it a waste of a full tub — they could have gone with a pitcher and a bowl in this case — but she went back and forth with herself about how soon she wanted him finished. Buas could not read the caits' minds, after all, and he was trying to please her. Plus, he was grubby; the water was probably collecting enough silt to turn the bottom muddy.

Oh, well. She'd have time to try again, maybe when her brother wasn't present.

The trader appeared a little smaller, more delicate, when he donned the white silk robe and took the third chair, now nice and clean. He seemed almost forlorn as the servants took away his regular clothes and brought their food.

The three waited for the servants to rinse out the tub — by the look on one's face, yes, there was a lot of grime — and take their leave before each plucking a small plate from the platter and selecting what they wanted from a communal assortment of favorite foods.

Ruk was either very hungry or was simply used to consuming all he could quickly before something happened to interrupt him. Azed seemed to be drawing just as much amusement from this as she. The siblings looked at each other, smiled mischievously, and waited for the moment Ruk realized his hosts weren't even halfway done and his first plate was empty.

"Oh, um," he began.

"Do that again, and I may find something else to fill your mouth while we finish," she teased wickedly.

His face flushed with heat. "I will slow down next time."

"Next time? You mean seconds? You can have more."

"At least if there's any poison in it, you'll show signs first," Azed commented.

Ruk's eyes went wide. Her brother laughed.

"No, actually," the First Son said, "that's why we have the shared platter with guests. Fewer poison-detection spells needed, and you know we're not trying to drug you. Although, you did not even give me the chance to show you."

The trader swallowed, but Rohenvi waved her hand. "Oh, I'm sure it's fine. You're paranoid, brother."

"I have reason to be," he drawled with a smirk. "I spent turns at Court, remember?"

They continued the charade that was only partly a charade, all with the purpose of quickly sending the message that the siblings of this House were allies and not to be driven apart by a temporary stud.

Ruk may have missed that. He only peered about the room without obvious greed, responding to questions in deference to her brother. Rohenvi was further reassured that she had made a good choice, and this could be a pleasant task on her path of ambition.

After they finished their sweets, Azed sighed contentedly. He signed a good eve, stood up with Rohenvi and Ruk following, and Rohenvi escorted him to the door.

Azed signed again with her body blocking the other bua's view while he spoke at the same time.

"I have a few things to look after then I will be retiring for the eve. I will make sure you are not disturbed, Matron."

★Not an obvious schemer,★ his hands stated. ★But intelligent enough to become one. Observant. Do not underestimate because he's acting the fool to put us both at ease.★

"Thank you, Azed. Rest well."

ROHENVI LET HER BROTHER OUT AND SECURED THE DOOR BEHIND HIM. SHE HAD only to half-turn to look at Ruk, who stood with his hands at his sides and a strange look on his face. She came closer to him, her hips swaying more as her confidence and interest rose, studying his expression, as he was clearly offering her one.

"What is it, Ruk?" she asked directly. "Were you sorry to see him go, now to be left alone with me, as you agreed?"

"No, Matron," he answered, trying to select any following words with care.

"Then why look as though you're surprised? You're clean, fed, rested. You might know what comes next."

"I might, Matron, but the flavor of what was coming I did not know."

"Oh?" She gently took his arm and led him toward the bed. "Tell me more. Be clear."

"Your comment about filling my mouth with something else while you and the First Son ate ..."

"Mm-hm?"

He watched her expression in return, trying to read it without saying more. She frowned.

"You are not being clear, Ruk."

He looked surprised, and he backpedaled. "Ah. In that case, I apologize for bringing it up."

"Bringing what up?"

"I'm sorry to concern you, Matron, forgive this fool."

"Ruk!" She turned him to face her using both hands as they stood beside the unruffled bed. "You are not forgiven! I —"

She stopped as something occurred to her, and she brought a finger to her mouth as she thought about it. "Wait. Our bargain. You agreed to be exclusive to me."

"And not rut with other females, yes," he said as if he wished they weren't discussing the details of the bargain right now.

Rohenvi was enough of her Mother's Daughter to see the hole she hadn't realized before, but Ruk apparently had. If he had seen it back at Hirai's shop, he hadn't even protested it. She felt more the fool for allowing him to confirm now that this unspoken part of the bargain hadn't even crossed her mind until he'd brought it up. *Sort of.*

It was too late to pretend to be anything else but caught flat-footed.

"No caits, but perhaps other buas," she said, her eyes narrowing at him as he tensed again. "Were you hoping I'd keep my own brother here to share you between us?"

Ruk had a strong somatic response, but he ignored his own body's flush to try and read her, as accurately and quickly as he could.

Azed was right, this one was observant.

"It's … not unusual among Nobles, as I understand it," he said warily.

Rohenvi exhaled irritably. Did every bua in Sivaraus know more about what other Matrons and their families did in their bedrooms than she did? Even though she was a Matron in her own right?

"What's not unusual?" she demanded, letting the irritation and insult show. "Matrons rutting with their own brothers?!"

Ruk's shoulders lifted as if he meant to cower at her voice rising. He started explaining, sounding rightfully desperate to speak now.

"No! I mean, no offense intended to you or the First Son, Matron Thalluen, I beg your tolerance, I'd never presume to know! I meant only that some matrons enjoy using their status to command some buas to rut with each other, especially to remind one or both … or more! … of his place. I thought you were suggesting you'd like to see my face in the First Son's lap while you ate, that my mouth would be filled with his —"

"Enough!"

Ruk snapped his mouth shut, and the room was blessedly silent as Rohenvi tried to collect her composure. She was furious — with him, and with herself — that she hadn't seen any of this coming. So much for her elegant, confident appearance as a sexually experienced Matron!

Azed was right, she bemoaned to herself. She simply did not know enough about sex to pull off playing games. Mother had not encouraged much exploration, and the First Daughter's tastes had never matched up with her Mother to learn many specifics from her.

Except in the one way.

Public shows of power were nonexistent at House Thalluen. All pleasure and breeding happened behind closed doors, even if some were suspected of peeking.

Are some Matrons so gleeful in letting others watch, then?

She supposed she could see this. To be naked and doing various things, even conducting the show, and being confident someone wasn't about to scrape a Matron with a poison needle or attack her without her armor on?

Mother would never have been able to tolerate that, Rohenvi thought with a huff as she sat down on the edge of the bed.

Ruk remained as he was, afraid to move at this point for fear of displeasing her further. Rohenvi felt her anger and embarrassment receding in the quiet. Her mind started working again.

"Have you ever been in that position, Ruk?" she asked curiously. "A powerful matron instructing who you fondled and sucked, even another male?"

He swallowed. "Yes, Matron. … She was one who included her brother in her play."

"Who was it?" she asked, nearly a demand.

"You would not have known her. She was from the fringe, like me. Not in your social sphere, Matron, and I'm not certain she is even still alive with how many enemies she made around her."

"She wasn't a Noble?"

Ruk's smile was wry, but now he was trying — in his own strange way — to reassure her. "I'm sure she told herself she was, Matron. Her mother had a creepy obsession with her own nephew, as I understood it."

Creepy.

Rohenvi had never really heard that word in this context before. The young Matron liked it. That was how this felt to her, to have the suggestion that Azed should remain here and laugh while Rohenvi commanded Ruk to do things to him …

As if her strong-willed brother would even sit still for it. Azed disliked being laughed at and had good reasons for it; as a result he rarely laughed at others. If nothing else, such a "show" would shatter the loyalty and respect he held for his sister, even being so young a Matron. She had listened to him when he'd told her how, at Court, his expressing any preference at all meant it would be used as a weapon against him.

Clearly, Ruk was used to the same expectation from his matrons, even if they weren't Nobles.

Rohenvi had not come up with a good reason to do the same as those at Court, and a better one to refrain. As long as she did not humiliate and laugh at him, Azed would watch her back, like Fintre did.

Rohenvi needed her brother to help observe things around her. Neither of them knew whether the House that Mother had attacked in her last mission had plans against House Thalluen or not, whether they would pay for the actions of their Mother.

Rohenvi pursed her lips and shook her head, her nose wrinkling. "Hmph. Well. Then let me be clear, Ruk. I will not ask you to 'play' with my brother. In fact, as an addendum to our bargain, I forbid you from rutting with all other buas, either. You will rut only me, Ruk. That is our agreement now, and that was our agreement back at Hirai's shop, whether you realized it or not. For the time you are here, you are to couple only with me."

He nodded quickly. "Yes, Matron. Thank you for clarifying."

Rohenvi took a deep breath and let her eyes trail over him. She was distracted, unsettled, flustered, a little too warm … and yet …

She blinked. *Is his member pressing up beneath the silk robe?*

"Are you aroused?" she demanded.

"And relieved, Matron," he admitted. "How may I pleasure you this eve?"

Rohenvi looked up at him, stared at his chagrin, looked down again at the bump of his groin, looked up again. Her jaw firmed. "Open your robe, Ruk. Drop it on the floor."

No hesitation this time; he stripped and did exactly as she said.

She watched the silk crumple onto her clean floor and drape partly across his bare foot, touching one of his ankles, and for some reason that one sight made her middle tight, her crotch tingling. She lifted her eyes up his legs to his genitals; he was partially erect. She watched his penis pulse and lengthen a bit more under her gaze, rising up from his tender sack.

Rohenvi had decided to wait for seeing the size and shape of his cock. She hadn't made him pull it out and show her when he'd become hard at the shop, although she could tell everyone there had expected her to. It didn't matter how it looked — straight, curved, bent, whatever — this wasn't for real breeding. She did not require a specific appearance.

In a way, she had wanted to be surprised, to save something for later. She liked his face, he didn't limp, and he was functional. What more did she need to inspect in public?

Now, she could take her time. They were alone and …

He's all mine.

Rohenvi eagerly smoothed her hands up his thighs. Ruk shivered a little, his erection pulsing again, as she took hold of his hips and positioned him just so in front of her. The bed, fortunately, wasn't too high off the ground, so her eyes were almost perfectly even with his crotch.

Letting go of his hips, she cupped his balls with one hand and wrapped her fingers around the other, massaging him, testing the impressive heat and vast array of textures — hard, smooth, soft, squishy …

Bua parts are so fun.

She was staring at these parts closely like a novice, as if she'd never seen them before. She knew she should be embarrassed.

"I'll remind you," she murmured, "the bargain includes not discussing my personal tastes to anyone outside this room."

He trembled. "I … I recall, Matron. Yes."

"You understand the consequences if I discover otherwise."

"Yes, Matron."

"Good."

She leaned forward, nuzzling his white bush first with her lips and inhaling through her nose as she still held him with both hands. She released his shaft and gently trailed her fingertips down his length, hearing him inhale in surprise at the sensation. She held just the tip, very delicately, and planted light kisses from the furry base all the way to the ridge of his glans, gently tugging on his scrotum.

The trader made further amusing noises as he struggled with how to express his feedback to her. She did not want to cause pain — he'd likely go limp on her — but she wanted to play. She left him to it, nuzzling and nibbling on his erection as it neared its apex.

She detected a change in his scent, too, an added musk to his groin as she manipulated him. This made her mouth water. She sniffed and licked him, stroked him once or twice at a time, and noticed when he began to leak clear fluid from the hole at the tip. Impulsively, she rubbed her cheek against it, smearing the pre-cum and causing both his glans and her cheek to glisten with the stretchy wetness.

"Mmm."

She opened her mouth and touched just the tip of her pink tongue to the dark phallus.

My toys. My tasty, tasty toys ...

"M-Matron, you do n-not have to —"

She closed her lips around just the head and sucked, her tongue slathering off the rest of the fluid, enjoying the taste. Nothing tasted or had a texture like this!

Ruk made a louder noise, a sucking breath of shock and he held perfectly still but for another quiver or two. He waited to see what she'd do next. Rohenvi gloated in her mind as she fed more of his member between her lips, stroking him again and again with her mouth, most of the way down, pressing her tongue hard along the plump underside.

Her trader had regained control of his breathing a short while ago and measured it. She glanced up at his face with her lips rolling wetly over the tip once again, and he had his eyes closed — but not squeezed shut. He looked stunned, or like he was floating. Drugged maybe. And he measured his breath, even as she could almost feel his quickened pulse through the cock in her mouth.

Rohenvi leaned in and took more, experimenting with how deep she could push him, whether it could be so far her nose was pressed to his bush and him lodged in her throat.

She'd thought about trying it, and so she did.

It took a few tries for her lips to reach his bush when she didn't gag but eventually, she got it. She had no choice but to hold her breath and tighten her stomach down to keep it in line. She held his cock this way for several moments, swallowing to squeeze her throat around his tip and he made a delightful sound.

"*Ngah!*" he garbled, quickly swallowing the drool in his mouth.

She had also successfully messed up his breathing, she noted with glee. A moan escaped him, and he shivered as she withdrew, taking her fill of every slurping finger-width until he popped out — soaking wet — into the open air. He exhaled and she took hold of his hips again when he wavered on his feet.

"Matron, I ..." he tried to speak. "Shall I reciprocate ... ?"

She was still catching her own breath after that. She shook her head. "No."

Leaning to grab the smooth covers and pull them back, bunched near her right hip, she pushed him to drop onto the clean sheets. "Knees and elbows, ankles and wrists crossed. Present to me."

Her trader was aware this was the slave position, but now he seemed dazed as he slowly but surely settled onto the bed as she'd instructed.

Rohenvi stood up immediately, admired his sack between his legs again — although this time it was drawn further up — and began running her hands along his back and flanks and buttocks, finding with her fingers all those scars which Azed had commented on.

Her sexy, common bua wasn't a perfect canvas, and yet he was a bewilderingly fascinating one.

She gently rubbed at his perineum, exploring it, and Ruk tensed, the little purple star of his anus clenching tighter. She chuckled softly, stroking her thumb along the tough ridge, exploring it.

She never had ... *explored* like this. Nothing so relaxed. Simple.

Slowly, she realized this was all she wanted to do for the first while: touch and taste him. He was only required to let her; he need do nothing else for the time being.

The Matron briefly rubbed at her netherlips through her gown, belatedly realizing that she was completely dressed while Ruk was nude in front of her. He had his face turned to one side, watching what he could.

"Are you comfortable?" she asked.

"Yes, Matron. This mattress is very easy on the knees."

She smiled, peeked at his stiff rod bobbing beneath his belly, and teased, "Are you leaking on my sheets?"

"I'd rather not … if I can use my hand — ?"

"Don't move."

Rohenvi reached underneath herself and stroked him again, squeezing out more of his pre-cum and drawing it across her palm.

There, he won't drip again for a little while.

She was sure to step out of his line of sight before she softly sniffed at her palm and smiled to herself as she looked at his ass.

She knew what she wanted to do next.

Dear Goddess, I'm not any less strange in my tastes than Mother was, am I?

She patted Ruk's left buttock with her clean hand "Move forward a bit. Make room for me."

He obeyed, remaining silent but his prick still hard, his back still a bit tense. She supposed, after what he'd told her about other matrons playing with two or more buas … that he probably thought she wanted to penetrate him with something.

He wasn't wrong, exactly.

"Uncross your ankles," she said softly, her chest growing hot in anticipation. "Spread your knees a bit."

Soon she could kneel comfortably behind him. She could also reach between his legs and take hold of his erection with her wet hand, using the natural lubricant for good purpose.

His toes curled as Ruk groaned again, and she grinned, squeezing her thighs together. Goddess, she was *aching*. And she hadn't even undressed yet!

Rohenvi squeezed his left buttock with her free hand, using it to part him a bit wider as she leaned down, again choosing to nuzzle some of his most tender of places with her lips.

He gasped. "Matron … you … ah, y-you … ?"

She kissed and licked very lightly, so dangerously close to his pucker, and it squeezed again in a most amusing way. She could feel a most intimate heat rising to touch her cheek; the blood was so close to the surface here.

"What is it, Ruk? You're clean, aren't you? You did a good job in my bath?"

He still sounded dazed. Maybe disbelieving. "Yes, Matron."

"Has anyone ever licked your netherhole, Ruk?" she asked crassly, loving the sound of the words coming out of her own mouth, and his reaction to them.

He thought about how to respond. Finally he said, "Not as you are doing, Matron."

"Certainly no one of my status."

"For certain, no."

"Do you like it?"

He swallowed.

"Be clear, Ruk."

"Yes, I like it," he answered.

"Do you want more?"

"If … it pleases you, Matron Thalluen."

She rewarded him with a few more kisses before flicking her tongue in light dabs here and there around the edge of that circle of delicate creases. He held his breath at one point without intending to, as she teased and hinted at licking him full along his dirt hole.

Her hand around his prick had stopped; she was merely holding him and checked again for dripping pre-cum. She caught what was there and, by a wizard's staff, he was still so hard in her grip!

Finally Rohenvi took the leap and swept her tongue, flat and wide, across his entire anus. Ruk sucked in his breath, his toes curling again. She did it again, and he moaned as his toes relaxed more. She kept swirling her tongue, around and around the tight ring as she confirmed he had indeed cleaned well, even there.

She could taste her soap but also something else distinct. A milder taste, no real odor. Inoffensive, she decided, but hard to pin down with this fun kind of skin. Such variety, texture, ridges and such sensitivity!

She loved his responses, the playful reflexes, especially when she stiffened her own tongue just like his prick, and pressed it into the tiny hole.

"AH!" he cried. "Matron … !"

She lifted her lips, her entire lower face a mess with her own saliva and whatever was left of his pre-cum from earlier. She missed the heat already.

"Do you like it, Ruk?"

He was gasping, his head turned to the right and now his eyes were squeezed shut. "Y-yes, Matron."

"Good."

Rohenvi went back to exploring him. She lost track of how long she had her lips and tongue between her trader's buttocks, even venturing again down and forward to his balls and back up, servicing him as determinedly as she'd heard some others required a slave to work at her snatch.

She never grew tired of his reactions or the sounds escaping him.

"Please, Matron, have mercy," he gasped at one point. "I-I may spurt over your sh-sheets soon …"

She lifted her head for the final time.

"Oh, no, you don't, Ruk. Get on your back."

With another groan, her deep trader rolled, watching her in awe as Rohenvi expertly unlaced her own dress until she could pull it down off her shoulders and down to join his white robe. The Matron stripped off her undergarments as well and tossed them impatiently aside. Her lubricant had collected so on her own netherlips that it smeared between her inner thighs the moment she brought them together.

He was cooperative, and quivering, as she crawled over him, straddling him as she planted her palms on his chest for leverage. Feeling confident, powerful, and not the least bit awkward — even if they were silent, staring at each other's faces — Rohenvi mashed her sex against him, grinding until his pubic hair was matted down with feminine moisture, his cock instantly slimy in her excitement.

As soon as she could, she reached with one hand to move his pole into place, and …

Oh!!

He sank in so easily!

Goddess, I've never been this wet before.

He was stretching her; his pole a snug, comfortable inside with her swollen, puffy lips wrapped around him.

"Mmnn!" she grunted, pleased as she leaned straight up, squatting as low as she could. She reached to play with her aching pearl, rubbing and pressing it as she kept Ruk's erection fully sheathed, squirming her hips some but without moving up or down.

Ruk bent his legs without being told, bringing his ankles halfway to his ass and settling her soft buttocks against his thighs. This helped to support her as she stroked herself harder and faster.

His hands rested lightly on her thighs, and his eyes were glued to her crotch the way hers had been to his. Odd, pained expressions passed his face regularly, especially when her cunt squeezed around him, but he laid still. Ready. *Waiting …*

When the Matron of House Thalluen felt herself on the verge of climax, she shrieked once and grunted the rest of the way, thrusting her hips down on her chosen bua to finally fuck him as she held on to her own crotch with one hand.

"Oh, Goddess … Matron … !" Ruk gasped, a clear warning that he could no longer keep it back.

"Yes!" she cried, fucking him harder as she hit her peak and started coasting. *I want that seed! Give it to me!*

Ruk's cock flexed and pulsed inside her as he lost control of his voice, barking in release as he clutched her thighs, spending his entire load inside her.

Warmth and satisfaction — and sleepiness — swept over her. Rohenvi sighed deeply as she flopped forward, feeling the ridiculous need to sniff and kiss his sweaty neck just after cumming.

Goddess, he smells good …

Ruk turned his head slightly away to make it easier for her, offering his throat. She grinned and sucked on his tasty neck, even as she berated herself for un-Matronly behavior inside her own head.

She hadn't wanted awkward silence while mating; she had chosen him for his stories and lack of connections. Yet they hadn't talked much beforehand, hardly at all during … and she didn't feel the lack.

"Wow … ." Ruk breathed then, and a giggle bubbled out of her mouth with the infinitely flattering and appreciative tone. "You must let me reciprocate, Matron."

"We'll see," she murmured. "Now roll with me so it doesn't spill out. I need to be on my back and put a pillow under my hips for a while."

"Mm," he hummed, also seeming sleepy but he rolled with her. "Why?"

"To keep your spending inside for as long as possible. Better chance of catching."

He looked modestly amused as he carefully withdrew from atop her. "Does that work?"

She lifted her chin. "My Mother did it. And I'm here."

"Ah-ha." He nodded, taking on what seemed a genuine smile. "Proof positive, without doubt, Matron."

She squinted, her suspicion blunted with relaxation as she fumbled for a pillow. "Are you teasing, Ruk?"

He reached up and tugged it closer, putting it in her hand. "Never, Matron."

"Hmph."

Soon she was in position, her butt propped on a thick pillow, and she had time to kill staring at her ceiling with her chosen sire lying next to her. "So I hired you for your stories as well as your erection, Ruk. Tell me a story while we wait."

"Anything in particular, Matron?"

"You said you didn't get a good look at whatever caused the claw marks?"

"I'm afraid not, Matron."

"What about another beast, then?"

"I can do that. Have you seen a drake?"

"They're small, aren't they?"

"About the size of a ten-turn-old child."

"Nothing bigger?"

"I try to avoid anything bigger."

She chuckled at his eloquent expression. "Coward."

But she didn't really mean it.

They talked for some time into the eve and there wasn't the least bit of awkward silence she had dreaded; not until Rohenvi had to get up to return to her own quarters. Even then, the awkwardness was only inside herself, hesitating to leave a warm, rumpled bed for a cool, crisp one.

Don't be ridiculous. No true Matron spends the sleep cycle in the same bed with a commoner!

CHAPTER 5

"SEE, I TOLD YOU," AZED SAID SMUGLY, AND SHE WAS IN A GOOD ENOUGH MOOD lately to let him get away with it. "You discovered your pleasure just fine."

Ruk had been a guest in the House for the last six spans, and there were times Rohenvi wondered whether she could pour her bones out of bed after another bedding with him. While she always could make herself do the things which needed to be done around her own plantation, it was easier than it had been to delegate other tasks that she did not have to oversee herself. And Azed had noticed.

"I take it the soldiers and servants aren't theorizing which direction I lean anymore?" she asked, cutting into her meal.

"No," her brother commented wryly. "Now they're theorizing how long you'll keep your consort around."

She frowned. "Three quad-spans. As agreed."

"They're taking bets for longer. You're glowing, Matron."

"*Peh!*" She ate a few bites. "No wonder Mother threatened them with tongue-swell potions."

"They're going to talk about something, Roh, it's better when it's you," Azed said quietly. "My opinion was that if they're talking about their Matron's sex life and betting on it being longer and better than before,

215

then they believe our House is stable and primed for growth. Just as you believe, yes?"

She nodded; her mouth was full, and it was unbecoming to speak right then.

"You're trying to conceive, they know it. We're all looking in the same direction, to grow. It makes them hopeful."

She swallowed, her belly feeling off as his called this out. "But they know it's just a test, yes? I ... can't keep it when it works."

Azed had his mouth closed, and he shrugged. "When were you going to call for two Palace witnesses?"

"When do you think I should?"

"Anytime, really," he said.

She stared at him. "What?"

"You've been eating more." Azed took a forkful himself. "And ... hard to say, but something is different about you."

"What?"

"Just a feeling."

"Don't give me that!"

Azed smiled a little. "Well, for one, I've called you Roh like three times now and you've barely noticed. Matron."

She scowled. "But ... it's only been six spans!"

"Two marks of sex every other cycle, regular as a foot march," he drawled. "And if the potions help, and Ruk's been *that* willing to please you, it wouldn't surprise me if you caught already. There's something to be said for Davrin willpower and being open to the magic working."

Rohenvi thought on it more than once following that conversation. *Open to the magic working ...*

Why weren't the potions she'd been taking the first thing to come to mind when Azed had said that?

"WELL, WELL. CONFIRMED, WITH WITNESSES, MATRON THALLUEN," THE

Palace representative said with a nod. "Congratulations. Do we record the sire now?"

"Hm? Oh. No. Thank you, officer. He's not here ... and I am not sure I'm keeping it."

The representative nodded, unconcerned as she packed up her scrolls with her smaller, male partner. Azed glanced at her but kept his face unreadable until after everyone had left and they had a private moment again.

"Not sure?" he whispered.

"You heard me," she responded stubbornly. "And in any case, I have over four spans left of my bargain. I wouldn't do anything until after that time regardless."

Azed's expression was one of refined, mock-bewilderment. "Well, the seed has been planted. Mother would have said you don't really need him anymore."

She poked his chest so hard he nearly yelped. "I will take my remaining time for pleasure, First Son. Do not tease me about that."

He rubbed at the sore spot. "Yes, Matron."

"ARE YOU SURE?" RUK ASKED AGAIN, PANTING.

"Yes!" she answered, arching her back a little as he pinched her nipple just how she liked. "I am sure, Ruk. Do it. Take me."

The crack of her ass was greased up so well it wouldn't dry out for a quad-span. Her consort's hard erection rolled around between her buttocks, teasing them both for as long as they could stand as his fingers played with her netherhole and stretched her out.

Now he finally had the head pressed to her own clean, purple pucker — one which his tongue was now as familiar as hers was with his — and she felt her hole relaxing, letting herself be spread open wider as his member sank into her ass. There was a little pain when she tightened up, which only encouraged her to breathe carefully, as he did, and stay relaxed.

Let him in. She wanted him to rut her this way.

It was one of the few "dirty" things they hadn't tried yet.

Ruk thrust in, and Rohenvi gasped. He paused.

"Do you like it, Matron?"

"I-intense ..."

Some part of her wasn't sure if she should *like* something so ... invasive. But then she relaxed for the third time, breathed out, and imagined him spurting inside this last, unexplored place, and felt her netherlips become sensitive. Her tight, straining ring seemed to tingle around his cock.

"Yes, I do," she whispered. "Fuck me slow ... for now."

Ruk's instincts on how to pleasure her had a sharp edge, and this activity was no different. He fucked her with care and plenty of oil making their skin shine; she didn't even care if some got onto the sheets.

Before too long, she wanted him to do it faster.

"Now it's your novice netherhole that's thirsty for my cum?" he whispered into her ear, holding her from behind as they kneeled on his bed.

"Yes!" she gasped, feeling her clutching, slippery hole trembling around his pole. Then she cried out and squeezed him involuntarily when his hand shifted from her breast to her lonely labia. "Oh, Goddess!"

He fucked her in deeper, longer strokes, mostly out and all the way back in. "And no one's pleasured you this way?"

"Ohhh ... .!"

"Well, Matron? I am the first you've commanded to open you this way?"

She twisted her neck back to ask without words for a kiss, which he did, pausing in his thrusts and holding himself deep inside so he could concentrate on kissing her.

When they finished their kiss, Rohenvi leaned forward slowly and held herself up on all fours, positioning her knees and ass to take his thrusts comfortably.

She looked back over her shoulder and smiled. "You are the first, Ruk. Look down, watch yourself plowing this Noble netherhole."

He shared a brief laugh with her but soon did just as she suggested;

he looked down, holding her hips as he thrust between her buttocks. The sight clearly excited him as she was rubbing herself, luxuriating in his energy and passion servicing such a tight hole for her. He was not only the first to do this to her, but the first to "open" her womb, as well.

I'm pregnant.

This time they didn't have to be concerned where his offering spilled; she wanted his glaze inside her ass, she wanted to feel it dripping out later. She wanted her hole loose from his cock stretching it, wanted to feel it shrinking slow after he pulled out …

"*Ahhhh … Roh …*" he whispered.

She knew his voice well enough by now to know he was about to peak. As it began, he took her deeply, and Rohenvi writhed with the intense joy of her clutching netherhole finishing his delight.

"Ohhh, Ruk!"

Before he left her House, she wanted to try quite a few more things that a Matron shouldn't want from a commoner.

One specific commoner.

"Has it worked, then?" Ruk asked less than a span before their bargain was complete.

He had finally noticed how tender her nipples had become to his touch, recognizing that she was eating more. Much more. He was dumbstruck sitting at her table.

She lifted her chin from habit, wanting to look elegant when she answered. "Yes, Ruk. I have caught, as I'd hoped."

"When?" he asked, at least understanding that these changes had not come on since last eve. "How far?"

She exhaled, taking another bite, chewing and swallowing before answering. "My healer says I am about eight spans in."

"You caught before I was here a third the way into the bargain?!" he exclaimed, almost too loudly.

She couldn't help but smile at the expression. "Azed suspected after about six. I only knew after taking my test."

"When was that, Matron?"

Rohenvi worked to keep that chin up. "Oh. The same span."

Ruk watched her directly, and for the first time since he had first arrived, she detected wariness in his eyes. "You've been keeping me here for the simple enjoyment, Matron?"

"Haven't you been enjoying yourself?" she responded placidly.

"I have, but …" He paused. "We still have an agreement, yes?"

She looked away first without meaning to, a strange discomfort piercing her chest. She snapped her gaze back to him immediately and shored up her dignity.

He still wanted to leave. He was just waiting for the time to leave.

If she had told him earlier and allowed him to go once he'd fulfilled his purpose, he would have taken it. Belatedly she realized their bargain had never specified what happened when she caught — only what happened if she didn't.

"Of course we do, Ruk," she said without much inflection. "You'll stay the full three quad-spans. And I should not need to call on you again in another three." She breathed out, trying to still nausea. "You can convince all your 'fringe' contacts you're still alive."

Fortunately, he didn't argue that particular oversight of the deal.

Their coupling over the next few cycles was much slower, lower risk. Ruk was even a bit too gentle, another reason she might have delayed telling him, and on their final eve together, he showed her he was still afraid of her power.

"Matron, please. Don't."

As much as he toed the line on matching her during sex, wit for wit, bold action for bolder still, and even as he teased her endlessly during his stories, relaxed a bit too much in casual, private conversation with her …

Her trader could be very humble when he fully realized he was in danger.

He had his head resting in her lap, and he was on his knees on the floor, his hands on the back of his head where she could see them at first, but then she moved them herself to place them at rest on her hips.

"My Matron, please," he whispered. "I can't."

"It's just a symbol," she said, trying to sound stern and powerful, not hurt. "It has no real magic. But wearing it would let others know of your contact with this House, and more of those females who might be troublesome would not pursue you. It will protect you."

"I can't," he repeated.

"Don't you want the connection?" she asked more loudly, her exasperation slipping through. "You've earned it, Ruk! I would like to do business with you again. Perhaps I will invest in some of your caravans. I'm sure that would make the various masters happy."

"You do not want to get involved in my trade, Matron. Please, if you'll keep anyone safe with your symbol, keep your own House unsullied by dubious connections."

She ran her fingers through his hair.

"You could just lie and take it, you fool," she whispered. "You need not make me so curious where you'll go, by not begging me like this. You could take my ring and toss it away later, how would I ever know? How would I even find you if you did not answer a message left with Hirai?"

"Because you're not lying to me," he said, keeping his eyes on the fabric covering her lap. "You haven't been, Matron. I've seen cruelty a great deal, but I agreed to come here because I didn't see it in your eyes. You haven't lied to me, Matron, don't force me to lie to you. I can't take your ring. I can't lead you on, thinking you can make any worthwhile connections through me."

She leaned back in her chair and gripped one of the arms of it, trying to stamp down the surge of heat in her chest. *How dare he … .?*

Her eyes stung, and she looked toward the ceiling when he did not move from his position, trusting that she wasn't about to pour acid or poison into his ear in retribution for the rejection. She knew what the other Nobles would say. He dared do this now because she allowed him to. Because she was lax and invited it.

Now look how she was acting toward the first sire she ever picked? Like she pursued a cherished First Son from a Top Tier House! Ruk had come from nowhere, from no House. His blood was worth nothing to any House!

She wanted to growl aloud in her frustration. Ruk didn't fit into her plans. She had almost forgotten about the Palace Consorts in her time with him. This had all been to prepare for presenting herself at Court!

How could you forget, 'Matron'?!

"Leave," she said. "Leave without my ring. Without any trace, if that's your wish. Fintre has your things, and Honaki will take you back to the city." Now her throat hurt, and her vision was blurry. "Just … get out and never come back."

Ruk left as quickly as he could, as if he was afraid that she would change her mind; a fact that didn't lessen the sting.

Later, in her empty, private quarters, she looked in a mirror naked, her hand covering her flat stomach. She couldn't even really tell. Not yet. Then she looked at the vial in her hand. The long-awaited test, the expulsion potion.

"Without a trace, if that's your wish," she repeated to herself. She began to pull the stopper, then paused.

Kill anyone when you're in blind-heat-anger, her Mother had jested once, *and they're guaranteed to draw a few shadowy pit traps around for you to fall into.*

Siranet probably hadn't meant this. She had meant anyone who would miss the one killed in a rage. Not even Ruk would miss it; he knew perfectly well that no Matron would ever bear his seedling as her first child. He knew what would happen, he just never asked for confirmation.

Still. Why do this when I'm so angry? It can wait until the next cycle.

She set it down on the washroom counter and laid down to rest.

CHAPTER 6

2822 S.E., HOUSE THALLUEN, SIVARAUS

"SO ... IF IT'S 'NOT UNCOMMON' FOR SOME MATRONS TO PERFORM THE TEST, then abort," she asked Azed a span later, "how many just ... let it continue?"

His eyebrows raised up very high at first, but then he wiped the disbelief and tried to think, to answer her seriously.

"Some might be offered to the Valsharess and the Priestesses in ritual —"

"No," she said flatly, scowling at him.

He blinked at her expression, taken aback by its clarity. "Ah ... well. Alright, if you believe the rumors, some of them end up in the Sanctuary, serving the Priestesses. Or the Palace always needs servants."

Azed watched her, trying to read her responses. She hadn't liked either of those, so he continued.

"Sometimes you can give one to serve in another House of your choice, but that can be ... troublesome if they ever come back to cause trouble for your true heirs. Everyone knows who they are if they become grown."

"None just keep them? Even being not true heirs?"

"Most would tell you it's not worth the trouble, Roh," Azed said soberly. "If the child is aware she is the Matron's child of the House in

223

which she lives, but is ignored in favor of younger siblings, it puts all of them at risk and in the worst cases can split a House if the true firstborn is female and garners enough military support despite her common blood.

"You can never know how it will turn out, sister, especially if you want more than one cait. Think very carefully before you decide to keep the offspring of a competent consort."

She felt like throwing something at him but suppressed it immediately. That was the early pregnancy making her more volatile. Azed had promised her he would never "double-speak" with her; he was only telling truths from his observant experience. She needed that right now; it wasn't his fault she felt so terrible.

"What if I waited long enough that we could tell from a spell if it was male or female?" she asked.

"To end a pregnancy at that point would be riskier to your health," he answered bluntly. "Possibly to your fertility as well. But ... if you have the healing to do it, and you were willing to risk it ..."

Azed couldn't encourage the risk, she could tell; he would be too worried about her.

"Your House might be nervous," he said instead. "Say it was male, Roh, what then? Do you think it will be any less disruptive to the peace of this House? You wouldn't have time to raise him, especially after your Daughters come. Who is going to do it?"

Rohenvi stared at Azed, and he blinked and put up his hands. "Oh, no, absolutely not. Listen, sister, please, it is a bad idea to keep a common blood in high living like a Noble. No good comes of it, not the least of which is respect for you from the other Matrons. The babe is a commoner, you realize that, right?"

"The babe is mine," she attempted to argue. "Noble because I'm Noble."

"The babe will also look less like the other Nobles, and they will be able to tell. You aren't doing the child any favors keeping it openly, Matron, male or female."

The siblings stared at each other for several beats.

"I'll think about it," Rohenvi said.

"By our beloved Spider Queen, Matron Thalluen," her honored guest cooed. "Look at you! I hadn't realized you were already breeding. Which House has the honor?"

Rohenvi wished she could get away with slipping sleeping drops into the other Matron's taze. She had not left her plantation since conceiving, hoping to stay out of sight of the majority of Nobles for the next two turns. But an odd number of them and the occasional Matron would come by, asking to visit. To refuse would only bring petty troubles she did not need, and there was nothing to be found peeking around her House; Azed had seen to it.

All the conversations went like this eventually.

"You have likely heard already, Matron Bovritz," she muttered before taking a sip of her hot drink to settle her roiling stomach. It wasn't the food; it was anger, and nerves.

"Then it is true?" she said with dramatic flair. "A common-blood sire."

"It proves my fertility, Matron Bovritz, and I will not risk something going wrong in taking too many potions. I will see it through to birth."

"Well! How charming. What have you decided to do with it?" This Matron of the Eleventh House, one just above Rohenvi, tilted her head. She was easily two hundred turns older. "The Sanctuary? The Palace? Or are you looking for an adoptive House?" The other Matron braced her chin on her palm, ignoring her taze. "I might be able to help you out, for a favor."

Rohenvi swallowed subtly. She already had a plan, but it might not hurt to have a cover story. And if Matron Bovritz was offering …

"What favor do you ask?" she asked.

2823 S.E., House Thalluen, Sivaraus

Rohenvi's birthing hurt enough to make it worthwhile to weep real tears, more than technically necessary, but she never cried out loud.

A healthy, young Davrin Mother carrying to fullness without complications experienced a birth which was nowhere near the level of agony some Nobles would have others believe. They acted as if the Nobles were an entirely different race from the commoners. They were more "sensitive," and the birth of their children was a much greater deal to be taken seriously.

All the Nobles knew how "common" Mothers could give birth without crying out once.

Her womb was strong, tensing up and contracting without her conscious control, and she concentrated on the sensation — the pain was nothing much, mostly abrupt shots of sharp cramping as the mouth of her womb opened. She felt how so many different muscles and parts of her moved and shifted inside her belly, and her birth canal would be ready to stretch to its limit soon.

Rohenvi pushed her bua out of her body with only Azed as her witness, in her own room with the doors locked. She didn't call her healer. It was better this way.

He is breathing, Azed signed to her after clearing the mouth and nose of mucus, as she gasped for breath herself.

She nodded, admitting to herself she was exhausted and glad Azed was here to manage the first few steps. Davrin newborns didn't tend to make noise, either; necessary for survival in the Deepearth, although she'd heard out in the wilderness, the fluids and blood would draw danger even without noise. She was glad to be safe here.

Even if tears still dripped from her eyes.

Azed rubbed down the little body in a blanket after cutting the cord, and her breasts began to ache in earnest when she saw tiny hands clutching at nothing.

Oh, Goddess, ow … She pressed on one breast, trying to massage the ache away, and milk squirted out, soaking her nightgown. *Shit* …

★Are you certain you want to go this way?★ Azed asked again, right on the cusp and she wanted to slap him for bringing it up yet again, and now of all times! ★We could still give him to House Bovritz.★

★No … I mean, yes,★ she signed, flustered and frustrated. ★Yes, I am certain! I will not give him to Matron Bovritz! If this works, he will be back under my House rule in two decades. Not long. He will still be a child.★

★If he survives.★

★Better this than knowing he's a Noble rejected by his Matron,★ she signed bitterly.

Azed nodded. ★Alright, sister. I will still help you. But they will want to see a body if you claim stillborn, and if you do not, the rumors will always be that he still lives somewhere. If you reclaim a child of about the right age later on … ★

★We've gone over this!★ she interrupted, demanding that he drop it. ★We have no Davrin infant body to swap. I will bring no servant in on this, and I will not kill another infant and mother to make it so! We'll burn the Pyte corpse in his place, no one must see … ★

Azed bowed his head, cradling the swaddled baby. He glanced at the tiny face. ★Will you feed him once, Matron?★

★No,★ she refused, and it felt like her beating heart would collapse. ★Get him out of here.★

⋆You won't come — ?⋆

⋆NO! I told you! Get him out before anyone knows he lives!⋆

AZED MOVED THROUGH THE SECRET PASSAGE USED ONLY BY THE NOBLE FAMILY and the Head of Guard, hoping that the other was still there, as he said he would be. If he was, Ruk had probably been waiting for a few cycles now, eating very little and trapped in a dark, closed space. He would be in need of a bath, but he would not have that luxury this time around.

The trader stood up and bowed to the First Son, smelling a little ripe and very nervous as his eyes landed on the bundle in Azed's arms. They transferred it quickly, before either could think too much about it.

⋆Thank you for answering,⋆ Azed signed. ⋆She will want him back, even as servant or a guard.⋆

⋆Understood,⋆ Ruk acknowledged, trying to balance the squirming babe, unfamiliar with the grip he should take as he signed.

⋆He's hungry,⋆ Azed said. ⋆You'll want to hurry. It's a long way back.⋆

Ruk nodded, still looking stunned, as if he wasn't sure what he was doing here. ⋆A name? Did she — ?⋆

⋆No. You choose something. Don't tell me what it is. Go.⋆

"I OUGHT TO KICK YOU STRAIGHT DOWN THE CLIFF FOR THIS, RUK," EYIN growled low in their meeting place a few cycles later.

Ruk had needed to make do with whatever livestock milk he could barter for. It was just enough, and for the first few cycles the new sire genuinely enjoyed caring for Rohenvi's son. He had never felt this way about anyone's infant, except this one. The fringe loner, the foreigner and outsider to Sivaraus, had accepted that he wanted to protect this helpless male.

Because no one else would.

His son was always hungry, and it was difficult to keep him clean without a stable home. Finally Ruk had needed to go to his superior in the shadows for help.

"What the fuck were you thinking?! Rausery's going to be … ! I don't even know what —"

"You can set me up in another part of Sivaraus, Eyin," he pleaded. "I'll take another name, a new background, one that includes Treyl. I only need twenty turns, then I can give him back to her. House Thalluen will raise him then as another servant."

"Only twenty turns," she snorted, glancing at the infant clutched to his chest. She thought for some very long moments. "So you need a long leave to be a sire."

"Just this once. I'll never do this again," he began.

"You bet your ass, you won't!" Eyin sighed in exasperation. "I can't believe the Matron Thalluen would even go to the trouble, even to want him back … !" She eyed him. "You must have really made an impression."

"I-I … was her first."

"First what? First male, as in 'ever'?"

"No. First sire."

"You were her first *something*, alright," she commented with heavy sarcasm, smiling dryly. She thought some more. "Treyl can't know you as Ruk. In fact, you can't use that name for a few centuries at least. It's compromised. Ruk's dead now, same as Hachyrr'ne."

He nodded in complete agreement, waiting and daring to hope for her final approval.

"A sire alone raising a baby is going to turn a few heads. A few females might think you need to join with one of them for protection."

"I'll do as I need to."

"We can do better, I think. We'll give the bua a mother from among the shadows, and you a common matron. Teyshuna is getting older, she needs to settle down, but you can both still be useful to us."

Ruk's attention heightened to blade-sharpness and Eyin continued.

"Easy story, the mother died shortly after birth, you took the infant and joined with an older female who could provide for you both. And she doesn't mind having the eye-sweet like you around or a healthy babe to keep her company." Eyin smirked at him in amusement. "You don't mind being a young trophy sire, right?"

Finally he felt enough hope that he could smile back. "Teyshuna's going to get a big laugh out of this."

"Fuck, yeah, she will. But she'll do it. Will you?"

He nodded, exhaling. "Yes. Anything that's needed. Thank you, Eyin."

Epilogue - 175 Turns Later

2998 S.E., House Thalluen, Sivaraus

Matron Thalluen braced herself tiredly against the washroom counter, hoping for herself a quiet, private moment undisturbed as she contemplated the future of her House. She wasn't sure what to do next.

She was always so *tired*, and she didn't know why.

It was as if just two Daughters was enough to sap all her strength, and she was old enough to wonder when her time to be replaced would come.

Matron Siranet had died around the age Rohenvi was now. *Maybe …*

Had her Matron's "bright and impressive Daughter" really done all she could do already? Rohenvi hadn't raised her House's status much at all; to do so at this point would take a military attack, something she had not the strength to muster right now, or anytime soon.

She had succeeded in all she and Azed had plotted so far. The Court respected her, the Valsharess acknowledged her. She had been granted the covetous honor of not just one but two Consorts to sire her heirs, and they had both been caits.

She even had Treyl back among her Guard. Her own First Son knew nothing of his origin, and Azed heard no whispers which would endanger him.

Rohenvi was more fortunate than any House below her, and several above! She had learned a lot, weaving in and out of the politics and the plots and the double-speak, learning because she had to. She had even squelched the plot of revenge instigated the moment her own Mother died, beating them with wit instead of might.

She was ambitious … *determined* … !

And always tired.

"Mother?" Jilrina asked at her outer door. "Queen's Blessing to you."

Rohenvi sighed. "Queen's Blessing, First Daughter."

"Open the door, will you?"

It seemed like a mistake to have sent her eldest Daughter to see the Sanctuary on her first big trip off the plantation a few decades ago.

Her First Daughter was already older than Rohenvi had been when she became Matron, and she seemed to be grasping toward the Priestesses as she grew bored. Their House remained stable, meaning there was no indication Rohenvi would be passing the inheritance soon.

Jilrina was never blatant with her impatience, but the Matron had learned to read a great deal at Court before the First Daughter was ever born.

Rohenvi peeked through the spy-gem first before opening her door. "Is there news?"

"No, Matron."

"A visitor?"

Jilrina smiled in a way that was indefinably chilling. "No, Matron."

"Daughter, I am very tired."

"I was wondering if you've seen Uncle Azed?" she asked. "I can't seem to find him."

Rohenvi stared at her daughter. *How oddly affectionate that sounds …*

Azed and Jilrina did not get along peacefully. He was difficult for the young female to manipulate or bend to her will, and Rohenvi herself did not punish him or force him to cater to the First Daughter any more than necessary.

Jilrina always wanted more, however, and she wanted punishments to be very public. She wanted the servants to see, to remind them of their place as she tried for "humility," she said.

It was really humiliation — the kind Azed had loathed at Court and had once come here to escape — for no other reason than she was First Daughter could get away with it much of the time.

The Matron was aware her eldest daughter blamed her Mother for not allowing her to fully sate her desires where Azed was concerned. It had been a constant source of abrasive tension for over a century, and sometimes she caught Jilrina's expression when the young cait did not think she was being watched — the contempt and derision, as she mouthed to herself, "Weak!"

"Azed is missing?" Rohenvi reiterated now.

"I didn't say that," Jilrina corrected, putting both hands forward with too much reassurance. "I'm looking for him and thought you might know where to find him."

"I … do not know where he is, Daughter. I'm sorry."

"It's alright. I know you're tired, Mother. Why don't you lie down? I'll let you know when I find him."

Her heart was beating harder as she closed the door again; pure unease and worry seemed to wake her up a bit. Soon she put on an outer robe and left through her secret passage to get to her brother's room.

She didn't make it quite that far before she tripped over his body.

"Azed … ?" she whispered, still feeling some warmth as she knelt by him in the close, dark space, shaking him. "Azed!"

She fumbled for a pulse.

Oh, no … ! No, Goddess, please, no … !

He had crawled in here on his own. He had known he was poisoned and had been trying to reach her …

Azed! Brother, please, don't leave me alone!

Sometimes it felt Rohenvi hadn't truly wept since birthing Treyl, but she knew she wept now. She tried very hard not to make any noise which would carry, but it only seemed to make it hurt worse.

Who had done this? She had her enemies, but how could she prove it? And he was male … less of a loss, most would say, than either of her heirs. The only true outcome was that there was no First Son at House Thalluen anymore. This was not a necessary role, but there was one who *should* be able to take Azed's place.

But I can never acknowledge him!

There were only females left in power at House Thalluen. This did not comfort Rohenvi in the least.

Her mind thought furiously on what she would do, who would pay, how she might cauterize the wound so viciously opened within her chest. Maybe her heart would leak for centuries, for how devastating it felt. Rohenvi slumped down in the secret passage as all her will seem to leave her.

She knew. She did not want to fight for House status anymore. *It doesn't matter … nothing at that Abyss-damned Court matters …*

What had she been forced to give up in exchange for all that she had scratched and competed for? Every male that could ever stand by her and comfort her. Every male who could know her and see as she could not show to the other females. She had lost all of them, given them up one by one. Ruk first, then Treyl …

Now Azed.

Fury flooded her limbs, giving her more energy than she'd had in turns, and she quickly dragged Azed's body back to his room before returning to her own and working every trick she had in her possession to hide the fact that she'd been weeping.

Her own Daughters must never see her cry.

Meanwhile, she must think.

Azed's death ritual will be at Court. He'll give me a reason to go into Sivaraus. There, she could leave one more message.

"WELCOME TO POLYNIA'S SHOP. MAY I HELP YOU?"

Polynia. Not Hirai. Alright, time moves on.

Except this wasn't Polynia.

"Yes," Rohenvi said, "I must speak with the shop owner."

The young Davrin nodded. "My mother, yes. Let me get her for you, Noble."

Not Matron. At least she wasn't so obvious. "Wait."

The young cait paused.

"What is your name?"

She curtsied. "My name is Gaelan, Noble."

"Are you the eldest daughter?"

"Yes, Noble."

Rohenvi nodded, letting her be off as she waited. Polynia would do what Hirai used to, she already knew. She might have to coax the same connection with this Gaelan if she was next in line to inherit the shop.

After leaving her message with the merchant, Rohenvi stayed in the central City for over a span praying to anything outside the Abyss for an answer. She could not leave House Thalluen in Jilrina's hands for long, but she had enough errands built up to explain her presence here.

The last time she had made any contact with Ruk was when they had smuggled Treyl back to her House, a short five turns before she gave birth to Jilrina. It had been a swift, head-whirling time, but Ruk had promised her — if he was alive — he could answer again if the need was dire.

The need was exceedingly dire now. And the wait, not even knowing if he lived to receive her message, was torment. Rohenvi could not rest in Reverie for longer than a few marks at a time.

Then, her prayers were answered. Like some beautiful shadow appearing from a magical summons, he somehow found her walking Sivaraus streets. He came to stand beside her without speaking.

★Come with me,★ she signed, and neither spoke aloud, both of them disguised.

Rohenvi had a filthy, lowborn room ready for rent and enough disguise for the proprietor not to care, as long as her coin was real. She could never have seen herself stepping over such a threshold when she had first become Matron, but now she felt she could do nearly anything with enough forethought and planning. Not having enough forethought or planning for contingencies was what had taken her First Son from her. Following in the footsteps of others was why she had lost both the son and the sire.

Now she had other ideas.

"Give me another child, Ruk," she whispered, putting her soft-gloved hands on his grimy face. "I know what I did wrong the first time. I know how to fix it. Bua or cait, I do not care, I will be able to keep and acknowledge the child as a Noble. I've already taken the fertility tonics ... please? There will be no burden on you, but ... I'd like to choose you as sire again."

He was nervous; he wanted her, but he was anxious. He tried to smile. "Not trying for a third Consort?"

He knew. He'd been seeking whispers on her.

The flash of anger on her face surprised him, and he nearly let go to step back. She clutched him to her.

"Never! *Never* another Consort! They are vain and stupid! I shall have *my* choice from now on. Spider Queen damn the Palace and the Court. Abyss damn the Consorts and their spawn!"

Ruk swallowed, taken aback by her vehemence, but they were alone, protected, and whispering. What was important was that he believed her.

"What has happened, Matr —"

"Roh. Call me Roh. Please."

His heart picked up. "What has happened, Roh? What's wrong?"

Rohenvi leaned to embrace him, resting her head on his shoulder. She wanted to weep yet again.

"Azed is dead. I-I do not know who killed him, but I suspect ..." She sniffed. "I cannot prove it ... and no one would care about him over ... over ... ."

"No one except you," he murmured, rubbing his fingers through her hair. "I am sorry, Roh ... I admired Azed."

"He admired you. He just couldn't say so."

She lifted her head to look at his face, holding her first true lover. She leaned to kiss him, gently. His eyes drooped as he accepted, seemed to enjoy touching her, smelling her again ... even if the place was much different, much smellier than their first time.

"Will you?" she asked again. "Please. Give me another child of yours. Your son is so smart, and much like you. I want an heir with your spirit and mind. You are worthy, Ruk — I am ... I regret so much what I did to Treyl … !"

"You could do nothing else," he said. "I know it. You were young, Roh. We are born where we are born, I can only imagine the pressure you are under. I don't hold a grudge." He smiled wryly. "How do you mean to 'fix it' this time?"

She swallowed. "After I am sure I carry … I must make arrangements with House Bovritz right after. Witness, register the sire, all that. Change the name, but the blood will be yours and mine, just like Treyl. No one need ever know."

Finally he nodded, accepting their plan and leaning to kiss her. He needed a bath so much, and she didn't care; she kissed hungrily back, wanting him inside her as soon as they could manage, giving her womb what it needed to begin again and grow her fourth child.

Four children, at least.

Just as she'd told Fintre she wanted on the eve her Mother died.

If only Rohenvi could begin everything again knowing what she knew now. Maybe she could have changed something, made things better for Ruk, acknowledged her First Son as he should have been …

It made her wonder about the secrets held at every other House, and if nothing was quite what everyone claimed it to be.

After all, her Mother had said it in her dying breath.

You can never show what you really are.

GAELAN

A TALE OF MIURAG
BY A.S. ETASKI

Chapter 1

3044 S.E., the Market of Sivaraus

"Gaelan! Wake up and get to work!"

Yes, yes, or you'll feed me to the Driders …

That was her one warning, as usual. The young Davrin yawned, stretching her arms and legs within her lumpy, hand-down bed. Another wake cycle, another twenty Nobles' servants demanding their potions for their mistresses and masters. Braqth forbid they skip one beauty salve or fertility tonic.

Most of them were very short-term effects anyway, assuming they even had any real magic in them.

"Why cheat them like that?"

She had asked her mother that once, turns ago, as she had been watching a demonstration of their current recipe to overcome wakefulness — something her mother repeatedly said Gaelan would never need. "Won't they just be angry at you?"

"You never want to be too successful in your vanity potions, Gaelan," her stern but balanced mother warned. "One thing you must always keep in mind is that the Nobles do not want lasting change. Anything which does not fade in a few spans or quad-spans at most, a little at a time so they won't notice …"

The potion merchant's dusky, red eyes observed a memory, briefly, before she blinked again and continued stirring her pot. "Well, I will just say if you make permanent any change they should ask for, you shall be noticed and remembered. Always, you will be blamed when that change causes some inconvenience for them. You must be wise about this at a young age, my daughter, or you will come to your end upon a Noble House's rack."

Gaelan was just five turns short of a century now, still living and working with her mother and siblings; she likely would be for a good long time. This was not unusual for the common class and the merchants within them. It took time, some luck, and inevitably some conflict to carve out a new place entirely.

Only the truly determined ones left the old den. Some had to remain behind to help keep the established one anyway, and Gaelan knew she was not the most determined of her siblings.

She tested the pitcher of water first, as she'd been taught very young, before using it to wipe down her body and face. Her outfit was one of three that she owned, and she chose the muted, dark yellow fold-over shirt with form-fitting, black trousers and her usual, slender but sturdy work boots. She wanted to stand out slightly this cycle.

There was always a light source in their shop, so her choice of color made a difference in her business. This was often how apothecaries were identified in the first place. Whatever secret trading of their wares went on in dark alleys and blackness, her family didn't care to know about them; all their activities were right there in the open.

Unlike other more necessary functions within Sivaraus, Gaelan's mother enjoyed a double-edged benefit from City Guards. They might stop by for a hot drink or free sample of the latest craze among the Nobles and hear some gossip. Since the matron obliged them every time, this apothecary saw less theft and disorder from elements of the darker areas in the Center. This also meant putting up with some of the guards' ill humors or occasionally needing to find a way to relieve their boredom.

Gaelan put on the yellow shirt because she felt a little bored herself and she hoped a decent ratio of the male guards would be with them. The all-female groups were the hardest to entertain.

When Gaelan got downstairs at last, her mother was giving last instructions to her younger sister and brother, Talade and Boqol, before spinning around to look at her. Polynia strode right toward her, her mouth tight. Gaelan started to ask what she'd done but snapped it shut when the older female gripped her arm and escorted her into one of the back stock rooms.

Her mother closed the door and pulled a small bottle out of her apron to set on the counter.

★Special delivery,★ she signed. ★The command word is 'd-u-t-h-e-l-r-e-n.'★

When her daughter frowned, she leaned forward and pronounced it precisely in her ear, glancing out toward the front as she did so. ★Understand?★

Gaelan committed the sound to memory. ★Yes, Mother.★

★Six silver. House Thalluen. Now.★

The daughter picked up the bottle. ★What is it?★

★Don't ask. This is for the First Daughter. She will meet you at their border, fourth place.★

Gaelan's eyes widened. ★Maybe I should change my shirt — ★

★No time! Go! Return immediately.★

Gaelan went with the bottle well-padded and tucked in her coat.

House Thalluen was one of their better customers, though Gaelan wasn't entirely sure why. Their plantation wasn't the farthest away from central Sivaraus borders but did require a quick coach ride at least out to the first fork, so trade with them always cost travel fare as well. From there, the merchant's daughter always made hand-deliveries on foot for privacy, as was the case with many Noble Houses.

For Thalluen, Gaelan knew all the meeting places around their lands, each with either wild or landscaped screens. There were enough so that it was difficult to watch them all at once or predict which would be used at a particular time. Some of this complexity might have to do with spies from other Houses, though Gaelan knew it had just as much to do with the two Daughters who lived there with their Matron-Mother.

Always at odds, so the rumors go.

It was unusual that Gaelan's own mother would refuse to tell her what she had made for a Noble, however. Most of the time it wasn't important, but Polynia would tell her daughter what it was. Gaelan had reason to feel a little nervous about this delivery.

What changed? Why the hurry?

★Don't ask,★ her mother had signed in warning.

The "fourth" meeting place required the young merchant to climb up a short, rocky side onto the plantation's land and disappear into a line of discarded boulders, naturally growing giant mushrooms and various other Deepearth growths along a well-kept wall. There was a single guard watching above, a bua. He knew she was there but did not acknowledge her. No doubt the First Daughter had told him to expect her, maybe to send his superior a silent message when the potion mage arrived with the purchase, so the Noble's precious time was not wasted.

Gaelan was surprised to discover that First Daughter Jilrina was already waiting. She had a small, bound bundle on the ground at her feet as well; that bundle was alive and trembling.

★At last!★ the First Daughter barked with her hands.

★Six silver,★ Gaelan signed, placid and waiting to receive a small pouch from the Noble before she handed over the potion.

★Too high,★ the Noble commented sourly.

★This was agreed.★

★Still too high.★

The covered bundle shifted, attempting to crawl away like a pincer-worm; it distracted Jilrina from her attempt at last-moment bargaining. The First Daughter turned and stepped upon what was probably the ankle, putting her full weight on it. The bundle whimpered and stopped, and Jilrina turned back to Gaelan to slap a leather pouch containing six coins of the correct size into Gaelan's outstretched palm. The merchant quickly passed the bottle to her in exchange.

★What is the command word?★

Gaelan took only a moment to recall, leaning forward. "Duthelren."

A smart nod. ★Now go! Until I summon you again.★

★My mother gives her regards.★

Gaelan turned to leave, not wishing to know more who was going on ... until she noticed that the male guard who'd been on watch wasn't there and there seemed to be no replacement. Jilrina and her captive were out of sight, but Gaelan could hear movement; there was clear struggling. The merchant might think herself good at minding her own business for the most part, but most of the time it was because somebody else was watching.

Was anybody watching now? Not from her view. She should at least find out what was bound up in the blanket, shouldn't she? Make sure it wasn't some secret dangerous to Sivaraus ...

That justification worked for any kind of eavesdropping one could name.

A young voice yowled, wordless and rage-filled, startling Gaelan as she tried to keep out of the sight. A slap followed immediately.

"Hold still, you little slit! Drink!"

Jilrina's hands must have been quite occupied to have spoken aloud like that. It gave the merchant the cover she needed to creep closer and peek from beneath a wide-base mushroom. The First Daughter struggled to hold down the thrashing, kicking, and biting cait.

"Ow! Braqth damn you!"

The sight and the curse were humorous enough that Gaelan had to bury her face from the nose down in the crook of her elbow to hide her laughter. Jilrina was getting the upper hand of the struggle quickly but not without consequences.

Looking between the two, Gaelan figured they must be sisters as they each looked like their Matron Thalluen, but there was a vast age difference between them. Two centuries, at least, maybe more. Gaelan had met Kaltra as well as Jilrina in her business, but until now she hadn't realized there was another surviving daughter.

This must be the youngest Third Daughter not yet brought out in society; Gaelan hadn't ever even heard a name yet. It wasn't unusual; Nobles often waited until a child survived to breeding age to make the City at large aware of them. Stories of their childhood followed them at that point but until then those tales usually stayed on the plantation where they were born.

Gaelan expected Jilrina to win eventually, which she did, pouring the potion she had purchased down her little sister's throat.

"Duthelren!" the Noble spoke with familiar command, her thumb pressed on to the tongue of the child.

There was a pulse of real, unsettlingly powerful magic; Gaelan could taste it on her tongue from here. Jilrina felt it as well and chuckled sinisterly, leaning down to whisper to her sister before the magic locked down with a final clamp.

Gaelan wanted to know what this was ... Why wouldn't her mother tell her?

She was shocked from her thought when the First Daughter lifted the skirts of her dress and mounted the child's face, lewdly moving her hips in domination as the little sister kicked and struggled. The nature of the fight had changed drastically. Gaelan covered her mouth in disgust and considered bolting right then and there — she didn't want to watch this — except she would surely be caught if she did.

Soon enough Jilrina pulled back and sat once again on her sister's torso, leaning down so close the First Daughter must have smelled her own personal scent on the young one's skin.

"Now talk. Describe what I just did to you. Talk!" The child tried to strike her, but Jilrina caught her wrists easily. She squeezed hard, hissing, "Say it!"

"M-mmuh ... guh —"

The youth's throat flexed, and her mouth opened and closed a few times, but she shook her head desperately, oddly mute as she tried to pull her hands free. Jilrina gave them that freedom and the little sister brought them to her head as if she had a splitting headache. She stopped kicking and was trembling in pain.

"Good," Jilrina breathed, sounding relieved. "Good. Now let us get you once again to the altar. You have delayed Braqth's Will long enough."

Gaelan realized she was biting on her fist to stay silent until they left, the larger and stronger sister dragging away the smaller and weaker. The merchant wiped the spit from her hand and eased back from her cover, planning to leave right away.

As she did, she caught the shape of the same guardsvrin who had been above to see her arrival. He was now on her level and watching her leave from another angle.

He smiled and signed high. *Nice yellow shirt.*

So someone else knew, Braqth damn it, though he made no motion to detain her. Gaelan fled, frightened that this might follow her back to the shop, though she was deeply troubled by much more than being seen as she made her way back home.

Mother does not make compulsion potions.

Or so Gaelan had believed.

These potions broke one of those few major rules their small family followed to be a profitable apothecary to the Nobles: never make anything permanent. Compulsions were permanent, at least until the one who spoke the command word was dead. Some other potion makers made sloppy compulsions on occasion, but not for long before the Red Sisters came for them when they royally fucked something up for a Noble.

To be known for this, even in whispers, put her family into a whole other level of politics, one they did not have a history of playing. They weren't powerful enough; they would just be squished by the giant boot of another sooner or later, and no one would care.

Why would her mother send her with something like that? And to be used against a child, no less, before she was even old enough to defend herself? It did not bode well for Jilrina's particular appetites that she felt she needed to silence her baby sister for the rest of her life.

Gaelan would be happy to never make another trade with this House again.

"MOTHER —"

"You shouldn't have watched. I told you to return right after."

"But we're in more danger now selling —"

"I had to, daughter, or we'd be in even greater danger this very moment."

Gaelan paused. Surely that purchased safety can't last. "Did you make that potion yourself? Are you being coerced to carry one made by another?"

The look on the matron's face warned her to be silent. "Only you will deliver to that House from now on. Be courteous and generous."

"Generous?"

"I've noticed you courting the City guards. Wear your yellow shirt next time. See if you can get any further gossip on the First Daughter, and tell me everything, just as you have now."

Gaelan's mouth was hanging open. When had their apothecary started trading in private secrets?

Her mother could read her face and she smirked. "Everyone must, sooner or later. You cannot be averse to it, my naïve, late-bloomer, or you wouldn't have stayed to watch."

CHAPTER 2

3044-3074 S.E., HOUSE THALLUEN, SIVARAUS

THOSE UNSETTLING DELIVERIES DID NOT ESCALATE AS GAELAN HAD WORRIED they might, perhaps to indicate that something larger within Sivaraus was bearing down upon her family. Instead she returned to House Thalluen with the usual short-term potions, some of which she even made herself.

She would occasionally wonder – but not wonder too hard – whether her mother had asked someone else to carry any forbidden compulsion potions for her elsewhere. An obedient child who didn't stop and question the outcome.

As time since delivering her last forbidden potion widened, Gaelan was tempted to relax. Maybe it was just the one time and it had stopped? One required favor, as her merchant-mother had said, but now she was wiser and had learned her lesson.

Polynia kept sending her eldest daughter to House Thalluen. As a perk, Gaelan enjoyed seeing the House's appealing buas in uniform; such dress was her liking, so tight and straight and clean. They appeared so much different from the scrabblers, the con artists, and the peddlers she usually saw so near her own neighborhood.

A few Guardsvrin were always nearby whenever Gaelan made her less secretive deliveries, including — every time — the first guard who had complimented her yellow shirt and caught her spying on the House

Daughters. This particular guard was there, the merchant's daughter slowly came to realize, just in case she wanted to linger after their mistress left.

It finally struck her. The bua was posing, inviting her to stay.

"Are you preening, soldier?" she teased after mustering the courage.

"We can tell you like to look at us," he answered, winking.

Gaelan started to smile despite knowing he had dirt on her. "A bit."

He smiled back as if that one disturbing eve wasn't when she first became aware of him. "My name is Treyl, if it pleases you to know, Merchant."

He was elbowed by another guard who shook his head in warning, whispering something about being presumptuous with a cait, but Gaelan didn't care. She cleared her throat, getting the three buas' attention.

"It does please me to know," she said, stepping closer and glancing at the other two. "And you two? What are your names?"

They answered her readily, Gaelan remembered, but the only name she mentioned when speaking with her mother later was Treyl.

"Hmph," Polynia said with a shrug and a smirk. "House Thalluen does have some enviable males for you to pick from. You're over a century old now. It's a good opportunity, is it not?"

Here it was again. Once a turn or so, since Gaelan had turned eighty, her mother passed her hints that they could use another daughter or two, another pair of magical hands to keep the apothecary strong and stable. As her one mistake of spying had become fuzzier in her memory, Gaelan felt a distinct tingle between her legs at the thought of regular sex from a source of her own choosing, not simply whomever happened to walk into the shop that cycle.

She also considered, only this moment, whether she wouldn't mind if she happened to catch her own baby during the fun.

"Opportunity," Gaelan repeated, nodding her head to her mother's widening smile.

It would be a quad-span more before an itching potion-maker's daughter had the chance to return and test whether Treyl and the other guards had been serious in their hints to "welcome" her back. By the time she did, the young female did not feel she would benefit from waiting for another opening. She must create it herself.

"Your fee," the First Daughter granted, this time deigning to meet the merchant in the tended garden and yet again, Treyl was Gaelan's escort.

She bowed to accept the pouch. "Braqth's Blessing on your House, First Daughter."

Jilrina smirked. "It already is. But go now. You are dismissed until next time."

"If you will permit me to rest here a time, First Daughter? It is always a journey to come. I will be harmless."

The Noble Davrin narrowed her eyes in wicked suspicion. "Do you ask for hospitality, Gaelan? This is a first."

"I would never presume the First Daughter need entertain me —"

"Good. Because I will not. I wish for you to go, merchant, now."

"If I might trouble the servants for only a few marks? Surely there is a bench somewhere out of sight —"

The First Daughter rolled her eyes and Gaelan had the sense she had pushed far enough without a compelling argument; any farther could see the start of an undesirable game. "You test my tolerance —"

Jilrina became distracted then, glancing over to a row of hedges. Gaelan realized belatedly someone was there spying — how could she expect otherwise? — and that someone mattered more to the First Daughter's attention than a mere merchant asking to sit.

"There is a bench in the barracks, First Daughter," Treyl spoke quietly, at just the right moment. "I will make sure she remains 'harmless' in her rest."

He spoke it in such a way as it seemed to settle in Jilrina's mind without resistance. Gaelan remained still.

"Very well, fine, do with her what you will, Treyl. Now get out."

The House guard slipped warm fingers around Gaelan's arm, and she readily fled with him away from the First Daughter. Permission was permission, however it was granted, although the young merchant had an unwelcome feeling that she knew who had drawn Jilrina's focus, to hers and Treyl's advantage.

Gaelan tried not to think about it as Treyl found them a small, private storeroom behind the barracks. The cramped, little space smelled of mushroom and smoked meat as well as old metal.

Grateful for the opportunity, Gaelan put her arms around the smartly dressed guard of House Thalluen without delay, sliding one hand down his back and over his tight backside. He grinned in the dark and his member grew swollen, pressing to her belly in what seemed mere moments, though he didn't put his own arms around her without permission.

"Hold me!" she demanded, pressing herself tighter to him and grinding against that eager erection.

Her attractive guard embraced her, lean, strong, and well-disciplined. He shuddered then he surprised her by kissing her mouth.

Bold bua. Maybe not so well disciplined ...

It was nice, though. She relaxed into it, letting him lead as she had more than enough confirmation to stroke her ego. She hadn't been wrong in the signals: Treyl wanted her; this older House guard, fixed to this one plantation, had waited more than once for the potion-maker's daughter to come back.

Why?

She didn't care because she didn't know how much time they had. She just wanted him to press that stiff member inside her while he tried not to ruin his uniform. There wasn't any place to sit or lie down here so Gaelan lowered her own trousers first and turned around, bending over and parting her legs.

She heard Treyl's deep inhale as her scent wafted to his nose and he swallowed a moan. Her guard went to one knee behind her, gripping her ass in his hands and burying his face in her cleft. He licked her to make her gasp, sucking on her netherlips before probing her sex again.

"Treyl!" she whispered, shivering, and working to keep her balance. "Oh, Goddess, I-I ... argh, just fuck me!"

He obeyed her quavering order, though Gaelan did not truly feel as the female in control once his cock penetrated her wet, greedy slit. Instead she felt helpless, impaled on him and not wishing to move until he was done.

The subtle sounds from her handsome guard, only barely contained, were what truly caused her sex to flush and swell around him. She only wanted him to use her as he needed to keep breathing like that, to keep making those alluring noises!

"As you will, Treyl!" she whispered, reaching between her legs. "As you will, as long as your cream goes in my belly ..."

He shuddered again, and Gaelan never recalled a better fucking than she got from her flirtatious male guard. He must be a good fighter, and clearly healthy, and—

The tempo as he rose toward his finish was quick. Hard. *Bold!*

Ohhh, Goddess!

Treyl held her up when she would have fallen forward; he growled in satisfied release, making the edges of her ears tingle as his hot pole flexed and spurted inside her. She caught her breath with her head still pointed toward the ground, not thinking for a moment how vulnerable she was, how distasteful her position might look to any ranking female.

"Come here again, if you can," he whispered, panting as he helped her stand vertical and held her from behind, only now daring to grope at her breasts.

"I shall," she had sighed, content to linger when he spoke next.

"Have some food and drink before you go. You can have some of my rations."

Gaelan received more than a small fright as, before she could leave, the Matron of the House, Rohenvi herself, visited the barracks in a surprise inspection. The elder female knew the young one was out of place standing among them and focused on her at once.

"Who are you?" the Matron asked, sounding as if she already knew and yet wouldn't offer even a hint of her displeasure, if there was any.

"Matron Thalluen. I am Gaelan, daughter of Polynia the Merchant." She bowed lower than she ever had for Jilrina, following Treyl's lead as well as the guard as a whole.

The Matron's impassive eyes and face did not help her to interpret the meaning in her next question. "You find entertainment among my Guard, Gaelan?"

Treyl's smart stance in the presence of his Matron did not have that same taste of reluctant duty as it did around Jilrina; there was genuine loyalty here. Only because of that was Gaelan inspired to be as bold as her newfound lover, daring to look up at least to fix her gaze on the tip of the Matron's nose.

"I do, Matron Thalluen. Your Guardsvrin Treyl has been my escort for each delivery. I find I enjoy his company and would like to pay a percentage of our fee back to see that he remains my escort while I am on your prosperous grounds, Matron."

The landowner barely arched one brow, her back perfectly straight and her face near expressionless as she inspected the traveling merchant in similar fashion to how she had her own guards. She was silent, as were all others, until she chose again to speak.

"The fee is Polynia's and not yours to barter, Gaelan," the Matron said at last. "But you are granted base hospitality nonetheless for your repeated journeys here at my Daughter's demands. Guardsvrin Treyl will oversee that hospitality. I will make sure Jilrina is aware of this arrangement."

Instantly, Treyl bowed at the waist. "Yes, Matron."

The young merchant blinked in surprise but quickly did the same. "Thank you, Matron Thalluen. Thank you."

Gaelan would come home to her mother with her guard's seed still staining her pants. Before too long she knew that she hadn't caught that first time, but both mother and daughter were pleased with the low price of being allowed to try again.

"Want to try a fertility potion?" Polynia asked.

Gaelan smirked and shook her head. "I'd rather just keep at it the hard way."

CHAPTER 3

3074-75 S.E., HOUSE THALLUEN, SIVARAUS

JILRINA MADE IT APPARENT THAT SHE WAS INDEED AWARE OF THIS NEW, MATRON-approved bonus to Gaelan's deliveries. She rolled her eyes in disgust and disinterest now that she understood why the two wanted to slip off somewhere private.

The disgust is mutual, First Daughter.

More important, however, was that Jilrina left them to it. Gaelan had noticed more and more over the next twenty turns that the First Daughter and even the Second would forgo opportunity after opportunity to interject power games between Gaelan and the House Guardsvrin — the one thing the young mage had expected to happen, sooner or later.

Finally, Gaelan had to accept that the First Daughter did not seem to like other adults, even to satisfy her clear love of power. Jilrina didn't even seem to care for males at all, though the House had no little brother for the eldest Daughter to victimize, to prove one way or another.

All Gaelan ever heard from her growing connections to the guards was that there was talk of an older brother, the actual firstborn of the house, but that he disappeared.

What do you mean? she had asked, quite engaged with the silent story in the barracks.

An ally of Treyl's, Sibron, had shrugged and signed back. *Centuries ago, when our Matron first took her mantle from her Mother, they say she carried a common blood's child to the end, but that it died in the birthing. No proof any which way, for or against, but story goes it was male, and he might not have died.★

The guardsvrin nodded, though they were all too young to know where the First Son might have gone, if he was indeed born alive and survived. His blood sisters may or may not have ever met him since, and the Matron did not acknowledge the rumors; to anyone's knowledge, Rohenvi had never tried to silence them.

★But is it true she carried a common blood child first?★ Gaelan asked.

Several guards nodded and Sibron continued. ★That's the only recorded truth, they say. Lots of Matrons do that, testing their fertility before bartering for a Noble or a Consort to breed with. It's expected among the Nobility, but most Matrons just end it before it goes too long.★

Matron Rohenvi had broken expectations there, attempting to give birth, so she was remembered for it even now. No doubt the thought of a mysterious First Son somewhere was too good a story to let go easily.

With repeated visits Gaelan learned that the youngest sister, the Third Daughter not yet announced to the Court, was named Sirana. She was a strange, quiet cait with blue eyes, the guards said, though the visiting merchant never saw the youth long enough in any light to be able to tell. Gaelan also didn't try very hard; she didn't want any connection to be made in the cait's mind between Gaelan's visits and the compulsion potion she had been given two decades ago.

If she's a quiet one, I know why.

The Second Daughter Kaltra agreed with everything her older sister said and asked no questions, but it was painfully clear when Sirana was near Jilrina that the youth raged against her forced silence.

The potion-maker had once spotted a murderous look in the Third Daughter's eyes one time when she thought no one was looking. Gaelan had felt frightened seeing it.

If Sirana ever learns what will break her compulsion, the First Daughter had better watch her back, no matter the age difference between them.

This decade, however, Gaelan was still trying to get pregnant while she had her choice of buas. She was having too much fun to want to stop exploring the stable of familiar guards.

"Mmm-hmm!" she hummed loudly now, forgetting to be quiet in the barn as she straddled Treyl, taking his willing erection within her slit. He was the only guard she allowed inside her breeding hole. When she caught, she wanted to be sure of the sire, but Treyl's cock was not the only one to join in the play.

Gaelan lowered herself down until her chest and belly were flush with her favorite guard, kissing his mouth as she reached back to squeeze her own buttock, exposing her purple star and encouraging the second male to mount her as well. Sibron was well practiced by now easing his greased phallus into her back passage and held no resentments at being second. He made the pleasure of being filled grow threefold, and he knew it.

This was pure indulgence for each of them, especially when they were high on the tonics Gaelan sometimes brought for them to share. It put their minds somewhere near the Great Cavern's ceiling as their base flesh humped themselves to a happy, tired heap. While the two males cycled their thrusts, Gaelan was in bliss with all their attention focused on her.

She felt helpless with sensation in a way she never felt safe expressing anywhere else.

She was willing to let the buas drive the rut, to forgo the commands she was supposed to give. She wanted to be passive as they took pleasure at their own pace, loving how the two took greater attempts at stamina each time, making it last as long as possible.

She enjoyed it, no matter how sore she sometimes got, but she didn't want anyone else to watch, as her males did well by her in keeping their mouths closed about her strange preferences.

Treyl and Sibron wanted to please her and wanted her to keep coming back. These times with her, Treyl once told her, were one of the few where he didn't have to be on alert, and he relished them. For each of them, it helped alleviate bouts of boredom better than anything else in her experience. One time, Gaelan even mentioned this thought to her mother.

"Persistent feelings in boredom means it is a good time to try for a child," Polynia said, perhaps to no one's surprise. "Your body is ready, and a Davrin can't just lie on her back and wait for it to happen!"

Gaelan snickered with a nod. Hopefully lying on her belly and being stuffed up the rear at the same time also improved the chances.

After a later visit, Treyl and Sibron had gone back to their duties and Gaelan was dressed. She was just leaving the plantation's grounds, a good distance from the manor, when Jilrina stepped out of the shadows to block her way.

Uh-oh. Gaelan bowed without missing a beat. "Thalluendara, my humble greetings."

Jilrina had her arms crossed beneath her breasts, staring curiously at her, and not for the first time that Gaelan noted the stylistic hints of the Priesthood in her clothing. They must've been custom-made and designed to be just short of presumptuous and insulting should a real Priestess see her.

When she said nothing, Gaelan said, "How may I assist you?"

Now Jilrina smirked. "The better question might be: How might I assist you?"

"I beg your pardon?"

"The guards tell me the purpose of your little trysts has changed. That you've chosen one of them as a sire."

That had happened long ago, but Gaelan still groaned inwardly at it being so plainly spoken by this particular female. "I have, Thalluendara. I try to catch my firstborn, yes."

"And you don't take your own fertility potions?"

"I might, Lady. Every merchant has their trade secrets."

Jilrina swayed a bit on her feet, somehow looking coy and imperious at once. "Have you prayed to Braqth for help? Have you gone to the Priestesses?"

Praying to the Priestesses was the last thing her family did in their own toils, but Gaelan knew to be careful in her answer.

"I pray for a child, and I give my tithing to the Sanctuary, First Daughter." Gaelan attempted another little humble bow of her head. "Perhaps if I grew desperate enough, I might see if a Priestess would give me an audience. But I would have to save up first."

"Ah, yes, 'save up.'" Jilrina looked extremely amused. "What if I could give you that same assistance in exchange for just a few of your regular potions?"

Gaelan felt a chill down her back. She might not be as devout as some, but even she knew that was blasphemy. "Um. I do not know what you mean —"

The Noble stepped closer to her, and there was a disturbing light in her eyes. A fanatic's light. There had been little hints before, but now it was in full view. "I am to be one of the next chosen for the Priesthood. Just wait until the next worship ball, you will see. I have been studying, and I know a ritual that would put your fertility at its pinnacle, Gaelan. A single rut afterward would guarantee the pregnancy for which you pray. It is called Braqth's Threshold, and it is a most potent divine spell. What do you think?"

Gaelan fidgeted despite looking weak to the older female. "I am content working for Braqth's Grace for the moment, First Daughter, but I thank you most sincerely."

Jilrina lifted a single, elegant eyebrow; the fevered heat in her eyes turned cool. "You will not lie upon my altar? I could summon Treyl right now. He is indeed quite fertile, I've checked. We need only come to an agreement on price."

Despite the protective rush she felt, wondering what Jilrina meant about "checking" Treyl's fertility, the merchant also swallowed a gasp of shock. It was worse than she thought. This Noble thought she had a divine altar?

It cannot be true, she's just unbalanced. It would've been destroyed by Priestesses with the help of the Sisterhood as soon as the Sanctuary learned about it!

There were many "altars" in Sivaraus used for various things, but none presumed to be divine; rituals Named explicitly for their Spider Queen were not one of those performed upon them. True divine altars only existed in the Sanctuary.

Gaelan spoke carefully. "I thank you for the most generous thought,

First Daughter. May I have some time to think about it?"

Jilrina grinned, placated for now. "Certainly. I will be sure to practice, and you will get the full benefit of my experience."

Oh, Goddess.

The merchant excused herself soon as she could, and on her trip home she contemplated the First Daughter actually having what she claimed. Gaelan also worried that she knew which pitiful soul the arrogant Noble might practice on first.

Sirana is barely of age to be considered possibly *fertile. Jilrina wouldn't, would she?*

Most mothers preferred that their daughter wait another score of turns or more beyond, as Polynia had, so it wouldn't be a dangerous birth the first time.

How might this 'practice' affect the poor youth . . ?

Gaelan shook her head, chiding herself for a fool. Despite notable charisma when she cared to use it, Jilrina had no true Priestess magic, and Gaelan bet she didn't have a real divine altar. Jilrina was still living her power fantasy, and Sirana would continue to bear the weight of it in silence.

So the game continues between Noble siblings. There is nothing any common blood can do about it.

A SPAN OR SO LATER, GAELAN WOKE FROM DEEP IN REVERIE, SENSING THAT HER mother had just opened the back door while the shop was closed. Only one other had come inside, and they weren't signing, they were whispering too loud to be subtle.

She knew that whisper; his lips had been pressed hot and impassioned against her ear quite recently.

Treyl?

Gaelan rolled out of bed and scrambled to put on the previous business cycle's trousers to add to her nightshirt, and quickly stuffed her feet into her boots before leaving her small room to head downstairs. She intended for both mother and lover to hear her coming, and they each noted her arrival with differing satisfaction.

"Here's the payment, madam," the Guard from House Thalluen whispered, brazenly taking the merchant's hand and pressing a dense little pouch into her palm. "We need something very strong. As powerful as you have."

"My strongest requires a magical word as well," she responded. "Do you trust yourself to carry that knowledge back to your mistress? If you tell it wrong, it will not work, and the potion will be wasted."

The handsome male in uniform pursed his lips and shook his head. "I'm not a mage. If I could beg an escort to carry that knowledge to my mistress in all accuracy, madam?"

Her mother turned her head to look at Gaelan, saying nothing.

"What is it?" she asked, lightly touching the railing as her stomach felt ill. "What do they need, Mother?"

"Healing," Polynia grunted. "Will you go?"

"If you instruct me, Mother."

"Come with me into the stockroom. Do not touch anything, Guardsvrin."

Once she closed and locked the stockroom door, Gaelan's mother clenched her fists in frustration. "It gets worse. I can't get out ..."

"Mother?"

She flipped a hand to bat away questions, searching almost frantically through her most valuable potions, handing her a belt of useful pouches as well. "If you are to have my granddaughter soon, Gaelan, you must go now. Do *not* let Matron Thalluen's Third Daughter die."

TREYL TOOK HER HAND AS THEY JOGGED THROUGH THE DARKNESS TOWARD THE single Uroan mount he'd ridden to get here. *Quickly.*

How long has it been? Gaelan signed one-handed.

Not sure. There was blood on the floor when I was summoned. A few marks?

Gaelan didn't like their chances, and she had already had a hand in doing something permanent to Sirana. Her mother was right again; having done it once, now Gaelan was remembered when the Nobility needed something else equally permanent, even thirty turns later. She would be blamed if it failed. Their shop would be blamed. It would only get worse …

This was why their family had played only in small magics, why they never exacted real change among the Nobles.

Where did that first compulsion potion come from?

Treyl brought her back to the plantation in the quickest trip Gaelan had ever made there. He jumped off the tall, burly beast and took her waist to help her down, then led her to an outbuilding on the grounds which she had never seen before.

The thing was no bigger than a shed and hidden behind an array of magically shaped rock growths and overlays and other storage buildings. There were no other openings but for a small chimney in the top, and until Treyl knocked low, in a certain, distinct rhythm and the door opened a crack, Gaelan could not smell the blood until that moment.

"Get in here," Jilrina hissed, her arm striking like a snake to seize Gaelan's wrist. "You took too long!"

The First Daughter closed the door behind them, leaving her guard outside. The interior was claustrophobic enough that the two of them were standing in the only area which was not marked by symbols. Gaelan felt her entire insides go cold as she saw the stone platform, one which could serve as an altar, lined halfway around with standing candlesticks and already stained on one side with blood as if a throat had been cut and the sacrifice had drained out all over the floor.

Following the blood, Gaelan saw the slender body curled up into a ball in the corner, eyes closed and face alarmingly ashen. Sirana did not seem to be breathing, but the blood hadn't come from her throat; she was covered only in a shift, and the youth was stained and sticky from the waist down to her toes.

"Heal her!" Jilrina commanded. "If my Matron finds out about this, I will see your shop burned to the ground!"

Gaelan had no doubt that she would. *Oh, Goddess, let it not be too late.*

Kneeling beside the adolescent, anxious with her back turned to the would-be Priestess, Gaelan checked for a pulse in Sirana's neck and breathed out slowly when she found one fluttering weakly. She might have to try a small, wakeful cantrip first to get the wounded Noble to drink the potion.

With a pinch of powder rubbed between her thumb and forefinger, Gaelan brushed Sirana's clammy forehead and sunken cheeks, drawing ash-grey lines on her dark skin. *"Leutrevaret."*

The youth's face had been more relaxed in unconsciousness with only her brows slightly drawn down. Now the pain returned in her eyes as they opened and she grimaced, every muscle in her face and body tight and trembling, unable to move from her spot.

Gaelan had never seen Sirana's eyes so close, pricked as they were now with tears, and the merchant ludicrously wished she had a shirt just that color of blue. They were beautiful.

"Drink this," Gaelan whispered. "It will make you well."

Sirana didn't believe her; she looked like an animal caught and waiting for the final blow. The cantrip also wouldn't last long; Sirana's lips were turning grey, and her pupils expanded and contracted in abnormal ways.

The merchant mage couldn't pretend she was surprised; she glanced back in her periphery and noticed Jilrina only just restrained herself, pacing and glaring at Gaelan's back. The merchant returned focus to the injured cait and lowered her whisper even more.

"Drink it, Sirana, and you will have the chance to kill her and break your silence. Only her death will loosen your tongue."

Sirana swallowed but Gaelan had spoken that which she wanted most, and with only the price of a small, piercing pain behind her right eye as the lid twitched. She barely nodded and reached for the bottle; the merchant helped to close her hand around it and unstopped it for her. The adolescent guzzled it down while Gaelan laid a hand on her thin shoulder and murmured the command word.

"*Iriseav'unal.*"

Sirana jerked and cried out, tightening her arms across her middle as the healing went to work very quickly. Probably too quickly, there would be some scarring. Gaelan took advantage of all her mental defenses being down to touch Sirana's temple and murmur a magical suggestion.

After this healing, forget my face, forget my actions, forget my name, but do not forget my words about Jilrina owning your silence.

Sirana closed those incredible blue eyes and fell asleep, her pulse beating hard and fast; Gaelan could see the hum of magic working within her.

Right then Jilrina deigned to step onto a bloodstain and hover over Gaelan's back. "Well? Is it working?"

"It is. You may want to give her time to rest before putting more strain on her."

"How much time?"

Gaelan pursed her lips in thought. "Two quad-spans? Maybe three."

The First Daughter was displeased. "You're lying, merchant."

Gaelan frowned and stood up, stepping away from Sirana but facing Jilrina. "She has lost a lot of blood. Too much to have survived otherwise, and the potion only took more strength from her to repair what it has. It will take food and rest and time for her body to be well again. I would start thinking what story you will tell your Matron why she is suddenly ill from loss of blood."

The Noble glowered at her so harshly, Gaelan automatically thought of a few protections she was prepared to cast.

"I will not share my gift with you, then," Jilrina spat. "Tell your mother to send anyone but you to deliver in the future. I will take nothing from you, and you may no longer visit the males of House Thalluen. They are forever beyond your reach. Find some low street bua to seed your cunt!"

Gaelan felt the rock land in her stomach but wouldn't give Jilrina the satisfaction of seeing her regret. She sought to take her leave but stopped when Jilrina spoke again.

"I do not need to remind you, Gaelan," the would-be Priestess murmured, "what will happen to your mother and siblings if you gossip about what you saw here. Do I?"

"No, First Daughter. I know what will happen."

"Good. Leave."

Treyl was outside but had heard nothing of the exchange, it seemed, as he was confused why Gaelan was leaving without even looking at him. He started to follow her, to reach for her, and she dared to pause and sign, *I am banished from here! No more, Treyl. Please.*

He hesitated but saw the tears in her eyes and nodded reluctantly. The intelligent male did not need further convincing. He signed to her.

I will miss you, Gaelan.

Her handsome guard stayed silent and dutiful at his post outside that horrid Noble's altar room while Gaelan walked off their land for the last time. She wept only until she reached the crossroad to catch a cart ride back home.

CHAPTER 4

3075-3092 S.E., THE MARKET OF SIVARAUS

GAELAN TOLD HER MOTHER MOST OF WHAT HAD HAPPENED, MINUS THE HINT she'd given Sirana how to take back her life. They waited for a turn to see if the wrath of House Thalluen came down upon them in some way, subtle or bold.

In the meantime, Gaelan discovered what her mother had already sensed: she was pregnant by Treyl, though she couldn't determine which coupling had seen her conceive. As long as she had tried for it, having it happen now was a mixed blessing with the uncertainty looming over her and her family.

It was a tense turn.

Nothing out of the ordinary happened, however; nothing which could be traced back to that insane First Daughter, and as the new mother's time neared and finally arrived after the full two turns, as Gaelan gave birth and was allowed a relatively peaceful first turn with her own firstborn daughter, she dared to hope no one was coming for them.

She could see Treyl in her child's eyes, much to her satisfaction, even if she would never see him again.

Within another turn, Gaelan could not help but hear the gossip that the First Daughter of House Thalluen was dead; she had taken a fall in the barn and broken her neck. Her mother and she sighed in relief.

"Kaltra's accusing Sirana Thalluensareci," her mother said. "The Matron isn't pushing for a full investigation."

"Mmm," Gaelan grunted noncommittally, bathing her squirming child with a sponge in the small tub.

"She'll have to provide proof, of course."

"Of course."

The Second Daughter never could, so the gossip in the moss-line went, and thus no one was surprised that Kaltra was caught in attempted murder within five turns. What did cause a bit of a stir at the markets, for a whole span, was that Kaltra was kept with the Matron while Sirana was the one sent to Court. The stories from there were about as titillating as one could hope among the Nobles at Court; conquests and games and lurid details.

Gaelan supposed that the young Davrin must have healed enough to still get pleasure from mating, even if she would never have a daughter of her own.

MORE THAN A DECADE PASSED AS GAELAN CONTINUED THE BUSINESS WITH HER mother. She thought very little had changed as she was kept very busy, not only raising Natia, but teaching herself more skills to benefit their own tiny stronghold at the edge of the central city.

It was those self-taught lessons which allowed her to find and identify the small clutch of compulsion potions well-hidden in their home.

"Mother! What is this? Not again! What are you doing?!"

"Don't you take that tone with me!"

Gaelan blocked the slap which was coming, glaring heated at her. "Where did these come from? Tell me!"

"Quiet down! And you cannot know —"

"You put all of us in danger! I won't let you ruin things for Natia — !"

"You don't understand!"

The way the door opened then, the way everything had gone quiet both inside and outside their shop called for each of them to go still, as if a predator was stalking them and they hoped to go unnoticed.

"Polynia," a commanding voice said. "Shopkeeper Polynia, please."

"Y-yes, Red Sister," Boqol stammered, and they heard his light boots coming toward them.

"Yes, yes, I'm coming," their mother said grumpily, flitting her hand at him to go away, desperate to hide her fear as she looked at Gaelan. "Go get Natia. Just in case."

Just in case of what?

Gaelan ran up the stairs where her daughter would be playing in her mother's room and knew as Natia lifted her eyes and stared behind her that something was wrong. Still, Gaelan was startled when a female warrior in red leather walked in right behind her. The young merchant spun around and lifted her child up, clutching her as if the Red Sister meant to take her away.

"Downstairs," was the only word spoken, and the Red Sister stood back and waited for her to descend first.

Darkness threatened to take her vision for a moment, and that terrifying red uniform would be gone, but Gaelan managed not to faint and headed downstairs clutching her daughter.

The whole family was gathered in the front room, any shades pulled, and the doors locked with the "closed" sign facing out. Three Red Sisters stood there, two looking alike but one of them was subtly different.

The quality of her leathers and her cloak were just a bit better, less worn. She was certainly the eldest female between them, and a sorceress whose aura was more powerful than any of them. Her gaze alone seemed to have the ability to hold them in their place as if turning them to stone.

"Elder D'Shea?" one of the other Red Sisters asked her.

"I will check the stockroom," she said, staring directly at Polynia's eyes, who looked down quickly.

It didn't matter that her mother had re-hidden the compulsion potions during their argument; the Red Sister found them again almost immediately, bringing them out. She nodded as if this was only the final piece which solved her own puzzle, and she set them down on the counter.

"Contraband," Elder D'Shea said. "Take these three for interrogation."

This Elder had just sentenced her mother and both her younger siblings with an ease as if she was requesting her evening meal. She ignored their protests as if she heard them all the time.

"No," Gaelan moaned, the misery she saw stretching out before her overwhelming as all but one of her family's faces disappeared inside black bags placed over their heads.

The Elder walked up to Gaelan holding Natia as they were dragged out, blocking any escape and the young mage's view of most of the room. Scarlet eyes both intense and calm drifted over the youngest Davrin, who barely reached mid-thigh when placed on her own two feet.

It was just the three of them now in the room.

Natia had buried her eyes in Gaelan's neck and clenched tight to her shirt. Gaelan couldn't remember the last time tears leaked down her cheeks in front of another female.

"Please ..." she whispered. "Don't take Natia to the dungeon. She won't survive."

The Elder Red Sister held absolutely no pity in her expression, but nor was she taking pleasure in the commoner's fear as almost any Noble would have been. If Elder D'Shea had been expressionless, Gaelan thought that would be better; she knew the Elder considered something specific about her daughter, but like Matron Thalluen, Gaelan could not tell what it was until she spoke.

"Give her to me," the Elder instructed, lifting her red-gloved hands.
Oh, Goddess, no!

Gaelan shook her head desperately, and D'Shea sighed as if she was slow in the head.

"Merchant, listen to me carefully. You have two choices: Refuse my order and cling to that child only to see yourself executed here, after which I take her anyway. Or show me the strength to hand her to me yourself and agree to undergo the trials. If you survive, you may see your daughter again. If you want it enough."

The … trials? Show strength to … ?

"Choose, Gaelan."

The young mage gasped at the power of her command, unable to think longer. "A-alright. Yes, a trial. Just don't hurt Natia. Please."

"That is no longer your concern, recruit."

Elder D'Shea held out her crimson-gloved hands with every expectation to have them filled with the child who'd begun to weep, begging to stay with her mother.

"Noooo!" Natia wailed, clutching the muted yellow fabric of her shirt and uncaring of the noise that might be irritating the Elder Red Sister. "*Maaamaaa!*"

"Shh, shh, be strong," Gaelan said while staring at D'Shea's intense eyes, willing her to hear her plea: *My baby. Just don't hurt her.*

When Elder D'Shea had her child and Gaelan let go of the small hands she'd just gotten to release her clothing, the young mage felt she had lost her grip while hanging on the side of a cliff. Her eyed blurred and she trembled, staring at the familiar shape of her daughter squirming in the Red Sister's arms.

The sorceress gestured and spoke a spell, placing Natia into an unnatural sleep against her shoulder, and Gaelan bit her lip so hard it began to bleed.

Voluntarily handing her daughter over to the Elder Sorceress was only the first of the trials. Though Elder D'Shea would tell Gaelan later that her first trial was a success, this proved instead to be the hardest failure to take.

I'll live to see you again, Natia. I promise.

The Sister Seekers Prequel is now available for free!

A century ago, one Priestess left for the Surface. She vanished. This is her story.

"What if …" Irrwaer began.

Jaunda leaned closer. "If?"

At least she wanted to play.

"What if Juliran authorized me to make a trade with you? An act for an act?"

The Corpora huffed through her nose, conveying all her skepticism for deals with the Sanctuary in one breath. Irrwaer was certain that sentiment should be returned in full, but she must work with what her Priestess had given her.

Prove useful to a Red Sister, and you will see her again.

That could be a warning or a promise.

Irrwaer is an acolyte serving in the Sanctuary, the religious seat in the underground city of Sivaraus. She's troubled no one, bedded no one, and seeks no higher service. She wants to be left alone.

Nowhere is safe in the Queen's web once the Priestesses know her name. To discover more of her betters is to risk tripping into their tangled threads, trapped as another's meal or amusement.

The subtlest path is to spin her own web before joining the larger with as few tremors as possible. The only place to spin unseen is between threads where Priestesses prefer not to walk.

As Irrwaer works among meek males, rowdy Red Sisters, and the sinister sons of demons, the acolyte must ask a troubling question:

In a matriarchy where power passes through daughters, why are the Priestesses only competing for sons?

In *Sons to Keep*, Etaski introduces the political sphere of Sivaraus through the eyes of the least ambitious.

These events occur one hundred years before the birth of the protagonist Sirana in *No Demons But Us*, yet their effects still ripple out from the center of a tightly woven tapestry.

Read *Sons to Keep: a Sister Seekers Prequel* FREE when you join Etaski's newsletter. Subscribe here! at https://etaski.com/about/

Begin *Sister Seekers* with *No Demons But Us,* a polyamorous dark epic fantasy! at https://etaski.com/sister-seekers/

My name is Sirana of House Thalluen.

When my eldest sister broke her neck, the Red Sisters suspected that I pushed her. They're watching me now. I'm afraid, but I'm also ready for them.

I am too young to be trapped in the most wretched spot of any scheme: accused of killing the Matron's heir. Dark Elves live for intrigue in our underground city of Sivaraus, and justice means nothing to the Red Sisters who enforce the Queen's edict. Yet, I know the rules bend for the cunning and the bold, if only I can seize on the aspirations of those who succeeded before me.

I must confront what lies beneath the ravening eyes of the Sisterhood, for they will give me no choice. I must discover that which is unspoken as they gaze at me. If I would thrive in pervasive webs of conspiracies, I must fight to reweave my place within them.

In *No Demons But Us,* A.S. Etaski spins the first threads of an intense and epic tale, in which the trials of a young Davrin test her resolve to rise from the depths of the fear and hatred tearing her down.

Sister Seekers is adult epic fantasy with an ever-broadening scope. Found Family is a core theme throughout. It's perfect for fans of entwined plots, challenging themes, immersive worldbuilding, and elements of erotic horror. Sexuality and inner conflict play into character growth with nuanced intrigue, intense action, and fantastical magic.

Follow Etaski's updates at World Anvil for extra lore and world-building treats! https://miurag.etaski.com

ACKNOWLEDGMENTS

Much love and gratitude to my Hubs, for believing in me and making this possible for us!

My greatest appreciation to Doc Kangey, who's taught me so many new skills to improve my books, and who works behind the scenes to improve my tools and options. Check out our hard work and lore yet to come at Etaski.com & Miurag.Etaski.com.

Lastly, thanks to my top patrons who support all my efforts and make new things possible!

Sir Cumference, Baelus, Jesse C., Does, John K., Julie S., Paul B., Carla H., Briana R., Josanna, RainbowNight, Lesley PLAY, Kalculyszero, NotSoWeird, Zenor, Kelly D, Lady Dia Meter, Raymond T., Lexanii, Zeroharas, Johnathon Matlock, Chris R., Daolord, and Roy Meyer, and in loving memory, Stacy Meyer.

ABOUT THE AUTHOR

Etaski has entertained herself with fantasy stories since the first day she sat on a school bus looking out the window. When hand-written letters were disappearing, she scribbled no less than five pages to be worth the postage. Her early stories were written by hand, and she had a writer's callus and three embarrassing novels before graduating high school.

She studied science, archaeology, history, and theater. Frank discussion of sexuality was rare growing up, so she wrote fantasies, theories, and observations within stories for deeper contemplation or just be entertained.

History speaks little on sexuality, yet biology demonstrates how it sways basic choices. Drama reveals our strongest bonds but may fade to black at its most intimate. In the *Sister Seekers*, the sex and the story are inseparable, and their discoveries will change the journey of Miurag without cutting away.

Etaski's Website: etaski.com
Etaski's Book Page: etaski.com/sister-seekers
Etaski's Series Lore: miurag.etaski.com
Etaski on Patreon: www.patreon.com/etaski
Etaski on GoodReads: www.goodreads.com/etaski
Etaski on BookBub: www.bookbub.com/authors/a-s-etaski
Etaski on Facebook: www.facebook.com/asetaski
Etaski on Mastodon: mastodon.online/@etaski

37000025R00156